CONNECT WITH CRAIG MARTELLE

Website & Newsletter:
www.craigmartelle.com

BookBub –
www.bookbub.com/authors/craig-martelle

Facebook:
www.facebook.com/AuthorCraigMartelle/

CONNECT WITH E.E. ISHERWOOD

Website & Newsletter:
www.sincethesirens.com

Facebook:
facebook.com/sincethesiren

Cover Illustration by Heather Hamilton-Senter
Editing services provided by Lynne Stiegler
Formatting by James Osiris Baldwin – jamesosiris.com

We couldn't do what we do without the support of great people around us. We thank our spouses and our families for giving us time alone to think, write, and review. We thank our editor (Lynne), cover artist (Heather), and insider team of beta readers (Micky Cocker, Kelly O'Donnell, Dr. James Caplan, and John Ashmore). It's not who we are as authors, but who we are surrounded by that makes this all happen. Enjoy the story.

ONE

West Wendover, Nevada

Buck woke up, opened his eyes, and saw himself in bed. "Why is there a mirror on my ceiling?" He blinked to clear the fog from his mind. The sleeper cab was nice, but sometimes it was best to get a good night's sleep in a real bed.

Even if there *was* a mirror on the ceiling and rates were by the hour.

Worth it.

"They must get clientele who aren't puritans like us," a voice replied from nearby. Buck tried to focus. Connie. The second bed was ruffled where she'd slept. Big Mac was still curled up over there with his head on the pillow. Buck had paid for two rooms, but they'd only used one because of the red wave. He closed his eyes.

"Anything different?"

"Not that I can tell. Not yet, anyway," she answered, smiling when she looked at him. He made to get up but stopped.

"Why am I in my underwear?"

"It was dark when we crashed. What's the big deal?"

Buck had to think about that. He sat up and scratched the growing beard on his face. "You're up early," he said. "What are you reading?"

Connie glanced his way and held up the atlas. "I think my internal clock is set to 2003 time. I woke up at four-thirty. While I was awake, I figured I'd try to understand the route you're taking to go east."

He pointed out the window, which was toward the rising sun. "We drive I-80 that way. I'm happy to say it is pretty much a straight shot to White Plains, New York. Then we'll hop in my pickup truck and find Garth."

"About that," she said. "It looks like our route goes near Three Mile Island. Will we get irradiated?"

Buck smiled and wiped the sleep from his eyes. "Boy, you get right into it in the morning. It is still over two thousand miles away. We'll know more once we get closer, but Garth said they told him it wasn't as serious an accident as they first thought."

Connie leaned back in her chair. "So, this is over? The storm on the East Coast is gone. The nuclear plant didn't spew radiation over everything. You find Garth and life goes back to normal for you?"

He detected the worry in her voice, so he slid out of bed, putting on his jeans while Connie giggled. He pulled out a clean Hawaiian shirt from his overnight bag and buttoned it.

"Are you kidding me?" she exclaimed. "Oh my God, it's terrible! Didn't your momma teach you how to dress?"

"What, this old rag?" He laughed. "What don't you like about it?"

His yellow and green shirt was decorated with AK-47s

shaped like palm trees and grenades dressed up as pineapples. The guys at truck stops loved it, and he wore it all the time on the road, although he didn't wear it much in the city because it did upset some people.

"It's so damned bright." She continued to chuckle between words. "People are going to see you coming from over the horizon."

He shook his head slowly. "I need to take a shower. Then we can catch some chow and hit the road."

"Only one towel," she told him.

Buck hesitated. "I'll use my shirt so you can use the towel."

She leaned back, wearing a confused expression. She pointed to herself with both hands. "You think I look like this *before* a shower? That's sweet. I already saved the towel for you."

"You shouldn't have."

"I'm kidding. I didn't save it because I knew what you would say, big tough Marine. How about you just use my wet towel so we can get some 'chow,' as you called it. I hope it looks like breakfast." She motioned for him to get moving. "And whatever you do, don't think of that towel all over my naked body. Now shoo."

Buck's mouth worked, but no sounds came out. He was rooted to the floor.

"Don't make me eat breakfast without you." She pointed one finger at the bathroom and returned to her study of the atlas.

He took three steps to the bathroom door and stopped, then looked over his shoulder and said softly. "I don't know what just happened, but I like it." He closed the door behind him.

When he finished, Connie had the television on.

Their eyes met for a moment, and she smiled in a way that was comfortable. For her. For him. A movement pulled Buck's attention away. The fifty-pound puppy was standing on the bed, tail wagging.

"All right, Big Mac, let's get you outside."

Buck was glad for the distraction. He needed time to think. He'd told her the truth about being glad he found her, because it felt like he'd known her for a long time already. Almost like they'd been friends all their lives, but they'd been away from each other until this disaster. It was strange but overwhelming. He was too old to be swept away. His mission was to get home to Garth, and that would take all his focus. It was true even in normal times, because the road was a dangerous place. One blown tire could be fatal.

When he came back in, he put some kibble in Mac's bowl and let him have his breakfast. Connie fiddled with the television while the pup wolfed it down.

The first thing that came on was a local news channel talking about Denver. She changed it immediately because they wanted something more local, like Salt Lake City news. That was the nearest population center.

However, when she found the next channel, the reporters were also talking about Denver.

"What's this all about?" he said aloud.

The talking head sat inside five or six graphics streaming across the screen. One was a ticker of stock prices, which showed nothing but red three-digit numbers. Another was a temperature ticker with numerous American cities and numbers behind them. Some cities were in triple digits, but others showed negative readings.

"Look at that weather!" Connie blurted. "It explains the snow storm yesterday. Well..." She hesitated, "Maybe it doesn't explain it, but it does confirm that it wasn't normal."

"No, it wasn't," he admitted. "This is unbelievable."

The other ribbons on the screen showed news around the world, but he focused on the anchor hemmed in between all the graphics.

"If you are just joining us, we are standing in front of the Search for Nuclear, Astrophysical, and Kronometric Extremes building, which is more commonly called SNAKE around these parts. We have every reason to believe this is where the red and blue waves came from. Aside from the multiple reports from nearby residents, we have eyewitness accounts from several members of the staff of the facility who have told their families what happened."

"Aw shit," Buck said with disappointment.

"What is it?" Connie asked.

"It looks like the scientists did it. Their crazy experiments ripped the world a new one, and you and I are the saps who are going to suffer for it."

Angry protesters held signs behind the reporter. Some of them had simple messages of doom, much like the guy he had seen back in Modesto, but one in particular caught his attention.

The hand-painted board said, You killed us!

"I've got to call Garth. I know he's half a continent away, but I have to make sure he knows not to ever go to Denver."

"Agreed," she said distantly.

Lewes, Delaware

His dad's nyuck-nyuck ringtone woke Garth from a dead sleep.

"Hello?" he said in a groggy voice. "Dad? What time is it?"

The shades on the motel window were almost pitch-black, so he had little clue as to the time of day.

"It is six in the morning here. That means it's nine there. What are you still doing in bed? You aren't fooling around, are you?"

Garth detected the "Dad tone."

"We're at a motel in Lewes, Delaware. We got off the ferry and went right here like you said." He thought about what was probably in the back of Dad's mind. "Lydia is in the other bed."

Buck sighed with relief but didn't press the subject.

"We're getting underway, son. I wanted to touch base with you in case I lose reception again. We'll be on some remote stretches of interstate today. We're shooting to be in Nebraska by nightfall."

"Nebraska? That's like halfway here."

Buck laughed. "It feels like it's still a long way to go. I want you to consider what you're going to do today. You have the taxi, right?"

He and Lydia had saved the cab from the mud yesterday. "We'll need some gas, but at least we have a means of getting around. I'd hate to have to walk.'"

Garth observed the lump that was Lydia buried beneath all the covers with a pillow wall around her head. She had been impressed with his driving skills and loved the ride, despite the broken window and the massive thunderstorm they had survived yesterday. She'd told him that despite all their issues on the road, it still beat walking.

"Good," Buck replied. "It looks like the radiation scare is over. The news isn't even talking about it today."

"Is the hurricane gone?" he asked in return.

"I don't see anything about it. All the news channels we have out here are talking about a science facility in Red Mesa, Colorado, near Denver. It looks like that's where the blue and red lights came from."

"Are they going to fix whatever they broke? I think Lydia might like to go back home." They'd talked about it briefly the previous night, but after she climbed into her own soft, clean bed, she found new enjoyment in modern conveniences. With no one waiting for her in the 1840s, Garth thought she might be more amenable to changing her mind, but everything she had known was gone, and almost none of it had prepared her for the twenty-first-century world.

"I don't know. We'll both stay away from there, okay?" Buck suggested.

Garth chuckled. "I doubt I'll ever be in Denver, Dad. I'm anxious to go home and wait for you to get here."

"That's probably the smart thing. While you are in the motel, make sure you watch the news. See what to expect when you walk out the door. Be safe, okay?"

"I will. Love you, Dad." He and his dad didn't typically exchange such emotional goodbyes, but the last couple of days made him realize how much he missed his father. They'd had their argument, and he'd been mad as hell for a little while, but seeing the plane crash and too many dead people had made him appreciate how lucky he was. Plus, Lydia was sound asleep, so he could speak openly, although she didn't seem to care about the things that teenagers of his era thought were important, like their social image.

"Love you too, son. Keep in touch."

"Will do."

He hung up his phone and wondered if he had remembered to bring a cell phone charger.

That could be a disaster.

He would check the bugout bag to see if his dad had remembered to pack one, but first, he used the clicker to turn on the television from his bed. He had to check on the world outside the motel's windows.

The first channel showed a metallic building surrounded by giant red-colored rock walls.

"SNAKE is off-limits to reporters, but there are now hundreds of protesters gathered at the front gate. Oddly enough, there is a contingent of Air Force police guarding the scientific facility. We've been unable to get any comment—"

He flicked the channel, careful to keep the volume low, so it didn't wake up Lydia.

"Protesters have turned over a car on Deer Creek Canyon Road, but so far, that has been the extent of their anger. We're trying to find the leader of this unruly bunch, but none have come forward—"

Garth went to five other stations—the motel had a full spread of cable channels—and they all focused on what was going on in Colorado. After a few additional channels of non-news programming, he finally found a weather broadcast.

A map of the east coast showed storm systems in random locations, including one apparently mislabeled as a snow shower on the coast of North Carolina, but there were no hurricanes to worry about.

"We can go home," he said to himself.

And Lydia?

He glanced at her, sleeping soundly. He started to consider how to get her home, but he became distracted by her appearance. She looked different without all the dirt on her cheeks, which had come off in another modern convenience last night: the shower. When she came out of the bathroom with a clean face and her blonde hair streaming over her shoulders, her natural beauty surprised him. Seeing her again reminded him of that.

The thought made him look away.

Stay on task, Garth. That's what Dad would say.

"Get gas for the car," he whispered. "Get back home. Wait for Dad. Lastly, I'll see if I can get Lydia back where she came from."

Garth took a long look at Lydia to make absolutely sure she was still asleep. Once he was certain, he scooted to the edge of his covers, then ran into the bathroom because he was only wearing his boxers.

They'd been soaked to the core in the rainstorm, and once they got to the motel, they took turns hanging their clothing to dry in the bathroom. They had used towels for robes.

He admitted he was a lot shyer about it than she was.

When he was inside the tiny room, he shut the door.

"I wish you were here, Sam, buddy, but I'm kind of glad you aren't."

He figured Sam's overbearing womanizing would have long since chased her away. She'd probably have preferred to stay under the overpass where he found her.

I've got to avoid pulling a Sam.

Garth looked in the vanity mirror and recited his day's mission.

"Gas. Home. Wait for Dad. Don't be like Sam." He

paused for a few seconds. "And help Lydia go back to 1849."

The thought saddened him greatly. As Dad would say, you create a bond with someone you've spent your life beside. She was his foxhole partner. Together, they'd pull through.

TWO

Search for Nuclear, Astrophysical, and Krono-metric Extremes (SNAKE). Red Mesa, Colorado

It was dawn outside, but the orange light peeking over the distant plains only served as a reminder of how little sleep Faith had gotten in the previous two nights. She looked longingly at the hogback close to her building and wished she could go out and jog for a couple of miles to wake up. On a normal day, that was part of her routine, but General Smith didn't want anyone to leave for any reason.

"Thanks for working all night, guys. I mean it more than I can say." She turned to her staff, who were assembled at the conference table. One of the computer guys sat where her name was scratched into the wooden tabletop, but he'd placed his laptop right over it. No one was joking around this morning, and they all looked as strung out as she felt.

Dr. Stafford replied first. "We have a better handle on what was happening before the beam was shut down yesterday, but we still don't know what to expect going forward."

Dr. Bob Stafford was the head of Computing, and he was in charge of the handful of computer men and women in the small room. He and Faith had butted heads in the past, but he'd been surprisingly helpful once he'd confessed to having a part in the secret experiment run by SNAKE and CERN. To her, his new attitude suggested things were worse than they seemed.

She nodded at him. "I was helping with the equations drawn up by the physics team. My mind is jelly after all the late-night work, but I can think straight enough to compliment your people, Bob. They were a big help."

Bob looked surprised. "Well, thanks. Glad to be of service."

"What did you find?" she went on.

"The beams were designed to pierce the upper mantle of the Earth and effectively dredge for residual dark matter locked into the atomic structure of the rock. Over thousands of miles, the experiment figured to encounter traces of the substance. However, it appears it struck a lot of it."

Faith took it from there. "And that's what our equations were trying to solve. Unfortunately, we don't know any of the properties of dark matter or dark energy, even though the blue beams appear to contain the latter."

One of the particle physicists on her team piped up, "The beams were co-opted by the new form of energy, almost like tapping into oil deep in the shale with a drill."

"Drill, baby, drill," someone said from the back.

"Exactly," Faith replied. "It jibes with what the computer guys and gals have found. There isn't enough energy in the entire Front Range power grid to produce the scale of energy bursts we've seen go out from our collider. It is being amplified in some way."

Another physicist joined in. "Without being able to observe and quantify dark energy or dark matter, we can only guess at their properties. We've had teams look at the remaining three beams, but we can't isolate their constituent parts."

"So," she began, "we know the beams go into the ground and travel to CERN under the curvature of the mantle, but we have no way of knowing what we've tapped into."

Bob broke in, "We'd have to dig a tunnel hundreds of kilometers deep to see what's down there."

"Well, that ain't gonna happen," she said in frustration. "We need to beat this thing. Keep working at it. Before those people get too feisty." Faith pointed outside, but then got up and went to the window again.

Protesters held signs at the front gate. They were still hundreds of yards away, but she saw a giant sign held high above the others.

"End Days," she read aloud.

Motion caught her eye on the parking lot two stories below. A man came out from behind one of the numerous school buses and threw something. She saw him plain as day.

The glass shattered a few feet to her left, and a small hole appeared.

"Shit!" she screamed as she jumped back. "The bastard threw a rock at me!"

She realized the sun on her blouse had probably made her a bright target for the guy.

A second rock glanced off a window farther down the row but didn't have enough force to crack the glass.

The rock-thrower sprinted for the edge of the lot. Guards came out of the front doors to chase him down, but in the few seconds she watched, it didn't look like they were going to catch him.

She was going to write it off as bad luck and resolve

never to stand by the windows again, but some loud cracks echoed from the lot below.

"Oh, fuck," she blurted.

Many of the others in the room came up to the windows to see the perpetrator. They reacted in almost the same way as her.

"They shot that guy," she said with shock.

It was now a spectacle. Her entire team lined up against the glass to watch.

The runner writhed on the pavement about ten feet from the rearmost edge of the paved parking lot.

"Is he dead?" one of the female computer programmers asked without looking up from her seat.

The man clearly wasn't dead, but he was injured. His arm was bloody, and his shirt looked like someone splashed him with ketchup. The guards dragged him toward the front door of SNAKE.

She realized she had to get involved before things got worse.

"You guys keep working," she said as she headed out. "And for the love of God, stay away from the windows!"

Canberra, Australian Capital Territory, Australia

Destiny rocked back and forth with the gentle swaying of the train, relieved to be leaving Canberra.

Once she had left Zandre's property, she'd ridden the four-wheeler until it ran out of gas, then walked the last two miles through the city until she reached the train station. She figured she'd have to spend the night on a hard steel bench, but a late-night train was departing for Sydney and allowed anyone who happened to be there to get on board.

She recognized the well-dressed people from her trip to Canberra earlier that same day. Zandre had said they were politicians. She had no feelings either way for the leaders of Australia's government, but those assholes seemed to look down on her because she was the only passenger besides them. It might also have been her dusty attire and wind-blown hairdo.

Those blighters can go fuck themselves, she thought.

After almost being shot, and then helping the Duck of Doom escape the hunters, she was in no mood for bullshit from anyone.

She pulled out her phone and sent a text message to Rodney at the Sydney Harbor Foundation.

Hey, Rod, I'm coming home from Canberra. Need a favor. Please message back.

She turned off the screen, figuring he would reply in the morning, but a message came right back.

Is everyone working late tonight?

What do you mean? she sent back.

The phone rang under her fingers.

"Hello?" she said quietly. The politicians were at the other end of the carriage, but she wasn't taking any chances.

"Hey, Dez. You doing all right? I know the Wollemi fire was a monster, but it seems to have burned itself out already."

"Yeah, I'm way past the fire. All good on that score. Hey, I wanted to ask. Does SHF still have access to the oceanography lab?" Her employer studied and preserved animals all over the world, but because they were headquartered in Sydney, they brought most of their work back home. They shared time and space on an old freighter that had been retrofitted with research equipment. She'd done a little time on it when they did a company outing at the Great Barrier Reef.

He sounded instantly skeptical. "The *Majestic* is moored in Sydney, yes. Why?"

Rodney was her equal on the company manifest, but he did most of his work at the main offices, while she was often out in the field. To her, it made it seem like Rod had an air of superiority when talking on the phone, so his manner of questioning tested her patience.

She drew a breath before replying. "Who has time booked? Is it us, or Fujitsu, or whoever?"

"Fujiyama," he corrected. "And we do. That whole group flew back to Japan a few days ago. They let us know before they left so we could take it out whenever we wanted. Ben Stephens and some of the tropics guys are sailing it up to Queensland starting tomorrow."

"Rodney, this is very important. I'm coming back from the A-C-T with some important photos. When you and the bosses see them, I guarantee they will want to give me time with the boat, okay?"

"Sure, Dez, whatever you say." He did not sound convinced, and she couldn't take the chance he would ignore her.

"Screw it. I'll text them to you. I have pictures of all kinds of extinct animals that I saw while I was out in the bush. Show them around, then tell me if anyone has a more important role for a naturalist to play than saving these things."

"I'll look for them, Dez, but I can't make any guarantees."

She sent him a picture of the Demon Duck of Doom.

"Crikey!" he said a few seconds later.

Her ego swelled for a moment when she heard his reaction, but she remembered the photo was necessary as a way to get his attention, not make herself look better. Before she could say anything more, however, the train jerked and began braking. She had to set the phone in her lap and hold onto the armrest to keep from hitting the seat in front of her.

The grind of metal on metal announced their unplanned stop.

"I'll call you back," she said to Rodney as she looked outside into the black of night. "Something is wrong."

West Wendover, Nevada

Buck and Connie listened to the news as they finished getting ready for the day. They tidied up the small amount of gear they had brought in, stowed Mac's food and travel dish, and moved around each other like a well-oiled machine.

"You would think we clear out of motels all the time," he said to her after they had most things organized by the door, including the rifle.

She smiled and chuckled but didn't reply.

"Do you mind if we skip the convenience store? I want to start logging some miles today. We can pick up what you need when we get to the next truck stop. Those places have everything." He eyed her dress innocently. "Except stylish clothing for women. I'm not sure where you'll need to go for that, but I do have some shirts you could borrow." He waggled his eyebrows and pointed at his Hawaiian shirt.

She exaggerated a frown. "I'll wear the same dress for a week before I wear one of those. I'll find something better, but," she paused for effect, "I won't let it delay us getting back to Garth."

"I didn't think you would. But you can't beat these

shirts," he remarked. "Nice pocket on the chest. Hangs down over your pistol to keep it hidden." He patted his hip where his PX4 Storm Subcompact was ready for action. There was no way to see its imprint under his gaudy, low-hanging shirt.

"If I get a pistol, I'll think about it." She traced a finger over her hip as if to show how her knee-length dress hugged her body. There was no way to conceal a weapon under it. At least, that was the message he took away from the gesture.

"That'll work," he replied.

She brightened. "I *would* like a toothbrush at some point along the way. I used some of your little bottle of mouthwash. I hope you don't mind?"

The whiteness of her teeth suggested she took care of them.

"What's mine is yours, as they say, although I'm running light, too. We'll both need to stock up at the truck stop."

Connie grabbed the rifle and made as if to put it over her shoulder, but they both turned to the television when someone mentioned an attack.

"Turn it up," she suggested.

They'd left the TV on while they packed to keep tabs on what was happening, but nothing had caught their ears or eyes until now.

"Reporters on the ground suggest a protester tried to get inside the SNAKE campus. The Air Force shot him for no reason."

"The military doesn't do anything for no reason," Buck commented, standing too close to the screen.

"Your backside makes a delightful wall but a crappy window."

Buck slid to the left so she had a clear view.

"Tensions are high here in Red Mesa, but no one in the SNAKE facility has come out to comment on the attack, nor have they said a word about any of the other rumors about what they do in there. Some people have said..."

He turned to her, suddenly overburdened by the heavy weight on his heart. "Everything that has happened the last two days has been wildly unpredictable. I hope we've seen the worst of it, but I don't think it's likely. Did I make a mistake telling Garth to go back home? Would you have told your son to stay at home, or would you want him to come to you? 'Meet in the middle' kind of thing."

"You didn't make a mistake," she said right away. "Stay home. Stay safe. That's good Mama Grizzly advice."

What if nowhere is safe?

He looked at the screen again, and had a sudden strange feeling that the research facility was filled with evil geniuses trying to destroy his world. Suddenly he understood why the protesters had gone there, although he could never condone going full-on idiot and attacking the place like the terrorist jackass they shot.

"Fair enough," he said as he clicked off the TV. "Let's go talk to our convoy friends and then get out of here."

"And let's avoid any motorcyclists in the parking lot," she teased.

"Those guys. If it weren't for them, we wouldn't be together, but then again, if we run across them again..." He didn't finish the thought.

He shared her laughter but checked through the peep-hole *before* he went out the door, nonetheless.

It was time to get back into sheepdog mode.

THREE

Lewes, Delaware

Garth had no idea how to wake up a girl from 1849. Maybe he needed a rooster or a mooing cow. Both sound files could probably be downloaded to his phone if he cared to dig for them.

"Lydia," he said in a soft voice, opting to stick with the traditional wake-up method.

"Hi, Garth." She yawned. "What time is it?" She looked at the darkened shades. "It feels like midnight."

"It says it right there on the clock." He pointed to the red digits on the motel's alarm clock.

She read what she saw. "Nine, zero, nine?"

"Nine minutes after nine," he said in a helpful voice.

"Wow. Those numbers are so colorful. How do they change?"

He had no idea how to explain the workings of a digital clock.

"I don't know." He laughed. "I've used this type of clock my whole life, but I've never seen inside one."

"Amazing," she exclaimed. Lydia strained to see

through the drapes, but they were solid save for a thin line of illumination down the middle. "And it is still dark at this hour in your time? I should have been up at sunrise."

There was no way to resist showing her, so he walked over to the shades and pulled them apart like a circus showman. "I give you...daytime!"

She recoiled at the bright light and shielded her eyes. "Oh, my word!"

"I told you," he pressed before remembering to be nice. He pulled the drapes almost all the way closed again to give her a chance to build up to it.

"Your world is beyond my wildest dreams. Your car. Your living quarters. Amazing."

"I wish I could show you my real house. This is just a sleazeball motel, probably not even one-star rated. And the car is nothing, too. You should see some of the hotrods my dad has brought home over the years. My favorite is the Mustang."

That captured her interest. "You have horses?"

He snickered. "We have Mustangs, Chargers, Broncos, and I think there are cars named after Colts."

"Wonderful! Horses are important in keeping our wagon train going. I'd see hundreds of them every day."

He let her off easy. "Well, these aren't real horses. They're the names of cars, except 'Bronco' is the name of a truck."

"Truck?"

"You saw lots of them yesterday. They are like cars, but look a little different. You might see them more as wagons because they have open back ends where you can store stuff." He wasn't sure if she would catch on, but she didn't ask for more. It was unclear if that meant she understood what he was saying, or she was too shy to ask for clarification.

She hopped out of bed wearing only her undergarments, but she showed no shame in the act. She boldly walked into the bathroom and shut the door.

Wow. What was that?

She came out a minute later wearing her mud-stained pioneer dress.

"Ready," she declared.

His shirt and jeans were also stained by the mud from the previous day, so he had no room to complain. "I guess I'm ready, too," he said. "Let's go eat, then we'll leave."

They had no gear other than the lone rifle case. He had made a big deal of bringing it in after it was dark outside so no one would see what it was. Dad often made a big deal about how it was dangerous to transport firearms in states with strict gun laws. He said crossing from one state to another could make you an instant criminal, depending on the laws of the new state.

However, Garth had no idea if Delaware was better or worse than New York and New Jersey, so he assumed it was worse. That was how Dad would play it.

He left the gun case in the room while he and Lydia went to the motel lobby for breakfast.

"I'm sorry this won't be very impressive, but it will be enough to fuel us up for the day and get us back to my house. They'll probably have a few types of cereal and some milk."

Lydia practically drooled when she saw the spread.

"Bread. Eggs. Bacon? This is just like home." She pointed at all the foods and beverages. "But we never had this much. We can eat as much as we want?"

He smiled and nodded.

Instead of grabbing a plate and loading up, she walked over to the tray of eggs and used the scooper to serve herself a huge mouthful.

"Whoa!"

He ran over before she managed to stick it back in for a second helping.

"You can't do it that way," he said in a low voice to keep from being noticed by the smattering of other diners.

"Are you sure?" she asked with surprise. "It seems so simple."

Garth grabbed the scooper and was going to set it on the counter, but he ended up tossing it in a small sink.

Lydia scowled. "I wasn't done!"

"No. You aren't done. I had to do that so no one would eat from it. They'll get your germs if they put it in their mouth after you've used it."

"Germs?"

"Hmm. That's going to be a tough one to explain. Remember how I told you yesterday that radiation was like little fires in each drop of water? Well, germs are like tiny crocodiles that swim around in drops of water. They also swim around in our mouths and all over our bodies."

She spat on the floor. "Eww. Disgusting! In my mouth?"

There were so many things he took on faith, such as germs being bad, but he had little understanding of how they worked. She'd have to take it on faith like he did.

"You'll have to trust me," he whispered. "Lydia, let me get your food, okay? We don't want to cause a scene." He didn't think it was too big a risk. There were only a couple other travelers in the eating area, and none of them seemed put out that she'd hocked a loogy onto the tiles. In any other scenario, that lack of concern for hygiene in an eatery would shock him, but not this time. He was glad to be ignored.

By the time he had her in a seat with a big plate of everything the motel kitchen had to offer, she seemed content.

"This is a feast fit for a king," she commented before praying over her food.

"Amen," he said when she finished the short verse.

Lydia used her fork to dig into the eggs and bacon, but something else needed to be said. "And I pray we and my dad all make it to our house."

She stopped eating and looked at him with her sparkly green eyes. "Amen, Garth. When we meet up with your father, do you think he will be able to help me find my way home?"

Just let me find a time machine, then sure, he thought.

He pretended to consider it before replying. "My dad is pretty clever. He's traveled all over the United States. If there is one person on Earth who knows how to get you back home, I'd be willing to bet on my dad."

West Wendover, Nevada

Buck called the members of his convoy together and had them meet in front of his truck. While he waited for everyone to arrive, he checked again to make sure there was no damage from hitting Connie's VW bug yesterday. On the front, there were deep scratches and streaks of yellow paint, but nothing serious. He made his way underneath.

"Looks like you had an incident," Sparky suggested when he walked up and saw Buck lying halfway under the frame.

"You wouldn't believe me," he called back out. "Yesterday was the most stressful day of driving I've ever done."

"Me, too," Sparky responded.

Buck was about to slide out when someone walked over his stomach.

"Son of a…" he bellowed, almost banging his head as he lurched upright.

The culprit had four legs.

"Mac! Come on!"

"Sorry," Connie laughed. "I gave him too much leash."

He slid out to her smiling face and immediately realized she'd found it hilarious.

"Uh huh," he said dryly while brushing himself off.

"We're all here," Eve interjected with mirth in her voice.

Buck stood and looked over the loose collaboration they'd put together. Sparky and Eve were nearest. Monsignor and Beans stood behind them. Mac sat next to Connie with what he imagined was a shit-eating grin.

He took it all in stride because it *was* funny—after the fact.

"Cool shirt," Sparky added politely.

"Thanks, guys. The news is consumed with that place in Colorado, but we don't have to worry about it because we aren't going to touch that state."

"Out here, we only have to worry about escaped prisoners and flooding," Monsignor replied.

"They didn't catch them yet?" Eve shuddered.

"Even if they didn't," Buck replied, "the point of being in a convoy is that we don't have to be frightened by one or two bad guys. I promise you, if anyone has thoughts about attacking one of us, they are going to run for the hills when they see five of us in a line. Convoys work, people."

"And the flooding?" Beans asked.

All eyes went to Monsignor because he'd brought it up.

"Well, they said Salt Lake has been filling with water

due to heavier than normal rainstorms the past couple of days. I guess it can become a hazard to driving, because the highway planners never anticipated the lake would add water again. It has been drying up for thousands of years."

Buck was impressed.

Monsignor went on, "That's what they said on the telly. I'm just repeating what they said."

"But the highway is open?" Buck asked.

"They never said anything about the interstate," Monsignor answered.

"Good," Buck said with relief. "Then let's get the hell out of here. If things go well and none of you need anything, I don't plan on stopping until Little America, Wyoming. I'll fuel up when we get there, but we also need to go in and buy some supplies." He pointed at Connie.

Eve interrupted before they could break away and go to their trucks. "Hey, before we go... Does anyone know what that red light was last night? They weren't giving any answers on the television."

She looked squarely at Buck, and the mantle of leadership hung heavy on his shoulders. Keeping his people informed about what was happening fell to him, although he had the same amount of information access as everyone else.

"I don't know," he began, "but I can tell you almost for certain what the blue light did. It affected the sky, so storms got worse and weather became unpredictable. It brought things back from the past, like missing planes and stuff like that. It also brought people forward in time, like my friend Connie here. She is from seventeen years in our past, but I've seen even older things, like a Model-T Ford I'm pretty sure was mint. The weird light broke time, if you ask me."

He had her attention.

"It is too early to say what's going on with the red blast last night," he went on. "I'm cautiously optimistic that it rolled back the effects of the blue light. Wouldn't that be nice?"

Eve flashed a frail smile. Her questions suggested she wasn't convinced about being in his convoy and pressing forward with her delivery. He'd have to treat her delicately to keep her from taking off.

"We'll follow you, boss," Sparky chimed in.

He stood there for a moment, appreciative of his good fortune in having found them. "Guys, you don't know how much it means to have you watch my back. I feel like we can do anything with the right people guarding our six, you know?"

"We feel the same way," Eve replied. "I'm happy you know what you're doing."

He laughed because he didn't know anything, not really. There was no way to know how to act during a time-crashing emergency like this one. He fumbled through it as best he could like everyone else. The only difference between him and them was that he *knew* he had no idea what was going on. They thought that because he was in charge, he had the answers.

I guess it's always been that way.

"Nice and easy, guys. We get on the 80, cross the salt flats, go past the lake, punch through Salt Lake City, and then we're in the mountains again. Once we pass the city, we should be clear of the threats created by people. That's when we have to really pay attention."

He didn't want to frighten them any more than necessary, but he didn't want them to blindly follow him without also paying attention to their own safety.

Buck turned to Connie, who still appeared happy to be

there. He spoke to everyone, but mostly to her. "And we stick together. That's the best way to get through any crisis."

After nods and grunts of agreement, the group broke up.

"Let's go see what the highway holds for us," Connie declared as she helped Mac into the cabin.

"Charlie Mike," Buck replied automatically.

"Continue with mission," she answered, nailing the military jargon.

FOUR

***Search for Nuclear, Astrophysical, and Krono-
metric Extremes (SNAKE). Red Mesa, Colorado***

"Ladies and gentlemen, for your own safety, please
vacate all offices and conference rooms at the front of the
building." The military police officials arrived a couple of
minutes after the protester threw his rocks.

"Kicked out again," she mumbled. Her whole management of the SNAKE facility had been upended by General
Smith and his men.

"I'm going to see if we're in any danger," she said to her
team as they cleared out. "We'll reconvene in one of the
interior conference rooms in thirty minutes. Bob, you pick.
I'll bring Donald if he's up to it."

She hurried down the hallway to her old office. The
door was ajar, so she knocked.

"Enter," the general called.

"It doesn't look like you're evacuating, Obadias," she
said in a slightly accusatory tone. After watching the red
light blast out from SNAKE last night with him, she and the
general were on more familiar terms. She wasn't afraid to

express her real emotions or use his given name when it was only the two of them.

"Hiya, Doctor Sinc...uh, Faith. Please come in."

"Aren't you afraid someone will throw a rock through those?" She pointed to the bank of windows behind him. The view of the Dakota Hogback and high plains had once belonged to her.

"My men reacted with valor and took the scumbag down. We won't see any more rocks come through the glass. Trust me."

We'll see.

"Does it mean we're safe to go back to the front offices? They just told us to leave."

"No, let's keep them empty. We don't want to give anyone a target."

She tried to keep her jaw from hitting the floor. "Wouldn't a general be a pretty big freakin' target?" she exclaimed.

He stood up. "My dear doctor, I'm touched."

"You know what I meant." She backpedaled to avoid ceding the point to him. "I'm worried about my window, not you."

He laughed a bit. "I'm sure. Rock-tossers don't scare me. I saw some grim scenes back in the Gulf War. Warheads on foreheads and all that comes with it. I'm not going to cower on account of a rock. It's not my style."

"But it's *our* style?" she parried.

"You aren't in my chain of command. If one of you got hurt, it would reflect poorly on me. Whether or not you believe it, I am sworn to protect the people of this great country. Better to keep the chance of you or your people getting hurt as close to zero as possible."

She shrugged. The whole facility was hers to have meetings wherever she pleased, and she would never tell this to the general, but the windows kept the walls from feeling like they wanted to smother her. Being inside the tunnels for days on end tended to make people go a little nuts.

He peered directly at her. "Your friend was right, it turns out. There *was* a military component to this experiment, but it wasn't easy to find. I had to report my suspicions directly to the President, and he had to knock over some huts to smoke out the department responsible. I got the call this morning."

"Who are they? What do they know?"

"I don't know, and I don't know," he said cryptically. "But I did find out *where* they were. We grabbed them overnight, and should have them here in the next six to eight hours, depending."

"Depending on what?"

General Smith tapped his desk. "It depends on whether the highways are safe to travel. Planes aren't moving, and trains don't run where I need them. The FBI went in and grabbed 'em, but now we have to see if the Bureau is similarly skilled at driving."

"This is a real mess," she said sympathetically.

He gestured outside the windows. "You have no idea, and you'd probably prefer it that way, wouldn't you?"

"No, general, I would not. If there's a threat to my people, I want to know about it. I mean, let's start right here. What's going on outside? Why are you shooting protesters instead of arresting them?"

"Deterrence, plain and simple. Your SNAKE is all over the news, and every one of those news reports paints your team as the villain. They're blaming the weather on you. They're blaming missing persons on you. Hell, probably the only people on Earth who like you are the passengers on that missing Malaysian airliner." He chuckled, but not for long.

"But, General," she countered, "we're the only ones who can make things right."

The man's eyes were sympathetic. "I know it. You know it. Everyone here knows it. But we can't go on the news and explain what's really happening."

"Why not? Isn't the press the best way to get our message out?"

He pretended to hold a microphone. "Yes, hello, I'm Dr. Faith Sinclair, and I run this facility. Well, I sort of do. The experiment that screwed you all was not my fault. I didn't even know it was running, in fact, but I'm sure I'm the one who can fix it, even though I have no idea what 'it' is."

The brutal truth pierced her soul.

"It won't sound that bad," she said without convincing herself.

"I take no pleasure in saying it, Doctor, but you were never going to win against the military. Your leadership was doomed as soon as the military work order was signed. I'm glad I followed my instincts and didn't sack you when I walked in. This was too complex an operation to blame on any one person."

"Thanks, I think."

"My instincts in keeping you around paid dividends, too. If you hadn't fought me, I would have turned off all four of the CERN beams, as you call them, and we'd likely all be dead right now." He took a short pause as if to chew on his words. "None of this can be said on TV, either. They would crucify us both."

"So, what do we do?"

"All the scientists I brought in are at your disposal. Put

them to work. Make them take out the trash if you need to keep them busy, but use them however you see fit. My job is going to shift toward getting better security for your property. That man should never have crossed the parking lot and gotten within throwing distance of a window. If he'd had a gun... Well, let's just say he might have found a juicier target."

She noticeably gulped.

"But to shoot them? Is it the right thing to do?"

General Smith smiled. "The more distraction we can sow among the television-watching public, the better. By shooting the rock-chucker, we've tossed down the gauntlet for all to see. It will be the only thing they talk about on the news today. As an afterthought, they'll be theorizing what you do here. It should buy us the time we need."

"Time for what?"

"For me," the general answered, "I've got more troops coming in to keep the peace on this property. I've got to stretch what's here until relief arrives."

"And for me?"

"You need to give me the answer to the only question that matters: how do we shut this merry-go-round down once and for all?"

She smirked. "And I thought you were going to ask something hard."

Ramstein Air Base, Germany

"How the hell did I get here?" Lieutenant Phil Stanwick demanded of anyone who would listen.

He wasn't in his command post. There were no explosions. No Phalanx auto-cannons. No soldiers screaming.

A man standing at the adjacent bed turned to him.

"They said you were medevacked from Bagram. Said it was a nightmare op. I heard them talking."

Phil concentrated on the man's insignia. It was the same silver oak leaf as his own.

"Thanks, Colonel," Phil replied. Then, realizing the surroundings, he took stock of his condition. "I'm not injured?"

"Well, I'm no doctor, but it seems to me that if you have to ask the question, you must be doing pretty well."

It didn't make Phil feel any better. "My men. I should be back there."

"Battle is over. Hell, the whole war is over. You were one of the last ones who caught a plane out of there, if what I'm hearing is true." He looked around at other beds in the ward. Some had men in them, but most were empty.

"That's impossible," Phil insisted. "We had thousands of men."

"Some went to Kabul, some were stuffed on other planes." The guy spoke in a quieter voice. "Some died."

"But the whole airbase? Why?"

"Didn't you hear? The Army is going back to the States. Our mission has changed."

Phil sat up and slid to the edge of the bed. "Colonel, you have to tell me what's going on. How the fuck did I get put in this bed? I'm fine."

"Have you looked at yourself?"

That caught him by surprise. "No."

His arms were bruised and covered in dried blood, but they otherwise felt fine. He got on his feet with no problem. "I feel a little beat up, for sure, but I'm fit for duty. I was pulled out by mistake."

"Maybe," the other man answered in an odd tone. "Or maybe fate brought you here for a different reason."

He didn't care about anything but finding a mirror. One hung on the wall a couple of beds down the row. Phil passed his fellow officer and noticed the wounded soldier in the next bed. "And sorry about your man."

"Thanks."

Phil walked in his socks. The floor was cold under his feet, almost like a morgue. That gave him a moment of panic, and for a couple of footfalls he imagined the other Lieutenant Colonel as Death come to collect him, but his doubt went away when he looked in the mirror.

"Fucking hell," he said when he saw himself.

He wasn't dead, but his face was bruised and swollen, as if a honey badger had taken out a lifetime of anger on him. The sides of his neck were blanketed with dried blood, and his uniform above the waistline was bathed in it. He patted around for tender injuries but came up with nothing. The blood wasn't his.

The image in the mirror jogged his memory, and he pieced together what must have happened.

"We were surrounded by Soviet, British, and mixed Afghan units. Our command post collapsed on us when a bomb struck. I did black out for a time. Medics must have thrown me on the plane with the others. Probably thought I was just as bad as them."

"Sounds like a one-in-a-million injury."

He didn't see it that way. "I have to get back in the fight."

"I told you, the fight's over."

Bonneville Salt Flats, I-80

Buck had driven I-80 numerous times in the past. He could compute how many times per year he went up and down the highway, and from there, come to an approximation of how many times he'd been over this particular stretch. Probably hundreds, at least.

And never in all those journeys had he seen a drop of water on the Bonneville Salt Flats.

"What's wrong?" Connie asked.

Buck wasn't driving at the speed limit, which raised red flags for his navigator. However, he had every reason to drive slowly and observe the new threat.

"You see the water too?" he asked, as if testing his sanity.

"Yeah, it's the Great Salt Lake, right?"

"No," he replied. "That's still up ahead. We're seventy-five miles from it, at least. This has always been a salt flat. It is fifty miles across, and I don't know how many miles it goes away from the highway."

The two strips of interstate were separated by a shallow median, creating parallel lines from his position to a tiny dot on the horizon. Instead of the packed white salt on both sides of the highway that should have been there, everything was now covered by water.

"It's like driving on the ocean," she remarked.

"Yeah, but why?"

She looked out her window, then out his. "Maybe the system threw snow on one side of the desert and rain on this side?"

"That must be it," he said without conviction.

Buck picked up the CB. "This is Buck. Anyone ever see water like this?"

"It reminds me of the bridges over the Florida Keys," Sparky replied. "A bridge over endless water."

"Is this another one of your changes?" Eve asked when the channel was clear.

During their brief conversations previously, Buck explained his theory about the blue light. As soon as it passed, he had started to notice odd things. The red light apparently didn't make things return to normal.

"Maybe," he replied.

"I don't want it to change again," Eve remarked matter-of-factly.

"We'll be fine," Beans said dismissively. "Right, Buck?"

"Yeah," he said, agreeing with Beans to instill confidence in the others. "We've got to push on."

They drove the first half hour without incident. Ahead, a grouping of hills rose from the vast stretch of flat water like an island mirage in the morning sunshine. Before the roadway made a turn and started to follow the rise in elevation, it seemed to dip down.

Ahead, water covered both sides of the highway.

"This ain't good. Look." Buck pointed a couple of miles ahead. A handful of vehicles lined up at the transition between dry road and wet. None of them seemed willing to wade into the water to get across the final mile of road before the incline.

"I'm glad we're among the first to see this," Connie said to him. "At least we didn't have to wait behind fifty miles of a traffic jam just to see that the road is blocked. Now we can turn around and find an alternate route as fast as possible." She got busy with the atlas.

He didn't want to say anything, but his survival instinct kicked in because of how things looked ahead. As he pulled up to the end of the short line of traffic, he felt confident he could tell Connie what bothered him about it.

"If there were more cars in line, it would mean the water has been there for a long time. Hell, they might even have blocked the highway back at Wendover. The fact that very few people are here tells me this water only recently started to cross the lanes."

"It's rising?" she asked, concerned.

"Or we're sinking," he said to play devil's advocate.

"I'll find you an alternate." She flipped pages of the atlas to get to Utah, which was near the back.

"Yeah, maybe," he allowed.

He hated the idea of going backward. It would be almost an hour back to Wendover, the last town, and from there, he had no idea where the backroads would take him. Each hour of delay might not mean much over the course of his trip, but if he got home an hour too late to save Garth, he'd never forgive himself.

"Then again..."

FIVE

Lewes, Delaware

"We'll get some gas at this station up ahead, then we'll get back on the ferry and go home."

"Okay," Lydia replied, distracted.

Garth wasn't pushy, so it took him almost an hour to get his teen friend into the taxi and away from the motel. She had begged him to let her take a warm bath, which was a luxury she'd seldom experienced back home. Then she fell in love with the blow dryer because it dried her long hair in record time. According to her, she had never looked better, although she admitted they didn't have many mirrors back home, so her comparison was only partly valid.

In the taxi, he showed her the mirror behind the sun visor, and she stared at herself some more. "Your grooming tools are truly from the future," she beamed. "I'm practically a woman."

No kidding, he thought, trying not to stare.

He allowed her to indulge herself because he felt bad for her. Getting pulled out of your time and stuck in someone else's would suck, he assumed, and having no parents or family only rubbed salt into the wound. She had to wonder if anyone from her time missed her. It might be impossible to get her back to where she belonged, but he could deliver a few modern luxuries to soften the blow.

Then again, everything in the twenty-first century was a modern luxury compared to what she was used to.

The motel breakfast soaked up the rest of the time. She'd never seen such excess, even in the dumpy little breakfast nook of the motel.

"I'm pretty now. And pretty stuffed." She laughed at her joke.

Garth pulled the car next to the gas pump of the filling station and turned off the motor. "Do you want to come inside or stay here?"

He wanted her to stay in the car, because of her appearance. She was still dressed like a bumpkin from an olde tyme farm, which was fine, but it did make him nervous that she would stand out.

"I'll stay with you, Garth," she said nervously. "I do not want to be trapped inside this machine."

"You won't be—" he started to say, before relenting. As much as he wanted her to stay, he knew she'd be scared by herself. "That's great. You come with me, and we'll go check the place out. We'll be back on the road in no time."

Minutes later, he realized nowhere was going to be an easy in and out with her.

"Oh, my gosh! Look at all this candy!"

The older woman at the register smiled as if a couple of suckers had walked into her store. "Welcome! We have whatever you need."

Garth had been going into gas stations all his life, and he'd never seen a reaction like that. The joke was on the woman, however, because she had no money to spend.

"What's your favorite?" Lydia asked him as they stood in front of a massive display of handmade candies in a glass case. There were chocolates and fruit chews of all shapes and sizes. "I don't think I could ever pick. We have candy stores back home, but we only have a few choices to make. This place...is like heaven."

Garth pointed to the rack of packaged candies. Her eyes brightened when she saw the colors on the packaging. She looked closer to see the pictures.

"It's like the best party ever."

He tried to see things through her eyes, but it was tough. To him, there was nothing remarkable about the store. Sure, it was filled with candy, bags of chips, and refrigerators for energy drinks and soda, but so was every other store.

"If we ever get to a Walmart or a Costco, you would shit your—"

He swung his head to see if she'd heard him, but she was engrossed with a giant Kit Kat bar.

"You would just die if you saw them." He walked away, hoping she didn't hear him swear. He figured it would be impolite to talk like it was him and Sam. Besides, he knew a whole vocabulary of curse words she couldn't possibly understand.

"I'm sure," she said distantly.

Dad's bugout bag had four hundred dollars in cash, so he had the money to buy her whatever she wanted, but he began to feel the clock.

"How about I pick one for you, and the next time you can pick whatever you want? I'm going to get gas and get on the ferry before it leaves." He didn't tell her he had no idea when that might be, but the most likely scenario is it would leave a few minutes before they got there, especially if they screwed around for the entire morning.

"Would you? I can't see what they are besides what's on the pictures. I'll trust you."

"Do you like chocolate or sugary hard candies?"

"I've had chocolate a few times," she said in a dream-like voice. "I really liked it."

There was no need to shop around. He grabbed the biggest Hersey chocolate bar they had, then picked up a second one for himself. "You are going to love these, but first we have to take them to the counter and pay."

"I understand," she reassured him.

"These two, and twenty dollars on Pump Five, please," he said to the smiling woman at the counter.

"This is all you could find, sweetie?" she said to Lydia.

"It's what he told me to get," she answered excitedly.

"Well," the clerk huffed, "He sure is a big spender, isn't he? Two lousy bars."

Garth understood by her tone that she wasn't too happy with what he had picked out, so he tried to head off some of the ill will. "We are buying gas. That's something, right?"

"I guess," the woman replied as he handed her a twenty and a ten.

She looked at the money, then at him. "License, please."

His eyes must have rolled around in his head as he tried to figure out what she meant because it made her even more impatient.

"I need your ID, son. Big spender like you getting a whole twenty dollars in gas? And you drive a taxi? I'm going to need to see your identification before I can sell gas. You look like you might be a minor."

It was his first time buying gasoline, so he wasn't sure how to act.

"I don't have ID," he replied, before thinking they probably thought he was going to buy cigarettes or beer. Asking young people for ID was probably standard procedure. "I just need a little gas, and this candy."

The woman turned her whole attention on him. Her brown hair was tied up in a ponytail, and her blue smock covered a T-shirt with what looked like a rock band on it. The name started with Super, but the smock blocked the rest of the name. "Son, the state of Delaware requires that I don't sell gas to anyone too young to drive. If you drove your taxi into my station, you have to have the proper ID, right?"

"Right," he replied. "Let me go get it."

He had no idea what to do next.

Canberra-to-Sydney train, Australia

Destiny sat on the stopped train for over an hour while the crew took care of whatever delay or obstruction was up ahead. It wasn't unheard of for a train to strike an animal, and she assumed that was what it had been, rather than a bush fire.

She had no interest in mingling with the political jerks in the front of her carriage, so she watched through the window. There wasn't much to see in the darkness, but eventually, she caught sight of someone walking below her beside the train.

I have to know what's going on.

She got up and headed for the exit from her car. Once she got there and made like she was going to go outside, one of the group finally said something to her.

"You can't go out there. You're supposed to wait until you're told what to do."

She looked at the well-dressed woman and could tell by her tone of voice what she was trying to do, but Destiny's respect for authority was jaded from working under bad leaders for too long. That was why she preferred working with animals. She opened the door while staring at the woman, then hopped down the three steps without looking back.

A man stood near the back of the train.

"Oi! What's the holdup?" she inquired as politely as she could.

The lights inside the carriage acted as a dim lantern, allowing her to get a good look at the young man's face.

"I'm just a trainee," he whined. "They said this might happen. It's been happening."

"What are you talking about?" Destiny replied sympathetically. "What did we hit?" She figured he was upset about hitting an animal. In her profession, she'd seen lots of pictures of trains and other vehicles after big animals had splattered all over the windscreen.

He pointed behind the train. "There's track back there. See?"

There was no denying he was right. The moon was only half-full, but it gave her enough light to see the parallel metal rails heading off a kilometer into the night. "I do see tracks, yeah."

The man hustled toward the front of the train, so she followed. The engine was only pulling one carriage tonight, so they didn't have far to go. When they reached the front, the giant spotlight on the nose made it possible to see well ahead of them.

"And what about this?" he said breathlessly, as if the short jog had been too much for him. "Do you see this?"

The tracks seemed to stop about fifty meters away. She also saw that the sides of the tracks were choked with trees and vines up ahead, like they'd driven into the edge of a rainforest.

"It looks like a tree fell. You guys can cut through it, right?" Was it unreasonable to assume a train company would have ways to cut trees if the service line went through a forest?

The man seemed unnerved. "Will you walk with me?"

She was touched that he wanted her to go with him, but she couldn't figure out why.

"There's a carriage full of political-types back there. You sure you don't want one of them to help you? They probably fund this line." She'd help anyone in need, and the guy seemed innocent enough, but she was wary about walking alone far from the train with him. The politicians were an easy way out for her.

"You came down first. I didn't think anyone was going to come outside all night."

She tried to keep the moment light. "You could have come in and asked for help."

He kicked the rocks. "They said we're not supposed to bother the passengers."

She was glad it was dark, because she rolled her eyes so hard, they banked off her eyelids. The guy was not too keen.

"Fine." She exhaled heavily. "I'll go with you."

"You're a life-saver," he remarked.

He took off down the path of light thrown out by the engine's high beam. It took her a few paces to catch up to him, but the guy didn't slow down until they reached what turned out to be the end of the rail.

She saw what had him shaken.

"How the fuck did you know this was here?" she asked.

"Safety systems, miss. I stomped on the brakes as soon as the warning came on. I had to come out here to see what it was, but then I didn't know what to do."

Ahead, where the train was supposed to cross a steep

ravine about twenty meters wide, there was nothing. No tracks. No bridge. Just a rocky crag.

"The bridge is gone," she said, amazed.

"And the tracks. There should be tracks on the other side, but there's nothing over there besides trees. How is that possible?"

Destiny was aware of all the changes taking place around her. Ever since the blue light had sent her running from her campsite, nothing had been normal with the world. Faith said SNAKE had time all messed up. If Tasmanian Tigers could come back from the past, then perhaps the land itself was restoring things to how they were before humans got too involved in reshaping things. If it snuffed out a bridge or the Sydney Opera house at the same time, then so be it.

She stood in silence, absorbing what it meant to see the change taking place so close to her.

Do we have time, or don't we? she thought. *I need to get hold of Faith.*

Bonneville Salt Flats, Utah

"This may be crazy," Buck said into the CB radio, "but stick with me."

Buck turned the wheel to the left and guided his Peterbilt into the breakdown lane next to the median. The emergency shoulder gave him room to pass the two lanes of stopped traffic. There were only about ten cars lined up ahead of him, so there wasn't far to go.

Connie braced herself on the front dash like he was going to try to flip the truck over. "What are you doing, Buck? There's water ahead."

He laughed. "I know that, Connie, and thanks for noticing. I figured you'd like to go for a swim." Buck revved the motor to tease her.

"I have to admit, I'm a little worried," she replied, sounding nervous for real.

"Trust me," he said in a soothing tone. "I'd never do anything to panic you, but I'm not willing to turn around until I have no other choice." He pointed at the long stretch of water ahead. "Look at the perspective of the highway as it goes into the lake. It can't be very deep."

"But no one else is going in," she responded.

That was true, but most of them were cars. They sat lower to the ground and from their point of view, it was more difficult to see where the pavement went. As he neared, the white and yellow lines under the water were distinct and clear.

He keyed the mic. "This is Buck Rogers. I'm going in."

When his tires first hit the water, he held his breath.

The yellow line wasn't visible the whole way.

SIX

Search for Nuclear, Astrophysical, and Krono-
metric Extremes (SNAKE). Red Mesa, Colorado

Faith banged on Dr. Donald Perkins' door and prayed he opened it for her. He was her mentor, but he had also become a close friend. Recently, he wasn't getting around as well as he had been, but his mind remained sharp. He often served as a sounding board for her ideas.

"Come in!" a weak voice replied from inside.

She went in, and was shocked to see that he appeared worse than the day before. He looked like he was now over a hundred years old, with ghost-white skin and sagging cheeks. Someone had given him a wheelchair, which completed the effect.

"I'm not going to say it," she exclaimed when she got close to him. The previous day she'd lied to him and told him that he looked fine. He hadn't believed it yesterday, and he would not believe it today.

"Don't listen to anyone who tells you these are the golden years, Faith. Life was golden when I could walk without a cane. It was a treat when I wasn't in constant pain." He coughed three or four times in a row. "And it was especially golden when my heart wasn't failing."

"Why is this happening to you?" Two days ago, before the Izanagi Project had shut them down, he'd been a spry old guy who was always cracking jokes and having fun. Now he would fit right in on a brochure for hospice care.

"It's because I'm lucky," he said in an expressionless voice.

His delivery threw her off-guard, and it took a few seconds to recognize he was joking.

"I was lucky to live to see what's been going on in your collider, Faith. Thanks for sending me the data last night." He pointed to his laptop on the coffee table. "I've been looking at it between naps."

"And?" she asked when he seemed to lose his train of thought.

"Oh, right. When we lost contact with one of the Four Arrows, as Bob called them, I checked to see if there were spikes at the other three boxes. I've studied the cameras recording in those chambers, and it seemed to me there was an increase in brightness in each one. I can't swear to it since we can't as yet measure the flow, but it's a best guess."

"They are picking up the load from the missing one to maintain an overall constant in regards to the total energy," she declared.

"My thought precisely."

"What do you think would happen if we keep destroying the boxes? Would the load get shared to the last device? And if so, what would happen if we destroyed that one?"

"I've been thinking about that too, and my conclusions are, uh…inconclusive." He coughed briefly. "We cut one leg off the table, and it is still standing. A table will fall if two legs are cut off. My gut tells me dark energy will find a way to compensate, no matter how many legs we cut."

"Quantum entanglement?" she suggested.

"Perhaps," he said sadly. "If that's the case, SNAKE and CERN are linked in ways current physics cannot explain."

She didn't want to go down that path yet. "So, let's focus on what we know. When we cut the first one, it sent that red wave of energy out into the atmosphere. Do you have any data in your laptop suggesting what it did?"

He smiled weakly. "Are the strange occurrences still taking place on the outside?"

She nodded grimly. The news was consumed with SNAKE, but there was still unusual activity elsewhere. The red blast of energy went all the way around the globe, just like the blue one, and seemed to double the world's problems. More storms. More extinct animal sightings. More disappearing structures.

And was SNAKE really immune to the breakage of time that was taking place everywhere else? If so, was there any way to get her sister and best friend to SNAKE all the way from Down Under? She'd have to figure that out at some point.

"You seem lost in thought," Donald noted.

"Oh, yeah. I'm worried about my sis."

"She's in Australia, right?" he asked.

"Yes. Sydney. She has a cushy job with some wealthy foundation. Goes around capturing animals for tracking and checkups. She loves it."

"You two must have made a funny pair when you were kids. The scientist and the animal lover."

She gave him a mock scowl. "I love animals, too."

He held up his hands and chuckled. "I should have known. You are both trying to save the world, I suppose."

That tempered the pleasant moment.

"Donald, how do I do that? I think the general will wait before destroying more of the devices linking us to CERN, but his patience won't last forever. We need to get someone to Switzerland and confirm if it is still there, although I fear what will happen if it's not."

"I think you've got it exactly right. You have to find the answer to that question, Faith. If there is no one at CERN and it was destroyed, you may have no choice but to shut things down here. However, if CERN survives, you may have better luck turning off the energy from over there."

He gestured to his laptop. "We can look at formulas and solve equations all the day long, Faith, but the answer is going to require someone like your sister. They'll need to get their hands dirty *out there* and tell us what's going on at the other end of the Four, uh, *Three* Arrows."

She put her hands together. "Will you come with me to a meeting with the other staff? I'll wheel you down there."

Donald wore a faint smile. "No, I don't want them to see me like this. That's another lie about the Golden Years, Faith. You see yourself through the eyes of others. People saw me as an old coot before. Now they're going to see me as a dried-up old coot."

She hesitated.

"Faith, you can do this without me. You came in here already knowing the answers you seek. Trust your instincts, okay? You'll make the right decisions."

His fatherly praise warmed her soul with the glow normally reserved for homemade chocolate chip cookies. She took pride in being smart about how she ran SNAKE. As the general said, it wasn't her fault she didn't know about the military aspect of the experiment she'd authorized. She'd had some missteps along the way, but also some victories. Most importantly, she still had an oar in the water to guide her team.

"I know what I have to do."

Bonneville Salt Flats, Utah

Buck imagined the famous words of Han Solo as he reached the halfway point of the water crossing.

Never tell me the odds.

The water was deeper than it had been, but he was sure he still saw the striped white line below him. He tried to keep his truck in the middle of the two lanes, so there was no chance of falling off the edge into a salty quagmire.

He had to wipe his brow to keep sweat from rolling into his eyes.

Connie sat up in her seat so she could see over the end of the hood. "Buck, are you sure? I'm having trouble seeing—"

"I'm good," he interrupted quickly. "We're going to make it."

There was still half a mile, and the water was certainly getting deeper, but it wasn't yet up to his side step, so that was a good indicator.

"Will you stop for a second?" she asked in a sensible voice.

He glanced over. "You okay?"

She smiled and held up her hand to show it wasn't shaking. "Cool as a garden tool, my friend, but there is something I want to do."

Buck put his foot on the brakes to stop them.

"I'll be right back," she said.

Before he could do or say anything, she opened her door and slipped out.

"Holy shit!" he screamed. "Connie?"

Mac hopped up from his bed, ran between the two seats, and immediately jumped into Connie's chair as if he'd been patiently planning a coup. Connie's boots were on the floorboard below him.

"What the fuck is she doing, Mac?"

For a few moments he didn't see her, but then her red hair appeared ahead of him. She waded into the water and found the white line, then moved a few more yards forward so he could see all of her. Her sage-green knee-length dress was soaked a few inches at the bottom.

Buck rolled down his window and held his head outside. "Connie, what the hell?"

She turned around and waved. "I'll guide you!"

"Damn, woman! Give me some warning next time," he mumbled. He was a little perturbed at her taking matters into her own hands, but a much larger part of him had a lot of respect for her because it was a great idea. He was upset that he hadn't thought of it.

Maybe he *did* need a partner. He'd made decisions without her input, so turnabout was fair play. "I will work on that," he vowed.

After watching her walk for half a minute, he hit the gas on the big engine to catch up to her. The water soaked the fabric of her dress, but she used her hands to hike it up and keep the rest of it out of the water. For the first time he could remember, he hoped a pretty woman wouldn't expose more of her legs—because that would mean it was getting deeper.

They'd gone about a hundred yards without her raising her dress, and he couldn't help but enjoy the view. Small waves crested in the deeper water, and the flatness of the giant lake went for miles to the north and south. Connie looked tiny, and almost seemed to walk on the water ahead of him.

His mind wandered as they made it another hundred yards, but he came to the conclusion she was slowly raising her dress.

Connie stopped, turned halfway around, and pointed around his truck. Buck looked in the side mirror and realized he'd been so wrapped around the axle of Connie's leadership methods he'd forgotten about the other trucks.

He gave her a thumbs-up.

The members of the convoy had stuck with him. Monsignor's rolling firebomb was directly behind him, followed by Eve and Sparky, with Beans at the back. They were the only vehicles in the water, but they looked like a fleet of battleships to him.

Buck hopped on the CB. "Connie is leading us across. She's almost there."

Everyone acknowledged, but he got back to focusing on his friend. There wasn't far to go, but anything that could go wrong...

His fully-loaded truck would probably survive still water three feet deep, which would be about up to Connie's waist, but he wouldn't push it beyond that. That much moving water could push him off the road, no matter how much his rig weighed. The only reason he had tried this crossing was that the lake water wasn't flowing in either direction.

He looked at Mac when he noticed movement inside the cabin.

"What the..."

The Golden Retriever had his back feet on the passenger seat, and his front legs were on top of the dashboard. He'd gotten himself up so he could see over the top.

He's worried about Connie.

He was impressed by his pup's ability to look after his pack, but when he glanced ahead to the object of their shared interest, Connie was in water up to her neck.

"Shit!"

Ramstein Air Base, Germany

Phil sat on the edge of his bed, facing his peer.

"I'm Ethan Knight, by the way."

"Phil Stanwick," he replied.

"I came here to see this soldier." Ethan pointed to the man in the next bed, who appeared to be sleeping.

"Is he going to be all right?"

Ethan's face hardened. "He's dead."

"Fuck, man, I'm sorry. What unit was he in? Where's he from?"

They were the same rank, but they didn't share much else. Phil was tall and muscular, while Ethan was thin and lanky. Both cropped their hair short, but Ethan's was a lot lighter. There was no contest between the usability of their uniforms. Phil's BDU's were wasted.

"Would you believe me if I said this man was from the Korean theater of operations?"

"Did the Norks finally go and cross the DMZ? Nothing else has gone right recently. After what I saw in Afghanistan, I'd believe anything could happen out there, including World War III."

"You get some credit. The Norks did come across the line, but the DMZ didn't exist when this man fought in Korea. He's—"

"Wait!" Phil broke in. "I know. He's from the 1950s."

Ethan nodded. "How the hell did you know? He's not

wearing a uniform, and I know he hasn't spoken since he came into this ward."

"I ran into similar shit back at Bagram." He thought for a few seconds about operational security, but if Knight was talking about the 1950s like it was real, he figured he could mention his own time-bending experience. "We picked up some Soviets from the 80s, and I heard British redcoats from the 1800s showed up during my last fight with the Taliban. Something is majorly fucked up out there."

"You saw them? I mean, up close and personal?" Ethan looked at the corpse again. "I saw this man's uniform as he crawled out of a World War II-era C-47 that crashed in Bavaria, but I didn't get to talk to him. None of the men in that plane survived."

"It's just like the Malaysia flight coming back," he replied. "People lost in the past are showing up in the present. I bet there are a lot of civilians from the past we don't even know about."

He thought about his mother. She had disappeared on a Nevada highway when he was a teenager. If time was wrapping itself in knots, maybe she would find a way to come through like all these others.

Ethan's jaw clenched before he answered. "It's only gotten worse since the red wave went around the world yesterday. That's the big reason CENTCOM ordered a complete withdrawal of forces. If this keeps up, we'll be fighting Nazis and the Kaiser's shock troops again."

"You think it's that serious? Shouldn't we fortify eastern France or Germany itself? Why send everyone home? I can't imagine that could be done quickly, and it has to be prohibitively expensive. We've spent twenty years building up our footprint in-theater. You can't undo that in a day."

Ethan considered the question. "Part of it is airlift

capacity. Planes are mostly grounded, except for military transports or those we commandeer, and they are flying by paper navigation charts. If things get worse and we can't fly at all, the bosses want all of our troops on friendly soil. As for the rest, I can't tell you, but I am interested to learn more about what you saw at Bagram. If you have experience operating with units from the past, maybe I have a job suited for you here."

His first thought was for his men.

"I can't. Really—"

Ethan cut in, "The active battalions of the 75th Ranger Regiment are scrambling back to the States as we speak. The wounded went first. The rest dumped their gear and got the hell out of there. I promise you won't be missing anything. Work with me now, and I'll get you back to the States to meet up when they get there."

He still didn't like the idea of being away from his command, but it could take a week to find and then catch up with them. The Air Force probably had them over Australia by now, if he knew their skills. It couldn't hurt to see what the guy wanted, especially if it got him better-informed for when he re-joined the battalion.

"I guess I'm free, for now."

The other man smiled. "Great! I think you've just volunteered for the same mission as me. Have you ever been to Switzerland?"

SEVEN

Lewes, Delaware

Garth headed for the swinging door of the convenience mart but realized he still carried the candy bars, so he set them on a shelf full of potato chips. "Lydia, could you come here for a second?"

The pioneer girl was infatuated with a display of hair barrettes, but she begrudgingly acknowledged him once she heard her name. "We aren't staying? I could shop in here all day. And the food! You have so much more to eat than hardtack."

It might have been fun to stand around and show her all the junk they sold at gas stations, and if she wanted real food, he knew exactly what fast food place he'd take her, but all that would have to wait for another time.

"Right now, just come with me, please."

She dutifully hung the barrettes on their proper hooks, then strode over to him at the front door. Her smile was impressive until she saw that his hands were empty.

"Aw..." She pouted. "You said we could get chocolate."

"We will," he replied, pulling her through the door. "But not here. We have to get back in the taxi."

His shirt clung to his chest as he walked across the hot asphalt. They got into the car, and he had a moment to wonder how much hotter Lydia must be in her dress and bonnet, but he didn't start it up when she slid inside. Instead, he watched the storefront.

"What are—" she began before he shushed her.

His heart beat like a racehorse sprinting for the finish line, and, at first, he didn't know why. However, the longer he sat there and waited to see if the woman would come out looking for his ID, the more he understood what had him worried. It wasn't just the clerk.

"Anyone could take this away from us, Lydia. They could decide I don't deserve it because I don't have a license." He paused for a moment. "And I guess it *isn't* really mine."

That was what scared him. Someone owned the car, and they might be out there looking for it. All it would take was one bad incident, and someone might report him to the police.

If Sam was here, we'd have already been caught. "Under the radar" wasn't in his vocabulary.

"We have to find another station," he reasoned.

"As long as we can get that chocolate, I'll be a happy girl."

"You can get that anywhere," he reassured her. "We can't risk losing this vehicle. Like you said, it would be impossible to get home if we had to walk."

"How far away do you live? I walked from Missouri to Wyoming before you found me."

"Damn!" he blurted. "That's amazing."

She seemed surprised. "Don't you ever walk? You look a little soft, but you still appear strong."

He tried not to take offense. While he could run and jump with the best of them, there was no way he could walk as far as she did. Garth had a new appreciation for the wiry girl.

"Thanks. I'd rather not find out how far I can walk. Not while we have a perfectly good car."

"I like riding in here, too. Let's keep it!"

Garth had every intention of keeping the taxi, at least until he got home, but he was wary at the next two gas stations he tried. Lydia stayed in the car while he went inside to pay, and he was ready to run back to her at the first sign of trouble. However, both clerks wanted him to show identification before they'd sell him gas.

When he got back in the car after the third refusal, he started to doubt their prospects. "It must be a Delaware thing. Dad never told me I'd need identification to buy gas, although I never bought the gas, even when I was with him."

Briefly, he thought about calling his dad and asking him what he should do. He'd no doubt have an answer, but Garth wanted to figure this out on his own.

"Sometimes the wagon would break, and Pa would have to ride to town and bring a part back to us. Is there any way you could do that with what you need for this tacks-see?"

He thought about it for a second. "There is no way to carry gas except in a container. I don't know if they'll ask for an ID when I buy one of those. I also don't know where to get one."

"Could you borrow the gas, like you did for this?" She patted the dashboard.

"You mean, steal it?" He chuckled, wondering if she

saw him as a liar and thief. By all appearances, she would be right. However, he tried to head off the accusation anyway. "Did you steal where you came from?"

She lost some of her friendliness. "Well, I don't like to talk about it, but there was that one winter where there was nothing to eat. I snuck into a farmer's field and ate some dry corn husks, but Pa said it was okay with the Lord because I might have died from starvation."

"No! I'm sorry. I wasn't asking you to 'fess up. I was only wondering...oh, forget it. It doesn't matter. This taxi was already stolen when I got it. I'll tell you the story sometime when we are safe. I have no intention of stealing. I have money, but I have to find someone who will take it."

Garth began to hash through a plan. He drove them around the small town of Lewes, with its three gas stations, but soon came to the conclusion it was too small to have larger stores. Rather than admit he didn't know what to do, he pulled into a small parking lot, turned off the car, and pretended to plan his next move.

He fiddled with his phone, hoping to get internet. That would allow him to search for a store close to his location. He tried to get his mapping app to come up, and it seemed like it was going to open a few different times, but then it paused for several minutes before saying the link failed. Minutes went by, then a half-hour.

After the frustration of technology failures, he decided a text to his dad couldn't hurt. It wasn't a surrender; it was using the resources at his command. If Dad had access to the internet, he could look up an address and tell him where to go.

When he punched in his message and hit Send, he got a "network is down" warning.

Eventually, Lydia got tired of waiting.

"Are we lost?" she said, cutting to the quick.

"Sort of," he admitted. "I don't have enough gas to drive around and look for the right store. It has to be somewhere that sells gas cans. I, uh, have no idea where to find a place that does."

"Well," she replied with enthusiasm for the challenge, "when Pa and I went into town, we always looked for the biggest, cleanest road. That was always the one that had the important buildings on it."

He looked around. "There's only one long road in this town. It goes from the ferry landing to who-knows-where in that direction." Garth pointed into the woods beyond the small town. "I've been thinking about driving out there to look around since I parked here, but what if we run out of gas before we get anywhere?"

She giggled. "We walk, silly. What else would you do?"

Call AAA?

She'd dispelled his indecision. They wouldn't get anywhere if they didn't take a few risks, and they couldn't be that far from the next town.

"Buckle up," he advised. "We're rolling."

Bonneville Salt Flats, Utah

"Connie!" Buck screamed out his open window.

He reacted on adrenaline-fueled instinct. He smashed the emergency brake down, flew out his door, and hopped down into the water.

"Connie!" he shouted again.

She was ahead, flailing in the churning water.

Buck did knee kicks to speed himself through the thigh-high water, and he arrived at the commotion expecting to dive in, but Connie's head was already in the clear. The look on her face was pure embarrassment.

He was breathless. "Are you okay?"

"Buck, I'm sorry. I stepped into a pothole and fell, then I guess I freaked out."

"But you are good?" In the few moments he'd lost sight of her, he had experienced a range of emotions, many of which caught him in the feels. "I thought I'd lost you."

She stood up, unsteady at first, and he took her hand. A tan shape paddled up to her at the same instant.

"Mac! Oh, thank you." She reached down and hugged the swimming Golden. "But I'm fine. Your daddy mistook me for a drowning woman."

He gave Mac a wet pat on the head. Garth couldn't have asked for a better dog.

"I should probably mention I can't swim," she continued. "In fact, you probably already figured out I'm afraid of water."

He laughed it off, happy to be having a conversation at all. He didn't think it was possible for her to drown in such shallow water, but he'd heard of people drowning in bathtubs, so he didn't take it for granted.

"Let's get you and Mac back to the truck. You've gotten us far enough."

"No!" she declared. "Let me finish the mission."

Mac still trod water, so he wanted to make sure he was good. "Mac, go back to the truck. Go!" He pointed to his idling big rig.

The pup looked at him, then at Connie, perhaps hoping one of them would pick him up, but then he dog-paddled his way back to the truck.

She held one of his hands with both of hers. "Buck, go back with him. I need to get this done."

His attitude softened. "You don't have to. I'm sure I can drive in a straight line to the dry road ahead." He gestured with an open hand to show how close they were to the other side of the new lake. "And you don't have to prove anything to me. You've got a spot on the team."

She beamed. "Thanks, really, but after all I've been through, I need to feel useful. I want to prove to myself that I can beat a little water."

It was the perfect moment to lean in and kiss her, but someone in his convoy chose that moment to blow their air horn. The obnoxious noise pulled him kicking and screaming back to reality.

"I'd better get behind the wheel. I have to dry Mac off. He's probably going to make a mess of your seat."

Connie laughed. "He's already in the window."

They both looked back. His happy face smiled at them from Connie's side, and his tail wagged furiously in the background. They couldn't see it moving, but his head tilted from one side to the other as it did when his tail went full throttle.

"Damn, he's fast," he said under his breath.

"Okay, get out of here," she advised. "The natives are restless." She let go of his hand and turned toward the near shore.

"And all I have to do is watch out for this pothole." She felt around with her foot, then took a big step over it.

Buck followed his guide for the next ten minutes as he slowly drove through the last section of water. It did get a little deeper, but it never went above Connie's waist, which was his cutoff. When she got about twenty yards from the dry road ahead, she began to walk out of the water like she was going up a boat ramp.

Several minutes later, the convoy was across the water

obstacle and parked in a line. All five of them, plus a drying Connie and Mac, held a celebratory meeting by the water's edge.

"No one was ballsy enough to follow us," Sparky announced.

"I think the water is rising," Connie added. She wrapped herself in one of Buck's blue showering towels, her red hair hanging limply on her head.

Beans motioned to Connie. "We didn't know you fell in or I wouldn't have sat on the horn. I was screwing around. Didn't mean nothing by it."

"It's no problem. I panicked. There's no way around it. Next time I'll know before I write myself off as drowned. Besides, he would have rescued me. That seems to be his role in my life." She pointed to Buck.

"This guy helped," he said, deferring to Mac. He was off the leash and running around in the median, probably looking for rabbits.

"I filmed the whole thing, Buck," Eve said matter-of-factly. "I'm going to use this for my company's recruiting videos. This is the kind of shit drivers do when they work for us. In fact, if you want to join a new employer..."

"I've already got a boss, and neither he nor the owner of my cargo would be happy to know what I just did." He laughed. "But really, you guys did the hard part. You followed me in, and you," he directed everyone to Connie, "made sure it was successful. That's what I call a team effort."

Monsignor snickered. "Buck, I was watching for your trailer to go under. Then I'd know we were beat. I'm glad it worked out, but there was a time I could have sworn my trailer started to float. Some nice Mormon family might have had a nice Christmas present wash ashore. Twenty-eight pallets of potato chips!"

A few of the others argued back and forth about how far a trailer would float, but Buck's mind wasn't following them. He hadn't considered the weight differentials in the other trailers. His was filled to the brim with cans of chili. Some of the other trucks were probably a lot lighter. He was lucky that hadn't bitten him in the ass. He reminded himself to take everyone's situation into account.

Cars and trucks had gathered on his side of the lake and would soon turn around and create traffic for his convoy. He wanted to get out of there.

"Okay, folks, we got over one hurdle, but we still have thousands of miles to go. I propose we head out and find the next problem."

"May this be the last," Eve suggested.

"Amen," Connie replied.

Buck took one quick glance back at the lake. Cars and trucks stacked up now at the far edge of the water, unwilling or unable to follow him and his friends. Some vehicles crossed the median and drove away. If his people had been a little later, they might have been stuck in the traffic over there instead of pushing forward.

Garth, don't do stupid shit like your old man.

They got on the road for Salt Lake City, and it wasn't long before they saw a giant plume of smoke rising from one section of the city.

"Well, we had our five minutes of peace," he joked.

EIGHT

***Search for Nuclear, Astrophysical, and Krono-
metric Extremes (SNAKE). Red Mesa, Colorado***

Faith felt like a pinball for all the running she did
between the general and her team, with side stops to places
like Donald's room. However, when she went back to see
General Smith again, he wasn't in his office. There was no
one there.

"Maybe I could take back my desk," she mused.

She went over to the window and immediately saw the
man's uniform as he directed his troops on the parking lot
like a traffic cop. For a short time, she deliberated whether
to go down there. Was it important enough to risk herself on
the outside, or should she wait for him to come back in?

"Screw it," she declared.

Faith went downstairs and onto the patio, but she ran
into a pair of uniformed guards.

"Miss, we can't let you pass through here," one of the
men said in a stern voice.

"We're prisoners?" She knew the general was adamant
that her team be protected, but she somehow assumed she

had the run of the place and if she wanted to sneak out, she could. But she'd clearly been mistaken.

I could take the tram and escape through one of the fire exits.

"General's orders," he replied as if it solved the impasse.

"General Smith!" she shouted. He was on the lot, but not that far away.

She waved when he turned around.

"I need a moment!" Faith waved him over.

She looked at the guard. "We'll see what happens, won't we?"

The general talked to a few more soldiers, and for a few seconds she thought she was going to have to eat her gloating words, but eventually, General Smith headed her way.

When he got near, he shushed her before she said a word.

Together, they went into the foyer of SNAKE. When they were inside, and the glass doors were closed, he spoke with his hand partway over his mouth. "The media is using directional mics to record everything I say. I need to be careful."

"Why were you out there in the first place?" she asked.

"Shorthanded," he said dryly. "Every man and woman has a job to do in holding the mob back until more troops arrive." He took a step closer. "If they knew how few guards were in this place, the crowd would probably swarm us. Some of them are outright pissed at your facility."

"Well, it's all the news talks about. Is it any wonder the public is up in our grille?"

"No, and this is what I told you would happen. We're becoming a bigger target every hour. I might have to put us on lockdown until further notice, Faith. You understand why?"

She fought the urge to complain because he was her only shield against the outside. It scared her to the core to think there were people who wanted to destroy SNAKE simply to prove a point. There was only one person who was more worried about it than her.

"I do, General, and thank you."

"I have to get back out there," he replied.

"Wait. There is one more thing—the reason I came out here instead of waiting. General, you have to send someone to CERN. My team believes that is the only way we're ever going to have a solid foundation for what our team needs to do at SNAKE. I know I said I was going to call someone there, and I did try, but no one picked up the phone."

"It sounds like everyone is dead," he said without emotion.

"Possibly, but my team seems united in their stance that CERN is still broadcasting the energy going into those devices. General, you have to send someone to Geneva, so we know one hundred percent whether their facility is still there. If it is, we need to determine if they are still feeding power through the supercollider's ring."

"You would have made a good general," he replied, "because you and I think a lot alike. The minute you mentioned those blue lights were linked to CERN, I sent a request to the European command asking them to go look at the lab in Switzerland. They should know more by the end of today."

"Are they flying? Can't you get an Air Force jet to go over the lab? Verify if it is damaged? We really need to know as soon as humanly possible."

The general ran out of patience as she watched.

"Faith, that is outside my area of operations, so it would have taken time to bounce planes between the major commands. It was a lot easier to send a small recon team in a wheeled truck. We should have eyes on the ground in about six hours."

"Six hours," she repeated with disappointment.

"It's the best I can do. Most of our existing air assets have been diverted to bringing our boys and girls back home. Bases are being evacuated around the world."

"Really? I mean, I know it's serious, but I guess I have to ask. Why now?"

"I can't say. The President of the United States gave the order. I presume my Commander-in-Chief has better intel than I do. At best, I would expect it to take weeks to bring them all home, but the process is underway. The resulting chaos has made it hard to assign units to side missions like this gamble in Geneva."

"It isn't a gamble," she complained. "Knowing what happened to CERN is crucial to our plan to fix things. Sir, we have to know."

He turned at a loud noise out on the parking lot.

"Car backfire," he said dryly.

"How do you know it wasn't a gunshot?"

"Lots of experience." He started to leave but turned to her again. "Faith, my men will get to CERN and report back. I've managed to track down a small unit of specialist Army boys who can get this done. I've made it clear how important this is to me, and to the President. They're on it."

She looked down at her watch and spoke gravely. "I guess we'll know the fate of the world in six hours."

He nodded seriously, then walked away.

. . .

I-80, Salt Lake City, Utah

Riding the ribbon of interstate through Salt Lake City was nerve-wracking for Buck. He kept the speed at seventy-five, but warily eyed the southern region of the sprawl. Several square blocks of suburban homes burned in one part of the city, and the giant plume of smoke rose to the sky and blotted out the morning sun.

"Could you turn the air conditioner down? I'm freezing," Connie asked.

It took Buck a moment to comprehend that she was talking to him. She'd wrapped herself in his shower towel, but it was now drenched.

"Oh. Right. You're soaked. My rig has dual climate zones. You can dial back the air conditioner over there if you'd like." Buck pointed to the controls for it.

His jeans and shoes were soaked, too, but he relished the chill. Summer had come back with a vengeance after the snowstorm the previous day. The truck's outside temperature indicator was stuck at 103 degrees Fahrenheit.

"Why didn't you say so?" she snarked.

He was glad to avoid watching the smoky scene outside, and he kept the speed steady with the other fast-moving traffic. It was as if everyone wanted to get through and out of the city.

I'm glad I still have her.

While she fiddled with the controls, he thought back to the moment he had almost kissed her. That brought up thoughts about what her life was like back in 2003.

"So," he drawled, "I have to ask..."

"Yeah?" she replied when he took a bit too long to say it.

"Are you seeing anyone?"

She laughed a little. "You mean in my time? No."

"You have a son. Are you married?"

Connie laughed some more. "Getting it all out on the table, are you?"

"No. Well, sorry. I'm not good at this stuff. If you disappear and go back to your own time, I don't want to complicate things. I also don't want to get my hopes up."

She turned from him and spent some time looking out her window. Salt Lake City was a broad, flat expanse of buildings and houses with a giant mountain range behind it. He had done a few drop-and-hooks there over the years, and the wide streets and friendly people always made him want to go back.

After a long pause, she finally replied. "My husband and I split a long time ago. Right after Philip was born. He was in the service—the Navy—and was out on deployments more often than he was home. I was able to handle it, but he confessed to some infidelities in some of his ports of call. We tried counseling for the sake of our son, but one time he went out on his tour and never came back. I got the papers in the mail."

"Ouch. What a fuckstick!"

She glanced at him. At first, he thought he'd put his foot in his mouth, but then she smirked. "Yeah. That's right. He *was* a big fuckstick."

"Sorry, I can't help the cussing. I've tried to tone it down, especially around my son, but after fifteen years, it is still a work in progress."

"Don't fancy it up on my account. If you keep driving like you have, you can use the F-word in every sentence as far as I'm concerned."

They laughed, despite the scene outside.

"I'll try not to. I want to be a better man—for my son, of course."

Buck drove with one hand on the wheel and the other

on his window sill like he was having the best day of his life. It would have cost her nothing to lie and say she had a man-friend back home, but she hadn't. He'd put himself out there, and she hadn't shot him down.

Buck picked up the CB microphone a short time later. "Goodbye, Salt Lake City. Hello, Wyoming." They still had seventy-five miles to the border, but they were as good as there.

The rising plume of ash haunted his side mirror almost the whole way.

Ramstein Air Base, Germany

"Gentlemen, that's all I have for you. We hop in an APC in fifteen, and we'll be on our way." Lieutenant Colonel Ethan Knight's briefing was about as thorough as he could make it, given that there was almost no intel on what to expect at the destination.

The eight enlisted men headed for the depot, but Phil stayed behind.

Ethan spoke quietly. "They are probably wondering what the hell is going on, working for two colonels on such a small team. These are strange times, huh?"

"Can't argue with that," he replied.

"These men are professionals, but they don't have much experience. You came from a hot zone, so I'm glad we ran into each other when we did."

They were both lieutenant colonels, but Ethan seniority based on time in grade. Phil was fine with it, though, since he was tagging along on the other officer's op.

"It's been a while since I've been on such a small team," Phil joked, "but I can't believe we're it. There has to be something more effective than two colonels and an ad-hoc squad that could go snoop around?"

Ethan shook his head vigorously. "I told you, everyone is jumping on whatever floats, drives, or flies to get to America. Most of the guys in Germany are heading north to the ports. I had to scrounge to find what we've got, including pulling a couple of men out of hospital beds."

"Is that going to be a problem?" he asked. There would be nothing worse than taking injured men into battle, himself excluded. His face still hurt, and it was bruised, but the pain was manageable even without pain killers. Nothing would interfere with his ability to fight.

"This is a simple recon mission. We're going to see some scientists, or, if they aren't home, see their bunker. If this were peacetime, I could have driven my car down there by myself, but my orders were to head out in at least squad strength. If we get into trouble, the 173d Airborne Brigade Combat Team is pulling duty as a quick reaction force for all of southern Europe. They're on standby in Caserma Ederle Army Base in Italy.

"Shit, how far is that?"

"Far," he deadpanned. "So let's not get into trouble."

"I didn't want to ask this in the meeting, but why not have the Swiss Army go in and poke around for us?"

"I asked that same question of the colonel," Ethan remarked. "You know what he said?"

He'd been in plenty of briefings where no one up the chain wanted to divulge important pieces of information for the men at the tip of the spear. He tried to be diligent about not doing that to his own men whenever possible, but there were times he had to keep them in the dark. However, he could tell by Ethan's tone what he was going to say.

"Go fuck yourself?"

Ethan laughed. "Pretty much. All he would say is the order came from a four-star in the States who told him this is an American problem, and it requires an American solution."

"Well, as long as I don't see ghost units from the past like back in the 'Stan, I imagine this will be a lookie-loo operation. This particle accelerator campus sounds like a university, not a hardened military site."

"Don't let the pretty co-eds mess with your head. We've got to get eyes on the hardware inside and report what we find up the chain. On paper, it is nothing."

"But no plan survives contact..."

Ethan frowned. "We're traveling light, but be sure to load up on rifle mags. We're not taking any chances. I heard fifth-hand that a couple of British Red Devils para-dropped into Arnhem, Netherlands last night. There really might *be* World War II crap showing up. Hell, Hitler himself might walk out of CERN, and then we'll have our hands full with SS stormtroopers and other douchebags."

Phil chuckled until he realized Ethan was serious.

"Well, am I cleared to shoot Hitler if he's there?"

That broke Ethan's serious demeanor. "Always. If you see that Nazi prick, you shoot him in the face."

They laughed together, but under the surface, Phil's nerves were at a boil. Ethan wasn't just planning for battle, he expected it.

NINE

Little America, Wyoming

"I feel like we've found a patch of grass on the Moon," Connie said as they pulled into the Little America truck stop. The tree-lined facility was an oasis on the endless flat scrub-brush plains of this part of Wyoming, and contained a small hotel, a restaurant, and two gas stations.

Buck pulled up to a diesel pump in the tractor-trailer section of the parking lot.

"Everyone stops here," he said. "Mostly because it is the only thing for thirty miles in either direction, but also because it's a nice place. Sometimes a clean can and shower are all it takes to get a driver to stop."

"Yuck," she replied before thinking about it. "I bet you've seen some nasty bathrooms on your trips."

"You have no idea. There was this one overflow situation in Mitchell, South Dakota that I—"

She held up her hand. "Why would you think I would want to hear that story? I don't want to know the details!"

They laughed as he pulled out his gas card.

"You want to take Mac for a walk while I gas up? Then

we'll go into the shop and see what they have for clothes. I'm telling you, John Deere green might be your color." He had razzed her the previous night about buying her clothes from the tractor company, mainly because their trademark green color was something she would know.

"I'll walk your little sweetheart." She brushed against Big Mac's flank. "Then I'll buy what I need without *your* suggestions."

"Hmm," he said nonchalantly. "I doubt your credit cards will be any good in my time. Are you sure you have enough cash? If not, I'm going to buy what I want for you."

She gritted her teeth and crinkled her nose like she didn't want to reply.

"Do you think a twenty will buy a shirt and pants? It's all the cash I have."

As he climbed out of the cab, he paused and glanced back like he was going to answer her, but then he shut the door and hopped to the pavement. He decided to have a little fun with her and make her sweat.

Monsignor's shiny tanker was parked at the adjacent pump. The youthful trucker was already out of his rig and had come over to talk. "This is crazy, isn't it?"

Buck looked around. The place was pretty busy, but not the worst he'd seen. "I guess. We'll have no problem getting a table for lunch."

Monsignor shook his head. "Not here. Haven't you been listening to the radio? Everyone is talking about how SNAKE is going to end the world!"

The TV and radio had been talking about SNAKE all morning. It had become repetitive to the point of agony, so he and Connie had agreed they needed to tune out for a while. They'd been listening to one of his books on tape for the last hour.

"What are you talking about? The news guys said the place worked with subatomic whatchyamajiggers, not end-the-world bombs and shit. They said that about a hundred times." When he was at home, he tuned into science shows to provide Garth with an example of programs he should be watching. Buck didn't always care for them, but he figured they would make Garth smarter and help get him into a good college.

"Everything has changed in the last couple of hours. The security guards at the site shot some people dead, then kept protesters from getting closer. They think terrorists have taken over inside."

Buck was always skeptical of the news. "Terrorists have taken over a super collider? How are they going to work it?" He sighed. "It sounds like something is going down, but I don't think for a second it could threaten the world."

The other driver looked more shaken than usual.

"Don't leave without me," Monsignor fretted as he trotted away. He tripped on the curb of the gas island but got right back up and kept talking over his shoulder. "I'm going to gas up and listen some more to the news to see if there's anything new."

Buck got the pump started and decided to call Garth. He figured his son was well on his way home by now.

The phone rang a couple of times, but then faded and disappeared like police sirens driving into the distance. He dialed again, but only heard a series of clicks. It was about what he expected, even when he had a line of sight to one of the cellular towers.

He turned and faced the giant tower at the corner of the big parking lot, which stood against the flat horizon like a lone metal tree. Even as close as it was, he couldn't talk to his son.

"Dammit to hell." He punched the buttons to text Garth, hoping he'd have better luck.

He sent a short text as a trial. **Hello G. All OK?**

Almost immediately, a message popped up. **Dad. Gas stations won't let me buy gas. Getting gas another way. More soon.**

"What the hell?" he said to himself.

What are you doing? he texted. Buck envisioned Garth trying to siphon fuel with a length of tubing because it was the only other method he could think of.

He watched his phone while the pump chugged diesel into his tank, but it finally clicked off because he'd reached maximum capacity.

"Fuck," he fumed. Whatever Garth was doing, he wasn't replying. Or he couldn't. Or the cell tower wouldn't connect. Or...

Buck calmed himself by taking a long, deep breath. The fumes of the pumps reminded him of innumerable other fill-ups in his career. Somewhere far to the east, his boy was trying to get gas for his own vehicle.

Good luck, son. I'm not sure I'd know what to do either. His thoughts returned to two days prior when the motel owner claimed he had counterfeit bills and Buck couldn't use his credit card. *I don't know either.*

Georgetown, Delaware

Garth had to pull over and park twice during his quest for gas. Each time he sat and debated going left, right, or forward. Each time he asked Lydia which road appeared larger and better traveled than the others. He was sold on the idea that the biggest road would take him to the largest town, and that was where he was going to find somewhere large enough to sell gas cans.

It seemed like hours before he found a place in Georgetown, Delaware. The standalone building was off by itself, although some houses were visible behind the store through some trees.

"The Dollar Palace will have what we need," he said with certainty as he parked the car on the little lot. "It has everything."

"Will they have chocolate?" she brightened.

"Definitely."

There were five or six other cars on the lot, suggesting it was open and everything was normal. He figured they would be okay going in together.

He patted the gun in his front pocket to remind himself it was there. He also double-checked his money supply, which he kept in the tiny front pocket of his jeans that wasn't used for anything else. It was a trick he had learned from Sam to keep pickpockets from robbing him on the subways.

The nyuck-nyuck ringtone announced that his dad had sent a message.

"What was that?" she asked.

"My dad sent me a text." He pulled the phone out.

Hello G. All OK?

Garth didn't want to get into a long discussion, so he shot a reply. 'Dad. Gas stations won't let me buy gas. Getting gas another way. More soon.'

"Let's go inside," he said to her.

She followed him through the automatic sliding doors. She oohed and aahed as she walked between them. "Wow. This is amazing!"

He gently tugged at her elbow to get her through. "They'll keep opening and closing if you stand there."

"What? How do they know?" She looked over her shoulder as he pulled her inside.

The elderly woman pulling clerk duties didn't even look at them. She appeared to stare at the floor or was daydreaming about being somewhere else.

"Oh my gosh! Look at this stuff! These food tins have cute kittens on the cans." She hesitated, then spoke with disgust. "Do you eat cats?"

He laughed. "No! Gross! Those are cans of cat food. They are *for* cats to eat."

She looked at it for a second, then back to him. "You have enough wealth to give your feral cats their own food?"

He shrugged. "It doesn't mean you're wealthy. Everyone feeds their cats this way. I assume so, anyway, since Dad doesn't let me have cats or other pets."

Her distractions only got worse from there. Lydia went into each aisle, and immediately found things that made her gush with enthusiasm at her good luck to see such wonders.

"If we ever get back, I'm going to take you to a shopping mall. They have a hundred stores with crap on the shelves like this. You'll never want to leave."

She heard him, but barely acknowledged what he'd said because she'd found a display of cheap cooking utensils.

"This one is plastic? How can it survive being in the fire?"

He chuckled. "You have a lot to learn. We don't cook on open fires anymore."

Garth admired how her emerald eyes seemed to get twice as big with shock. "Oh, I have *got* to see you cook, Garth. Will you show me?"

There was no one else in their row, so he stepped up

next to her and spoke softly. "I don't know how to cook, except using the microwave."

"What is a—" she began to say before he cut her off.

"Wait a sec. What's going on back there?" He saw two men walk by at the end of the aisle, each pushing a full shopping cart. A second later, three more men walked by pushing another pair of carts.

If he wasn't already on alert, he might not have thought anything of it, but the fronts of the aisles were all empty. Someone had to drive those cars parked outside, and there was no way all of them would naturally go to the back of the store.

"Hey, I see the gas cans," he added quietly. They were most of the way down the aisle, but the red plastic containers were hard to miss.

"Stick with me," he advised. His heart rate, as if it was warming up for a hasty retreat. The gun in his pocket threatened to drop his pants right off his hips because it suddenly felt like it weighed a hundred pounds.

A pair of shifty-looking women trundled carts by the end of his aisle, and one of them looked at him for a second before continuing on.

"We have to hurry," he told Lydia.

"Why? I have to see all these sundries. I'm sure I need something here."

"I'm sure you do too, but right now this is all we need." He grabbed one of the medium-sized fuel containers, figuring it was about the right size to carry around. As soon as he had it in his hand, he shoved Lydia back up the aisle.

"Go!" he ordered.

"But..." she complained.

"No." He shoved her toward the exit. "Go!"

He felt bad for pushing her, but there was no reason to

stick around a second longer. When he reached the end of the aisle, he was relieved to see the old woman, but he realized that was premature.

Someone shouted in the back of the store, but he couldn't understand what they said.

"Ma'am, we want to buy this." He plopped a ten on the counter.

The old woman seemed to come to life, but not at top speed.

"Will this be all? Did you find everything all right?" They were the two things she was probably trained to say, because every checkout person in history had asked him the same two questions.

"We didn't find chocolate," Lydia replied dutifully.

He couldn't take the delay. "You know what? Keep the change."

He grabbed the can and made for the entrance, but stopped before leaving. "Ma'am, they are stealing from your store back there. I'm sure of it."

"Oh, dear," she replied in a voice as slow as molasses.

"I love your store," Lydia added.

"Come on," he said again. This time he made sure she didn't dawdle at the magic door.

"What is the hurry?" she said, finally showing her anger. "I want to explore everything this future world has to offer."

Garth jogged to the taxi, praying she kept up. He was inside and had the car started before she got inside.

"Close the door!" he barked.

"Oh, my. Garth, I don't know—"

As soon as the door was shut, he put the car in reverse. Two seconds later, he shifted into drive and smashed the gas again.

When they drove to the far side of the store, Garth saw the looters. A line of twenty people pushed shopping carts of stuff out the back door to a waiting box truck. Empty carts went back into the store. A couple of guys with shotguns stood near the rear dock, watching him.

"Drive safely," he said to himself. This was no time to slip off the road.

Garth fully expected the rear window to explode like they always do in the movies, but as he got onto the two-lane road, no one shot at him.

He breathed wildly in and out as the panic abated.

Lydia seemed to zone out for a short time, but then she looked at him. "You are sweating, Garth. Were you really that scared? Were we truly in danger?"

His slippery palms slid along the steering wheel as he got the taxi up to speed.

"I'm sorry for being like that, Lydia. I didn't have time to explain. Those were thieves. The worker in the front was too lazy or too old to know what those people were doing in the back of her store. If we had gotten caught, they might have hurt us for seeing them. They also might have taken this cab, especially if they knew we had guns."

She chewed her lip as she worked through it all. Garth thought she looked cute in the pose.

"So you protected me?" She gasped.

"Of course. That's what guys do. We protect."

His dad taught him to look out for the weak and stand up to the bullies. Lydia wasn't exactly weak, but she had the street smarts of a newborn infant in 2020. It fell to him to watch over her.

She reached over and gently touched his wrist while he held the wheel. "Then I should say thanks. I did not see the threat, and I was more enchanted than I can say about the products you have in this world. Next time, I'll listen to you."

He leaned back in his seat, proud to have won her over by doing what came naturally, but all his pride went out the broken window when the engine sputtered once before sounding normal again.

"Oh, shit, we're finally running out of gas."

TEN

Canberra-to-Sydney Train, Australia

After surveying the missing bridge, Destiny and the engineer went back inside the carriage.

"Hi, everyone. Sorry for the delay. My name is Becker. I'm afraid the bridge is out. We have to hike across the ravine."

Destiny noted Becker didn't tell them he was an engineer trainee.

The politicians looked put out, and they huddled together rather than get up and move for the exits.

"What do you think they're doing?" she asked Becker in a quiet voice.

"Fuck if I know," he shot back. "Oi, sorry, mate! I cuss when I'm nervous."

"Me too," she assured him. "You're doing fine."

After a short deliberation, a woman replied. "The other representatives and I will call for a van to come get us. We're not going through the jungle on some nature hike." It was the same woman who had yelled at Destiny earlier.

They were hundreds of kilometers from any jungle, but

Destiny had to concede the point. Outside, the trees were thick and vine-covered, exactly like the jungles in Queensland and Borneo.

SNAKE messed this up.

Her sister's text message weighed heavily on her. Everything was changing, and she didn't want to waste time arguing with assholes.

Becker wasn't happy about their decision. "But I've been told to get you to safety. I called back to the station, and they are diverting a second train to pick us up. All we have to do is walk to the far side of the ravine." He hesitated for a second. "The other train can't reach us all the way because the tracks are out."

"They could send one from that way," the woman huffed, pointing back to Canberra.

Becker shook his head. "The tracks end at the station. We are the only train on this side of the ravine. Nothing is available to pick us up from behind."

Destiny had heard enough from the blowhards. "Screw 'em, mate. If they want to sit here and rot, let them. Let's hike out of here."

"Hey!" one of the men said too loudly. "Fuck you, too!"

The anger swelled within her. Politicians, the bane of everyone's existence. Wankers and blighters all. "Come on, Becker, they're carrying on like a bunch of, well, politicians. All talk and no do! Ha! We'll clear out to safety while they're still discussing it."

She went out the door and down the steps, praying he would follow her. She figured he'd stick with the larger group of riders inside rather than go with her.

I'm not afraid of the dark.

The giant spotlight still pierced the darkness ahead, but it didn't do much to light up the trees next to the tracks, and they seemed particularly sinister, as if they'd been painted with ink. For a minute or two, she was completely alone outside the train with the fauna in the dark.

A bat winged its way across the moon, and a rustle suggested movement in a nearby tree. The longer she stood there, the more she heard. *Buck up. It's time to save yourself.*

"What a bunch of bastards!" Becker grumbled as he hopped down off the train.

"They aren't coming?" she asked, trying not to sound relieved at the trainee's appearance.

"No."

"Are you?" she added hopefully.

"Trainlink said they were sending another engine to pick us up. There can't be many engines left, actually, because they keep getting lost or cut off from the main lines, like mine. If the trains stop running, I want to end up in Sydney, not Canberra with that fucking lot." He pointed inside the car.

She smirked in the darkness, happy to have one ally. "I like the way you think, Becker. I want to be in Sydney, too. Besides, we can't have that far to walk. The tracks have to start on the other side of the gap, right?"

"And we have the biggest spotlight in the world backing us up," he said confidently.

They walked past the engine, then jumped in between the rails and strode toward the ravine.

"How long have you been doing this?" she asked to break the silence.

"Just under three weeks," he said like he was embarrassed.

"Well, I'd say you did pretty damned good in this emergency. We—"

A wave of nausea washed over her, and she crumpled to

the tracks. Becker fell next to her. The train's headlight extinguished, leaving the area as a big pit of darkness.

Search for Nuclear, Astrophysical, and Kronometric Extremes (SNAKE). Red Mesa, Colorado

Faith was glad General Smith already had a team going to CERN to confirm what was happening on that end, but she didn't plan on sitting around for six hours waiting for a report. She put out a call to her computer and physics groups and requested the leaders meet her in the tunnel where the first box was moved.

She rode the *Silver Bullet* with Bob and Sun, giving her a few minutes alone with them.

"Do you think this tram is safe?" she asked, absently looking out the window at the white blocks of light shooting by.

"You mean, will it crash?" Bob inquired. "I don't think so. It seems pretty safe to me."

He knew about her irrational fear of being in cramped quarters, although she hid it fairly well from everyone else.

"No, I'm talking about the energy bursts and time-shifting weirdness. Maybe the *Silver Bullet* will run over someone who appears on the tracks out of nowhere. Or the three of us will disappear and wake up in a dinosaur nest."

There was no consistency to the news broadcasts. Some things appeared from the past, but modern people also went missing.

"What are you saying, Doctor Sinclair?" asked the always-formal Indian scientist.

"Oh, just a theory I shared with General Smith and the NORAD jerks when I was trying to stop them from removing that box. I think I confirmed it later. I saw the red wave shoot out from the ground with my own eyes. It came out exactly in line with the collider ring. The energy then formed a growing ripple broadcasting outward from SNAKE, but it did not come inward. I think that is significant."

The three of them fell silent. Faith was sure she was right about that one small piece of the mystery, but she still didn't know what it meant.

A quiet chime announced their arrival, and the car decelerated gently. Seconds later, they pulled into the well-lit station and stopped. Three guards greeted her and motioned them from the car. NORAD scientists and some of her people gathered along the collider ring where the Four Arrows box had been pulled out of service.

"I'm glad to see the research is ongoing," she said quietly.

Sun gestured to the device sitting about ten feet from where it had been. "My team has been working on isolating the power supply inside the box, Dr. Sinclair. If we knew what it was, we might have a better understanding of the nature of the energy flow."

Faith turned to Bob. "Do you have anything to add?" She was still upset at him for not telling her earlier about his role in setting up the secret experiment between CERN and SNAKE, but her goal at the moment was learning what she didn't know about the strange devices and using that to extrapolate the cause of the blue and red blasts of energy.

"I don't know for sure. I'm being honest. My understanding of these links was that the Four Arrow project was designed to test the viability of quantum entanglement. It was supposed to project energy from one point on Earth to another, kind of like a wireless internet connection. They told me the goal was to power both boxes with the colliders and link them with their proprietary technology."

Faith groaned but didn't say what she wanted to. He'd let the project go forward without a full understanding of the science or the hardware being used.

"Well, that at least tells us something," she replied. "Can we open the box?"

Bob breathed in through his teeth. "I don't think so, Faith. They sealed the cabinets by welding them shut. If we cut in, we might destroy something important."

"At this point, does it matter?" Sunetra deadpanned. "I would like to get a better look at what inspired this project. It might give me a nudge in the right direction on how to stop it."

Faith agreed, and saw the connection with their earlier conversation. "And it might help us piece together how these boxes are affecting the direction of the energy bursts."

It might also answer a question she'd been dancing around since that early conversation with Donald.

Was it safe inside the ring?

Little America, Wyoming

Connie sat next to Buck at the restaurant. She was done with her chicken sandwich, but he was still working on the half-pound burger he'd ordered. She had her arm slung over the top of his chair and gently rubbed his back with her fingernails. It was like she knew he was wracked with doubt about not being able to make contact with Garth.

She made it easy to get distracted.

He glanced at her from time to time without being too obvious about it and admired her new outfit. After joking about buying her something tasteless, he had let her buy whatever she desired in the truck stop's clothing department as another payment for his role in destroying her Volkswagen. She bought faded blue jeans, something she described as a "darling leather cowgirl belt," and a long-sleeved white blouse that exposed both her shoulders. As before, he thought she came right out of a country and western lifestyle catalog, but it made her extremely happy to find what she wanted.

"Thanks, Buck," she said when their eyes met. "This all fits perfectly. I'm proud I was able to eat without dumping chicken on myself. That's what usually happens with me and new clothes."

"I'm a little disappointed I couldn't get you to buy something more truck stop-y," he mused, "although for a fifty-four-year-old woman, you sure do dress like a young'un."

She pulled her arm off the back of his chair and smacked him on the shoulder. "You should never talk about a woman's age!"

Monsignor, Eve, Beans, and Sparky sat at the table with them. They'd been talking among themselves while they ate, but Connie's jest focused their attention on Buck and her.

"You're fifty-four?" Eve asked. "You look amazing."

"Yeah, I would never have guessed," Monsignor added.

Buck laughed. "It's an inside joke. She's from 2003, so I added a few years to her real age. I have it on good authority that she isn't a day over thirty."

Connie rolled her eyes and laughed. "They aren't stupid, Buck, but it was a nice try. They know I have an eighteen-year-old son."

"Did you have him at twelve?" the young Monsignor asked after subtracting numbers in his head.

"No, you fool," Sparky interjected. "She's not thirty for real. She only *looks* thirty."

Connie melted. "Aw, that's so sweet. Thank you."

Buck was impressed with the older man's political savvy. He had said exactly the right thing.

She put her fingernails back on his Hawaiian shirt, signifying their friendly sparring was at an end, but her sympathetic touch immediately reminded him of Garth again.

Come on, son, check in.

"All I know is, I didn't realize truck stops were this elaborate," Connie continued to the group. "I'm going to have to remember this place when I write a book about my journey. It really does have everything a normal person needs."

Buck focused on chewing his burger while she discussed her background and writing career with the others. He'd already heard her backstory. However, he couldn't help but notice people running to the front counter of the restaurant and waving others to check it out.

Danger, Buck. Danger.

He put down the greasy slab. "Hey, guys. Look."

Everyone turned to the front where Buck motioned.

Beans dropped his knife and fork on his half-eaten plate of ribs with evident frustration. "We finally get a decent meal, and something else goes wrong."

"Hang tough, Beans," Buck replied. "I'm going to check it out."

Connie stood with him. "Me too."

He smiled, glad she was anxious to stick by his side.

They went to the front of the restaurant together. He let her lead because she was better able to cut through the onlookers. She directed him to the far-right edge of the serving counter where the crowd was thinnest.

An old-style boombox radio sat on the shelf where meals were staged before going out to diners. The staff was huddled around it, listening to the news.

"We say again, Network 5 has learned from two sources that Malmstrom Air Force Base has been placed on lockdown. This site is important because it controls Minuteman III intercontinental ballistic missiles."

"Oh, no," Connie blurted.

One of the other truckers smiled at her. "No shit. This is heavy-duty fucked up." The guy noticed Buck's rifle and grenade shirt. "Nice shirt, man."

"Thanks," Buck replied, smiling to Connie.

"Is this happening in our time?" Buck asked the man. He'd heard enough out-of-time radio broadcasts to be wary.

"Yep, it is happening right now," one of the restaurant managers replied. "The hotel staff is watching this on television, and they called over here to let us know."

"What does it mean?" Connie quietly asked Buck.

"I don't know, but we've got to get back out there so we can drive on."

He and Connie backed away from the radio, but when Buck turned around, he was face-to-face with a few other drivers who had the same idea as him.

First movers.

He nodded at one of the white-bearded truckers, who returned the gesture. The man then walked away at high speed, but he shoved another guy, who dropped a plate on the hard floor. The plate breaking and clink of silverware made everyone aware that something was amiss.

Connie waved to get Sparky's and the other convoy drivers' attention. Buck twirled his finger in the air to signal that it was time to spin up the engines and go. Beans and the others stood as one, which undoubtedly compounded the confusion in the room. Several others who had been listening to the radio now gestured or shouted for their associates to get up and leave.

Panic rippled through the restaurant as the news spread. Truckers and travelers sprang from their seats, tipped over chairs, and ran for the doors. His team was on the move, too.

"Go!" he yelled to Connie.

ELEVEN

Georgetown, Delaware

"C'mon, car, don't fail me now." Garth let up on the gas, hoping it would get them farther down the road.

"Why is your tacks-see behaving this way?"

He sighed with frustration. "I told you, it needs gas. It's a liquid, and it goes in the red container we bought." The gas can tumbled around the back seat. "I need to find a place that sells it."

"What does it look like? Perhaps I'll spy one on my own."

How to describe a gas station?

"There are pumps on the ground, like big boxes lined up next to each other with hoses sticking out of one side. It usually has a large shelter over it, like a flat metal tent."

She seemed satisfied and began to look around, but there was nothing besides trees. Since they left the Dollar Palace, it had seemed like they were driving away from civilization rather than toward it.

"It has to be soon, or we'll have to pull over." No good could come of parking on the side of the road in a taxi missing a window. The weather was much better, so people were out. People meant trouble. Plus, the looters had already seen the taxi. If they came along in their box truck full of stolen goods, it wasn't a stretch to imagine them pulling over to look for more contraband in an abandoned vehicle.

I have to do something.

The car sputtered again as they came around a curve through the woodlands. He spotted a small gravel driveway off to the side of the road, so he decided to take a chance.

"We'll pull off," he declared.

He turned downhill into a long driveway, and the motor died on the way. After a slight bend in the path, it came out at the side of an old log cabin. Garth guided the dead car as far as he could, but it ran out of momentum about fifty feet from the isolated house.

"They'll help us," she said in a comforting voice.

He gripped the wheel, contemplating them being at the mercy of whoever was inside the wooden shack. When no one came out or shifted the drapes of the windows, he let out the breath he'd been holding.

"I don't think anyone is home."

"In my time, it is not that unusual to pay visits to neighbors or spend the night with strangers. People are very friendly, usually. They'll give you some food and a place to stay for the night."

He chuckled. "Things aren't like that anymore. If these people were home, they might have come out with a shotgun to tell us to get lost. Dad taught me never to open the door for strangers. If someone came to the door asking to use the phone, I was supposed to tell them I'd make the call for them if they'd give the number."

He'd tested that advice with the visitor ringing the bell back at Sam's house.

"You are talking about your phone?" She pointed to his pants pocket.

"Yes, and he also said ten times out of ten, those people will run away before you get to the phone because they are scammers and jagoffs."

"Jagoffs? I like that."

"It's not polite. I don't think we're supposed to use it."

She smiled, and he thought she was going to push him to explain it. He was glad she didn't. His dad used the word a lot, and he thought he knew where it came from, but he wasn't sure he could explain it. He wondered if bad words were similar in the 1840s.

"Let's get the can and walk to find a gas station. With a little luck, we can be back here before anyone comes home."

His dilemma was what to do with the stuff in the trunk. If he got out and hid the guns, anyone laying low inside the house would see him and maybe go snoop for them. If he left them in the car, he took a risk that someone would happen along and break in.

"I'm happy to walk with you, though I prefer the comfort of this." She patted the leather seat.

"Me too. Once we get some gas, we can make good time and get far away. Maybe all the way to my house."

"I would like that. At least one of us can reach home."

He heard the anguish in her voice, even though she probably hadn't intended to reveal those feelings. She was as far from home as anyone could be.

Garth reached over and patted her shoulder to console her. "One step at a time. Gas is what we need now, so let's go get it, okay?"

She smiled, but her watery green eyes betrayed her deeper feelings.

"Come on," he insisted with as light a touch as possible.

"I'm coming," she replied with resolve.

He dropped the keys in his pocket but didn't bother locking the car. One window was permanently open, so there was no way to secure it. Speed was his best defense, and it was also the reason he opted to leave the gun case in the trunk. Someone could be hiding inside, or someone could accidentally come down the drive, as he'd done.

It was a roll of the dice either way.

"Garth, I understand your words, but I also saw them refuse to sell you this gas you need. Why are they going to sell it to you just because of a little red container?"

He smiled because he'd been thinking through that very problem.

"Come on, and I'll show you."

Ramstein Air Base, Germany

"Gentlemen, welcome to the Fox."

Phil strode up to the six-wheeled armored vehicle with the other men in the unit. He carried a regulation M4 rifle and all the mags he could stuff in a pack. While he loaded up on gear, he'd also found a set of clean BDUs, so he felt like a proper soldier again. He transferred his rank tab and his hook and loop shoulder patches but could do nothing about the name tape. He hoped the group didn't think of him as Sargent, the unfortunate name attached by the uniform's previous owner.

Ethan spoke like a used car salesman. "The Mercedes-Benz V-8 liquid-cooled diesel can spit out 320 horsepower without sneezing. This ugly monster was upgraded with the

Military Operations in Urban Terrain or MOUT package. Reinforced hull. Spall liner. Everything to keep your privates safe from external hazards."

The multicolored camouflage paint and its battered appearance made it look as if it had recently come back from duty in a dense forest.

One of the soldiers leaned against the hull. "This is a fine piece, sir, but why are we driving German armor and not a good ol' Stryker? Doesn't this mission rate a Bradley with a twenty-five-mike-mike bolted on top?"

The other colonel slapped the hull of the German-engineered armored vehicle. "Guys, I'll be straight up with you. The US Army is in full-on bug-out mode. They're heading for home."

"Sir?"

"Anything not bolted down is making its way to Antwerp, Rotterdam, and Hamburg to get on a boat. They're cycling everyone stateside, including us when we wrap up this mission. We were lucky to get this thing from the Germans, although you've already noticed it doesn't have any external armaments."

Phil raised his hand, and Ethan nodded to him. "We have to make time on paved roads. A Bradley would be fine for any mission except highway driving. This hideous thing will get us there as fast as possible."

The others nodded but were unsure of the mission.

"Plus," Phil added, "the seats are comfortable." He had trained with one during a joint military exercise.

Ethan pulled at the rear door, and it sprang open like a jaw. The bottom half flipped down to become a ramp with steps, and the top half became an overhead shield.

"Stop your bitching. This is what we've got. We're going to drive south, punch across the Swiss border at Basel, then see what's shaking in Geneva. This is Task Force Blue 7. We've got an important mission to accomplish, and we'll do it in a Yugo if we have to. Understood?"

"Hooah!" they said in near-unison.

"Load up, monkey asses, and let's get this over with."

Phil climbed in. It was like walking into a dank cave because of the cramped quarters and humidity trapped inside. The passenger compartment contained two rows of five front-facing seats, with two additional seats up front for the driver and navigator. He sat at the front of the passenger compartment next to Ethan and settled in.

One of the enlisted sealed the back door.

Two seconds later, guys started coughing like they were dying.

Holy shit! he thought. The Fox was outfitted with nuclear, biological and chemical-scrubbing hardware, but maybe the hardware had failed?

Phil spun around to find the guys laughing.

"Jackson just shit his pants, sir. We're going to need the air filters kicked on high."

He smelled it, too, coughing once and covering his face with a sleeve.

"It's going to be a long six hours," he said under his breath.

Little America, Wyoming

Buck and the others ran for their rigs, but the lot was huge, so it took a little time to get to his. Faster runners made it to their vehicles and started them up while he and Connie were climbing aboard his Peterbilt. Some a-holes in sportscars screeched their tires and left in white clouds of smoke like it was the start of a race.

The instant panic caused by the radio announcement was irrational and unwarranted, and he told himself not to get caught up in it, but the sight of other people running to get away sparked his own flight response. The threat of death could drive men into *Mad Max* territory, and it was dangerous to be around that mentality for too long. His books about the end of the world had taught him everything he needed to know on the point.

Once he was behind the wheel, he took a long, slow breath.

"Think, Buck," he said quietly. "Don't fucking panic."

Connie laughed nervously. "I didn't think you knew how to panic."

"I'm not, yet," he assured her, "but people here are wound up tighter than a drum. Everyone is looking for answers, but there aren't any. They fill information voids with the worst things they can imagine." He gestured out the window as the big diesel warmed up, then ruffled Mac's ears. Connie gave Mac an ear massage as well. They smiled at each other. "But not us. We know where we're going."

"So, what are we going to do?" she asked.

"Not what everyone else is doing," he declared.

He picked up the CB microphone. "Guys, follow me. We're not going into that mess."

"We're on you like glue," Sparky replied a second later.

The other trucks and cars scattered like roaches in the sunlight, all desperate to get back on the interstate, but he didn't turn right on the outer road and drive the quarter-mile toward the interchange with everyone else. There was a four-way stop sign in front of the motel destined to catch everyone in a huge cluster-fuck of delay.

To Connie, he clearly stated he knew what he was doing. "We're going to cut a new path."

He drove off the parking lot and went into the grass at the edge of the highway.

"Holy shit, Buck, you can't ignore traffic laws," Beans complained.

"Just follow the guy," Sparky barked. "He knows what he's doing."

We hope, Buck thought.

The ground was pancake-flat in all directions. There was a slight rise where the concrete lanes had been poured, but it was simple to drive over the grass and cross over the pair of westbound lanes. There were no cars coming from the east.

After a quick glance back to ensure that his friends were tagging along, he looked forward and planned how to traverse the scrub-grass median. The sixty feet between the lanes dipped lower than the pavement, so there was a minor tip-over risk if he hit it at an angle, but the larger threat was bogging down in the loose dirt and rock if he slowed or stopped.

"Hang on, guys," he said to his cab mates. His faithful dog sat in front of Connie's seat, facing her like an attentive student. She used both of her legs to steady him while she grabbed the truck's "oh shit" bar on the glove box with both hands.

The Peterbilt's nose dipped as they left the westbound lanes and went into the gravel. Buck goosed the motor and shifted like he meant it.

She looked out her window. "Buck! Cars!"

It wasn't random highway traffic. He'd done a cursory glance to make sure the roadway was clear before he left the grass of the truck stop. "Are you sure?"

"They're coming onto the highway right now!"

He hadn't expected the fleeing cars from the truck stop to

have reached the highway yet, but he had misjudged their determination and speed. Several sports cars raced off the ramp and jockeyed for positions in both of the eastbound lanes.

For a few seconds, he thought he'd made a huge mistake by rushing into the no man's land between eastbound and westbound sides, but he wasn't going to end his journey stuck in the gravel.

"They'll move for us," he reasoned. "The law of gross tonnage is on our side."

Buck angled the truck across the median and aimed for the breakdown lane at the leftmost side of the highway. He hoped the incline onto the pavement wasn't steep enough to tip over his load. Over the years, he'd been off-camber more times than he cared to admit, and every close call had taught him more about the limits his trailers could handle. This time, he thought it would be within tolerances. He hoped.

A bright red Dodge Hellcat roared by, its driver hidden behind privacy glass. The speeding sports car swerved and missed his front right tire by only a few feet.

"Good night!" Connie exclaimed.

The Peterbilt hopped onto the highway in the breakdown lane and it came up at a diagonal, so the entire trailer swayed on the fifth-wheel behind him.

"Hang on," he begged his payload of chili.

The left side mirror filled with dust as the rocks and dirt of the median rolled off his eighteen wheels. Three other rigs came out of the haze moments later, duplicating his maneuver.

"Fuck, yeah!" he shouted.

After merging into a proper lane, he picked up the mic. "That was great driving, guys. We saved half an hour or more not sitting in the traffic jam."

Truck stops were notorious bottlenecks, and he'd spent his share of time getting in and out of them. The sports cars had made it to open road first because they got in front of the traffic snarl. He made it out second because he skipped the jam altogether. He watched the tach as he accelerated, smoothly gliding through the gears. He had every intention of running wide open as long as there were cars passing him to keep the Highway Patrol busy.

Connie rubbed Mac's ears but glanced at Buck. "I was joking when I said I could drive your truck. There is no way I could have performed your escape maneuver."

He laughed cautiously. "That was what we Marines call a high risk, high reward maneuver. I should have waited with everyone else, but a half-hour could become two hours could become a whole day. Garth is somewhere out there, and sitting in a traffic jam burning our precious diesel doesn't get us any closer."

A dozen cars cruised past them as he merged into the right lane where he could resume his normal cruising speed of seventy-five. Once all the dust cleared and he got a good look at his convoy, he realized they were one short.

"Beans?" he called out. "Where you at?"

"He's not behind me," Sparky reported. "I thought he was."

"This is Beans. Sorry, guys, I'm in the mobile parking lot." He laughed. "You did a good job going around it. I'll be here for an hour. Some dickhead t-boned a pig-hauler. It's a fucking mess."

"You going to catch up?" Buck asked with reservation in his voice.

"Nah. I can't follow you; driving in water was more than I was comfortable doing. Going for broke over the median was one step too far. If the world is going to shit, I'm headed back to SoCal. I've got to get to my family."

He wanted to say it was only a rumor and no nation on earth would really use nukes, or that the effects of the blue light couldn't stop any of them if they stuck together, but he couldn't deny the guy an opportunity to get to his family. It was what Buck was doing.

"All right, man," Buck replied. "Take care of yourself. Thanks for riding along while you did."

Everyone else said their goodbyes, then Beans was gone.

"It looks like I've lost one," he said to Connie, wincing at his own words.

"That's some serious bullshit right there!" she stated in no uncertain terms. "You didn't lose anything. An adult made an adult's choice. You have your truck, your dog, and me. Maybe you can be droopy-faced if you lose one of us, but until then, you're doing what you need to do, and they're following. You are this much closer to your son. Look back there." She pointed to his side mirror. "There aren't any trucks on the highway but us. They're all stuck on that lot. Your instinct was right on the money."

"This time it was," he said in a more cheerful tone. "But I need to talk to Garth now more than ever. This country is spiraling out of control."

She reached for his phone, while he thought about what to say.

TWELVE

Search for Nuclear, Astrophysical, and Krono-metric Extremes (SNAKE). Red Mesa, Colorado

Faith worked with Sun and Bob down in the tunnel for a couple hours. She talked briefly with the NORAD scientists and asked if they could cut into one of the Four Arrows boxes, but they claimed General Smith had advised against it.

She wasn't in the mood to go begging to him again, so she focused on her laptop and the data generated by Bob and Sun's research efforts.

"Guys, let's assume what Bob said is true. The cabinets on both ends are linked via quantum entanglement. Why do you think the energy from inside this box jumped to one of the others? Why didn't it turn off? To me, it suggests there isn't a one-to-one relationship between the boxes on each end."

"Right," Bob replied. "If the energy was relegated to a certain container, it should have shut off instantly when the box was removed. The fact that it moved to another one would suggest what you say is true."

"Can we assume, then, that shutting down additional boxes will not stop the flow completely?" It was the working theory she had expressed earlier.

"We can't disprove that," Sun said in her quiet voice.

Faith took a deep breath, not sure how her theory would be taken. "I believe the Four Arrows were designed to ensure the energy *joined* between the two colliders, but they aren't necessary to continue the relationship."

Bob's face was riddled with question-marks and his brow furrowed above his nose.

"Hear me out," she went on. "I believe the first box showed us the way out of this mess, but not for the reason the general and his people think. While it is true we tracked the energy flow increasing at the other boxes, it doesn't make any sense whatsoever if there is entanglement between the containers themselves."

"Faith, I know what they told me. I saw the readings between both sites when it was active for those few seconds before the telemetry went bust. There were four links. Four arrows, just like it says in the name."

Her experience with particle physics ran deep and wide, as anyone in charge of the world's most sophisticated piece of hardware would need. However, most of the past few days had been spent in damage control mode after having her project usurped by another group. Now that she had time to look at the data and think, she came back into her element.

"It might not matter if we turn off the other boxes. That's what I think."

"But Faith, didn't you beg the general not to turn any of them off?" he asked. "Are you now saying your caution was for nothing?"

"I wouldn't yank them at the same time like Smith was

going to do, but we know more now than we did yesterday."
She let out a fatalistic chuckle. "I've said it before: everything we do here reveals more data, no matter how we get it.
Kind of like peeling back the onion. Maybe it worked out
for the best that he turned one off, because Sun's data
collection revealed this to us."

She typed in a few things on her keyboard, then turned
the screen so they could see it. A sophisticated graph
appeared on the screen, with what a bystander would see as
a tube drawn at a forty-five-degree angle. One open end was
about twice as wide as the other, making it look like a traffic
cone with an open top.

"You've drawn SNAKE on one end and CERN on the
other," Sun acknowledged.

Faith painstakingly mapped the data onto the graphing
program. It required a black box in the middle, since she
didn't know the nature of the dark energy well enough to
represent its effects. Instead, she was forced to guess, based
on observed results on her end of the equation.

"This isn't to scale, nor are the dimensions correct.
Because the beams cut into the mantle of the earth and
because CERN isn't directly below us on the other side of
the planet, the real circles would appear more like ovals
relative to each other. Still, this is a crude representation
designed to show what I believe will happen when we
remove the other boxes." She tapped a button on the
keyboard, and it began to play.

At first, it was a tube with four points assigned to the
circles on both ends. A blue line connected each box to a
companion on the far loop.

"First, we have the initial experiment, Four Arrows as it
was set up to run. Then, this." She pressed another key.

One of the boxes was removed on the larger end of the

oddly-shaped tube. It represented the cabinet pulled aside using the winch. The animation showed the blue line splitting in two, then getting pulled to the two nearest boxes.

"This is where we are now. The energy of Box One is being shared with the others." She pressed the button. "And this is where we're going."

The simulation ran through the scenario she had set up.

At the very end, she spiked the flow of energy by a factor of one hundred. She had to make a host of assumptions, including the designed capacity of each of the four boxes and the broadcast power of known energy sources on the CERN end. She also took into account a best-guess for the amount of energy shooting out from SNAKE in the blue and red waves.

The result was a new shape.

"I think this explains it all," Faith concluded.

Near Georgetown, Delaware

Garth decided to take his chances and headed in the direction away from the Dollar Palace and the looters. He and Lydia walked next to each other for about fifteen minutes before they saw the familiar shape of a gas station.

They were headed into the business district of the town.

"Well, we finally got some good luck," he told her. "Now we need it to hold while we buy some gas."

"Your time is strange, Garth. You are a man, apparently in good standing. There should be no reason you cannot buy what you desire."

Her kind words made his head swell to hot-air-balloon size.

"Would a fifteen-year-old be a man in 1849?"

"Sure. At that age, his parents would seldom insist he

was to be seen, not heard, like younger boys. It would be unusual, I suppose, to marry that young, but I know the elders of the wagon train were trying to find me a husband among my peers. Girls marry younger than boys, usually. If I did get married, then I would be *his* problem."

"Wow." He looked at her. "Amazing. You were going to be married? At fifteen?"

"I'm sixteen, to be accurate. And, yes. If a suitable man was found for me, I would probably be married off. Once my pa died, you know, I was a burden."

"That's harsh," he admitted. "You're not a burden."

"It just is," she conceded.

He looked ahead as they approached the gas station's parking area. "I'm close to being sixteen," he said as if it were no big deal. "Here, I think you have to be older to get married. Maybe eighteen? I'm not sure, because I've never thought about it. I also don't have any friends who are married, not even at my school, and there are hundreds of girls and boys there."

"Incredible," she gushed. "I would love to go to school with that many kids. My school has eight, but seldom are we all together at the same time. Often, the boys have to help with the wagons. Back in Pawnee, Indiana I was in a proper school for a short time. There were ten pupils of all different ages."

"I have two hundred in my sophomore class in high school. All my age."

He held the door open for her as they went inside the combination gas station and convenience store. The wafting aroma of wood-fired pizza greeted him when he went inside.

"What is that?" Lydia asked. "It smells wonderful."

He walked fast, because she would be overwhelmed by

the rows of treats, chips, and candy if he lingered. However, before he could get near the cashier to pay for his gas, she dragged him by the elbow to the aisle he wanted to avoid.

"Can we buy our chocolate now?" she said, clapping her hands with anticipation.

Hurry, dude.

"Okay," he replied. "You'll still want this one." He picked up another pair of Hershey bars and handed them over. Her green eyes twinkled.

"Thank you, Garth," she said as she studied the packaging. "This is amazing. It looks so clean."

"It's nothing," he said, walking farther down the aisle. A flash of red caught his eye on the top shelf of the next row, so he went over to check it out.

"Wouldn't you know it?" he said with dry humor. "Gas stations carry gas cans, too."

She seemed let down. "We could have bought this a long time ago?"

He thought about it for a few seconds. "No, not at the first place. That clerk had it in for us. But I bet the other two stations sold these."

The aisle was filled with automotive and household goods, as if offering a small selection of frequently-used items to drivers. One object caught his attention.

"This could be useful," he said as he picked up a can of black spray paint. Lydia came over to see what he had, but she didn't look for long because it wasn't nearly as interesting as the chocolate bars.

"Actually," he continued, "I'll need a few more." He stuffed his arms with six of the cans. "Now, let's get out of here."

They walked together to the front of the store and set the cans and candy on the checkout counter. He also deliberately set his gas can in front of the clerk, like he did it every day. The fake story was on his lips, ready to be told.

The older teen girl in a red vest looked up at him and smiled brightly, then scanned his purchases.

"You want two-and-a-half for your can?" she asked in an offhand way. "You didn't have to bring that in, y'know," she added.

"We ran out of—" he started to say before going silent.

He'd prepared a long story about how his parents pulled over on the highway and sent him to get gas for them. He built the tale as a way to get around the questions about his ID, because obviously he was getting gas for his parents. However, her friendly demeanor short-circuited the need to convince her of his plight.

The clerk stopped the checkout process, brushed aside some of the blonde hair blocking her eyes, and looked at him seriously. "Sorry to hear that. I'll set you up on pump five. It will put two and a half gallons in your container. You and your pretty girlfriend will be home in no time."

The clerk spoke up so Lydia would hear. "I love your Laura Ingalls dress!"

Girlfriend?

"Thank you!" Lydia curtseyed a little.

The blonde girl smiled at him again in a friendly way.

Garth looked sheepishly at Lydia. All of his complicated scheming was supposed to impress her, but the girl behind the counter had other plans. Not only did she not require his story, but she'd also seen him as boyfriend material, even if it was for a girl dressed like she was from the frontier.

"Thanks for helping us," he said.

He paid for the gear with cash, then it all went in a plastic bag.

"Good luck, you two," the clerk said in sing-song.

After holding the door for Lydia, he paused on the front walkway.

"The lovely woman seemed pleased to serve you, yet you appeared uneasy."

Garth nodded. "I expected to have to talk our way through the gas-buying process. Instead, she didn't ask me anything. I guess it took me by surprise."

Lydia smirked. "Your time is not that much different than mine. She saw you were a man and treated you as such. It's obvious that was what it was."

She grabbed his hand before he could read anything into her words. "Show me what we do next."

He was going to shake off her hand out of pure reflex, but he didn't. They were doing great as a team and were having a streak of good luck. If she wanted to hold his hand in the process, he was happy to do it.

"C'mon, we have to fill up this can and then get back to the taxi. When we get there, assuming nothing goes wrong, I want to show you the next part of my master plan."

"Is that when we can eat the chocolate?"

He chuckled and respected her single-mindedness. "We'll eat those on the way. Maybe they'll help us maintain this winning streak."

"I hope!"

I-80, Wyoming

Buck and Connie didn't listen to any books on tape after leaving Little America. The only thing that mattered was learning more about the situation in Montana. Even the problems at the SNAKE laboratory took a back seat to the threat of a nuclear war.

"This is unreal," Connie declared. "America went over to fight in Iraq, and I guess I was afraid of chemical weapons, but I never thought I'd hear of countries using nukes. It's madness."

"Saddam didn't have shit, as it turns out, but you are right. It has been decades since anyone seriously discussed using nuclear weapons. I still can't believe what we're hearing."

The news was all over the place. They often repeated the role of Malmstrom Air Base in managing and possibly launching the big missiles originally designed to crush the Soviet Union, and then the talking heads debated the why of it. There didn't seem to be a consensus. Enough time had passed that Buck expected they should have already heard about a retaliatory strike if the missiles had truly been launched.

Outside, balls of weedy green appeared randomly and in clumps over the dry, flat land. Gashes of white rock and sand appeared where the foliage didn't grow and made long intrusions in the otherwise uniform scenery.

"Ladies and gentlemen, the President of the United States is speaking from the Rose Garden. We take you there live."

"Turn it up," Buck requested.

Connie cranked up the radio, then removed her boots. She drew her feet up and put them on the dashboard as if hot lava were below her. In reality, it was the sleeping Golden Retriever.

"My fellow Americans and fellow humans of the world, I'm here today for one purpose. I want to reassure every nation of Earth, including anyone who may have been less than a friend previously, that we have no intention of launching our nuclear arsenal. There has been chatter in diplomatic circles explaining how changes in the Earth's geomagnetic field, as well as the loss of many tracking satellites, has made it impossible to target anything smaller than a continent. Some believe the time to use ICBMs is coming to an end and will soon be gone. As God as my witness, I will not give the order to launch unless we are attacked first.

"The recent voluntary evacuations of New York and Philadelphia because of the Three Mile Island nuclear plant have reminded us of the dangers of radiation. The specter of all-out nuclear destruction should terrify us all. Mutually assured destruction is not what I want for the citizens of this or any country. Please follow my lead. If these weapons are soon to be obsolete, then let's let them die."

The President talked about the events taking place around the country and the world, but Buck and Connie already knew about those. The only thing new was an admission that troops from overseas were coming back home.

When the President was done, she turned the radio back to dull background noise.

"You think anyone will attack us?"

Buck laughed. "We have a lot of enemies, but I don't think any of them are dumb enough to light us up."

"Don't politicians still excel at being dumb, or has that changed in the seventeen years I missed?"

Buck was silent for a long time since he couldn't come up with a good counter-argument.

"That's what I thought," she quipped.

THIRTEEN

Canberra-to-Sydney Train, Australia

Destiny woke up on the train tracks. The dizzy spell was gone, and it was still the dead of night, but the spotlight of the train no longer pierced the jungle.

Becker was nearby. "I was three parts gone for a second, there," he confessed.

"No, we weren't drunk. I've felt the wobbly sensation before." She looked for the train, thinking the light had gone off by accident, but the moonlit scene showed no evidence of the engine.

"They went back!" Becker cried out.

She got to her feet and brushed off.

"But that's impossible," he declared a moment later. "None of them could get into the front compartment. I locked it. I swear. It's protocol."

There was nervousness in his voice.

"I'm not going to report you if that's what you're worried about." She helped the engineer get off the ground.

"Uh, thanks. It means a lot."

"I blacked out this time," she volunteered. "That's never happened before."

"What does it mean? Did I black out, too?"

"Not sure," she replied.

Faith's message about SNAKE was now overwhelming her mind. Whatever changes were going on in the world, good and bad, they stemmed from the experiments her sister was running at her place of work. If the effects were this serious in Australia, were they worse in America? Or were they better the closer one got to the source?

A train whistled in the distance. The crush of trees on both sides of the railroad grade made it difficult to tell which direction it came from.

"Is that the train arriving to pick us up?" she inquired.

"I—I don't know. Maybe. I think it's coming from across the gorge."

She breathed in and steadied her exhale. "Okay, mate. Neither of us wants to end up in Canberra, so we need to get across this gorge."

Becker had a small flashlight, which helped immensely when they went into the ditch where the bridge should have been. It did nothing to fend off the gloom of the darkened trees. They dropped about five meters into the dry creek bed, then scrambled up the far side. She was tempted to point out that the bridge hadn't fallen in disrepair. It was gone, exactly like the Sydney Opera House.

Becker didn't seem interested in anything but moving forward, so once they were on the far side, he started into the dense jungle.

The high-pitched train horn blew three quick times in the distance.

"They won't leave without us, will they?" Becker worried.

She chuckled. "You tell me. Would *you* leave if you'd come to pick us up but we didn't show?"

He thought about it as they walked. "If I was ordered to depart, I guess I'd do what they wanted."

"You wouldn't break the rules?" she quipped. "It seems like you're breaking them right now."

Her snarky tone got the serious young man to laugh. "Yeah, maybe. Trainlink is pretty rigid about keeping everything moving on time. They said I might see some weird shit out here, but no one said it would be like this. When tracks end like they'd never been there, even though I just traveled on them earlier in the day, what good is protocol?"

"They knew it was bad but sent you out anyway?"

"I thought the other engineers were me mates, but I guess they used me on this route to see if I could make it out and back. Though, to be fair, a lot of them went missing, too. Still, a few of the last ones think the sun shines out their asses. They'll probably be there when I get back."

"Yeah," she agreed. "Every organization you ever work for will have that type of people. For what it's worth, I'm glad it was you out here and not one of them. They would have played it safe and stayed on the stranded train all night."

"I feel a little bad about losing the engine, but if they figured out how to get it back to the Canberra shed, all's good."

They walked for a short time in the heavy jungle, but they had no path to follow. The train tracks stopped where the bridge should have been, but they didn't resume on the far side. The steel rails were gone completely. Even the raised rock bed of the grade was gone. She had assumed it would be there and easy to follow. Nothing made sense, just like everything else she had seen in the past few days.

Sounds of beetles, crickets, and a thousand other insects made the forest seem to vibrate with energy around them. The flashlight often revealed little creatures scurrying to get out of their way.

The trumpet-horn of the passenger train sounded again.

"We're going in the right direction," she reassured him. "It has to be the pickup train, but we need to turn a little more. We'll go that way, through those tangles." Destiny pointed and Becker shined the light in the same direction.

"I sure don't remember this mess on the ride in," he said. "Maybe we went off on a siding and got lost, but the jungle shouldn't be anywhere around here. There aren't this many trees on the entire Canberra route."

She knew why.

"The night makes everything look different, you know? I'm sure if we waited around until first light, we'd probably both look at this and remember where we'd seen it before. Things don't magically appear out of nowhere."

Oh, yes they do.

She bent the truth like a pretzel because there was no point in speculating and freaking the kid out of his mind. She hadn't accepted the truth until she had seen the Duck of Doom up close and for real.

"Yeah, maybe," he finally agreed.

The rescue train's horn belted out again and sounded a lot closer than it had been a few minutes before. "Time to pick up the pace," she encouraged, but with the brambles and dense undergrowth, they could go no faster.

As they walked, the horn continued to blare, mostly in short, repeated bursts.

Becker high-stepped into the bush, using his hands to pull him through.

"What is it?" she asked, keeping to his heels.

"They are in trouble. I think they're leaving."

"Bollocks," she exclaimed.

Becker broke free of the worst of it and started to run.

I-80, Wyoming

After the President's message, Buck and Connie settled into a long period of silence. Mac slept on the floorboard in front, probably because he was tired from his water rescue, and the radio continued to spew out the same old stuff about SNAKE, the blue light, and inexplicable phenomena across America.

Outside, the dry scrubland of western Wyoming faded into low hills on the horizon. It was a lot like the boring nothing of Nevada, except the rock was white instead of red and there was greenery scattered in small, weedy clumps. However, there wasn't a tree in sight.

They made it an hour outside of Little America before he noticed a change on the horizon ahead.

"What's that?" Connie asked when she noticed it. "Another storm?"

The brown dust was more reminiscent of sand storms back in Iraq, but not quite as high.

"It reminds me of a column of tanks," he stated, "although I know it's impossible here."

"Hmm," she replied. "Maybe they are tanks headed for the base in Montana?"

"Blue on blue fighting? I don't think so. Besides, there's no way a bunch of tanks could end up out here in the middle of nowhere in such a short time."

They watched it grow for the next several miles until they came over a small rise in the roadway and encountered a line of brake lights.

Connie pulled her feet off the dashboard and sat up straight.

"What now?" he said with frustration. Between the admission by the president a nuclear strike wasn't in the cards, and the weird things he'd seen since the blue light kicked off the fun, nothing would surprise him on the highway. However, it was a relief not to see a column of tanks.

"What are they?" Connie asked.

"I think they're buffalo," he replied with wonder. "About a million damn buffalo."

Ahead, a line of fifty cars waited at the edge of a galloping herd of shaggy brown beasts. They crossed the highway as if it wasn't worth an ounce of their attention. The head of the line was to the left, although it was miles in the distance. The rear of the procession was nowhere in sight. The animals came from the right, and the dust cloud created by millions of stomping feet went thousands of feet in the air, so it was impossible to see the end.

Buck picked up the microphone. "You guys won't believe this. We have to stop to let the buffalo cross the highway."

He guided his Peterbilt to a halt behind the last of the cars waiting at the blockage, and Monsignor rolled up next to him on the right. Buck touched his forehead in the young man's direction, acknowledging him.

"This would be a good time to get out and stretch," Connie remarked. "I can let Mac out, too."

"That would be awesome," he replied, pulling a treat out of his stash. "Give this to him after he's done."

She woke up Big Mac when she clicked on his leash. "Come on, boy. Let's go for a nice, dry walk." The dog nosed around sniffing for the treat, but Connie had it stuffed in her back pocket, so he couldn't find it.

Buck watched them get out but didn't follow right away. After pulling the phone from its cradle, Buck typed out a message and tried to take a picture of the herd to send to his boy.

Garth. You won't believe what I'm doing. Watching the buffalo roam!

He hit Send, hoping to get a reply back so he could get an update on Garth's gas situation, but the screen stayed quiet. It didn't disappoint him too much, because disruption was the norm. If it didn't work while sitting next to the cell tower at Little America, it was unlikely to work fifty miles away. But he would never stop trying.

Once it was in his pocket, he climbed out of the cab to stretch his legs.

Monsignor was the first to reach him. "That was a great idea getting us out of Little America ahead of everyone else, but I bet you didn't expect to stop again so soon."

"Nope. I don't suppose we can drive across this river of buffalo," Buck remarked while watching the spectacle. "Could be fun."

The young man pursed his lips, then spat out some chewing tobacco. It reminded Buck of being back in the Corps.

Sparky evidently overheard the question as he strode up. "I think even the great Buck Rogers is going to have to wait for nature to take its course on this one. The water crossing was brilliant, and I'm glad we're not stuck back there, but I think this is a deal-breaker. It looks like they could push a truck over on its side. Eve is already on the fence about going on."

"She is?" he replied with concern.

Monsignor nodded.

"Yep," Sparky replied. "I don't know her that well, of

course, but she seems to always be somewhere else when you talk to her. I get the feeling she's looking for an excuse to give up. This won't help her stay." The other driver pointed from right to left in front of them.

The herd of trotting buffalo had to be a mile or two across and dozens of miles long. He'd seen such things in the movies, but he had never imagined how big and powerful it would seem up close. The ground shook under his boots. A person would be trampled instantly if they tried to cross, and vehicles wouldn't fare much better.

"We'll be fine as long as nothing shows up while we're waiting for the end of this parade. Hey, maybe we should shoot one of them for the meat. That could feed us all for the entire trip." Buck imagined himself walking up to the edge of the herd and using his 9-mm to bring down one of the giant animals. It would be a challenge, but he guessed he could do it.

"We have no way to store or cure the meat," Sparky remarked. "Most of it would go to waste, you know?"

Buck laughed inwardly at all the meat he could stuff in his mini-fridge, but hundreds of pounds would indeed go to waste. However, the thought entered his mind that if he and Garth ever needed to escape together to somewhere with lots of food, the windswept plains of Wyoming would be a good choice, given the return of the great creatures.

One man and his son could live a lifetime by feeding on the herd, but he'd read enough books to know that was not how reality worked. A thousand civilian hunters would probably destroy all the buffalo in a few weeks. A Marine division could wipe them out in an afternoon.

Behind them, more big rigs and cars came over the rise and joined the line of parked vehicles. He was part of a herd too, and it was growing.

It brought back the memories of years of stopped traffic and being at the mercy of others. He was going to be trapped, precisely as he had been when those bikers wouldn't let him reverse. The risk he had taken at Little America would be for nothing if he ended up in a huge jam anyway.

Buck surveyed the land, desperate for a way out.

FOURTEEN

Near Georgetown, Delaware

Garth and Lydia walked along the two-lane roadway with the gas can and his other supplies. He made sure they moved as fast as possible because he imagined criminals stripping the cab down to the frame while it was out of his sight.

However, no matter what their speed, he made sure Lydia got her candy bar.

"Take it slow, Lydia. You're going to want to devour this. I always do."

Garth showed her how to open the wrapper and break off one of the rectangles of chocolate. He tried to be mature about it, but he wasn't one to talk about taking his time. He usually gobbled them down in seconds.

She broke off one of them, then put it in her mouth.

"Amazing!" she said as she chewed.

"I like to keep breaking them off," he started to say.

Lydia ripped off all the paper wrapper and jammed half the bar in her mouth.

"It is *so* good!" she mumbled. "Thank you!"

They walked in silence as each chewed through what was left of their candy. Once he saw she wasn't interested in portioning it out like his Dad might do, he followed her lead and shoved it in his mouth.

"We should have bought more of these," Garth admitted.

The food experiment was over too soon. Using the sugar rush, he practically power-walked the final hundred yards when he recognized the hard-to-see driveway.

"That's the place," he whispered. "Let's head through the trees so no one on the street sees where we go. I don't want to get shot or followed, if you know what I mean."

"Back on the wagon train, we had lookouts to keep watch on the cattle and other valuables. Sometimes Indians would raid us."

They waited until there were no cars on the road, then jumped into the dense woods. They had to stop moving a few times and hide behind brushy undergrowth when cars went by. Nothing would get a driver's attention faster than two teens sneaking through the trees.

He came out about halfway down the driveway and decided to walk in the middle. While he wanted to avoid being seen by the cars on the road, he didn't want to surprise the owner of the house if they were hiding inside. His dad had often cautioned him about sneaking around on other people's property, although Garth always thought it was to persuade him not to toilet-paper the neighbor's houses.

Sam was the one interested in TP missions. He laughed to himself.

"Come on," he insisted.

They fast-walked down the incline and made it to the

car, but he never took his eyes off the house. Garth was convinced someone was in there watching them.

"Get in," he said in a hurried voice.

They both opened the front doors, but he realized that was stupid because he still had the gas can in his hand.

"Oops. I have to fill us up first." He laughed out loud, but internally his stomach was twisted in a hundred knots.

"Can I help?" Lydia asked in a similarly quiet voice, as if she shared his worry.

"This is a one-man job." He tried to sound casual as he scanned the house, but seeing it made him think of a task for her to do. "Just tell me if you see anyone. You know, in the woods. On the drive. In the house."

"Okay," she answered.

It took him a couple of minutes to figure out there were two locks on the door for the gas tank. The first one was a release button below the dashboard. The second lock on the door itself required the use of a key on the cab's keychain.

He dumped the two-and-a-half gallons into the tank, all the while casually studying the windows of the house for any sign they were being watched. Even after the can was empty, he stood there fighting the certainty someone was in there.

What would Dad do?

It was tempting to get in and drive away, but nothing besides his gut feeling suggested the house was occupied. If he could fight that for a few more minutes, this was a safe place to enact the next step in his master plan. He might not get a better chance for privacy than what he had there.

His phone vibrated in his pocket and his dad's nyuck-nyuck ringtone blared.

"Shit!" He groaned. It was a terrible time to get a call. He fumbled with the gas can, spraying droplets down the front leg of his jeans. After putting the container on the pavement, he wiped his hands on his pants, making them smell even more like gasoline. Finally, he yanked out his phone.

The text said, **What are you doing?**

It still wasn't the time to engage in a long discussion, so he replied with the single word **Spraypainting**.

He put the phone back in his pocket, then threw the empty gas container in the back seat. Finally, he pulled out the bag of spray cans, popped the cap off the first, and started shaking.

The spray paint rattle echoed loudly off the nearby garage door.

"What is that?" Lydia asked.

He stopped for a second and handed her his can, then prepared another.

"Shake this for a minute," he said dryly. "We need to use it on the car."

Lydia looked at the can like it had three eyes. "Like this?" To her credit, she shook it exactly as he wanted.

He and his dad had once spray-painted some old lawn furniture they kept on the back patio. Garth had taken away a couple of lessons from the experience. One, it took more spray paint than you thought. And two, your hand got tired pressing the spray button faster than you'd imagine.

"You got it." He finished shaking his, then pointed it at the yellow taxi. Black paint shot out of the nozzle as he steered the jet onto the trunk.

"Oh, my," she said with amazement. "I never imagined you could change the colors like this."

She watched him while he went back and forth over the top of the trunk, then a little onto the sides. He ran out of paint even faster than he had anticipated.

Lydia had stopped shaking her paint.

"Do you have the next one ready?" he asked.

She glanced at the can in her hand. At first, she shook it vigorously, but then she stopped and looked back to him. "May I spray this one?"

There wasn't time to teach her, but he had to admit his experience wasn't much either. Dad had done most of the painting back on the patio because he said it was important to have an even hand so the chairs looked professional. However, after looking at the mess he'd made of the trunk, he didn't think she could do any worse.

"Knock yourself out," he deadpanned.

"How would I do that? Should I hit myself?"

He rolled his eyes and laughed.

"No, please don't. It means you should do the thing you asked. I won't stop you."

She struggled to get the lid off the second paint can, and once she had it off, it took a lot of time for her to line it up where she wanted. However, when she hit the spray button, the paint went on in smooth, even streaks on the driver's side doors.

"You paint better than I do," he admitted. "You're hired."

"I never get the chance to paint back home. This is boy's work, to be sure."

"Hmm, I never thought of it that way. The chore should go to whoever can do it better. In this case, your painting wins."

"Yay!" She giggled. "I really enjoy this!"

Garth was proud of himself for letting her paint the taxi. It was an adult thing to do. While she did that, he climbed up on the hood so he could reach the boxy-looking taxi sign affixed to the roof. It required a Philips screwdriver to get it off the car, which he didn't have, so he did the next best thing...

He kicked the plastic box as hard as he could. The taxi sign shattered on contact, sending pieces all over the driveway, including on Lydia.

"Ouch!" she yelped.

"Holy shit!" he blurted at the same moment. "That hurt!"

Lydia laughed a second later. "And my head." She picked out a large piece of plastic wedged in her blonde hair.

"I am so sorry. I guess I didn't think that through." He could tell she was more surprised than hurt, because the piece was small. The taxi sign was gone, which was what he wanted, but he downplayed the painful way he had done it. "Now I can paint up here."

"You have a strange manner of doing things, Garth. You destroyed that marquee. Won't you require it again in the future?"

He laughed but didn't respond.

Behind her, the garage door of the house slowly opened.

He stood on top of the car like a deer caught in headlights.

I-80, Wyoming

Buck knew better than to get his hopes up, but when Garth sent a text saying that he was spraypainting, he immediately texted back. He waited for about a minute, watching more and more vehicles stack up in the line behind them.

"We can't stay here," he said aloud, hoping the right people would hear.

"Well," he said to himself, still looking at his reflection in the chrome around his exhaust, "it's time for more bold action."

He made his way over to Connie and Mac, who were standing at the side of the highway.

Connie saw him holding his phone. "Hear anything from Garth?"

"Yeah, but I think our texts are out of order. After he said he ran out of gas I asked him what he was doing to get more, then I told him about this buffalo situation. His reply just now told me he is spray-painting. I'm not sure what to make of that."

She laughed. "You are talking to a teen boy, Buck. I'm sure you already know they seldom make any sense."

He let her laughter infect him. "Yeah, I guess you're right. If he was unable to gas up his taxi, I'm sure he would have texted to ask for help."

She didn't look his way. "Unless he wants to prove he can do it all on his own."

After she said it, she spun around. "I'm not suggesting he can't."

"I know. You're right. He can figure out how to get gas. I mean every dummy driving on the road today can figure it out. My boy is smarter than the average bear." He played the past over in his head, and couldn't recall a single time he had explained point by point how to get gasoline at a filling station. He'd showed him how to turn on the pump and stick the nozzle in the tank, but he always did the credit card, closed things up, and, if necessary, went in to pay the cashier.

The buffalo showed no sign of finishing their crossing. The dust rose higher than before, and the direction of the wind made the debris seem to float alongside the giant animals. It was like watching an endless freight train at a railroad crossing.

He thought for a minute, then typed, **Call me ASAP**. He couldn't spend his whole day wondering about missed texts. It was time to hear his son's voice.

Once his phone was pocketed, he got Connie's attention. "Hey, if we can hurry up and get through this mess, what do you think about meeting my son somewhere out here on the road?"

Her blue eyes studied him intently, and he saw the inner workings of her mind behind them. "You're worried about the nuclear threat. You know, I think that's overblown. I believe, deep down, that you do, too."

"Three Mile Island was a mess that turned out to be a mistake, but this doesn't feel the same. If there was nothing to worry about, the President wouldn't have gone on national news to say everything was fine. He's the President, for fuck's sake. He doesn't need an open channel to broadcast his message around the world."

Connie didn't seem convinced. "Maybe he's lost communication with other countries."

He expressed his doubt. "He's the President. I'm sure his comms are better than mine, and despite the mixed messages, I've mostly been able to communicate with Garth on the other side of the country. I think there is something more going on."

Now he was scaring himself. More cars and trucks came in behind them, adding to the pressure.

"Do you have any idea what it might be?" she asked.

"The Marine in me says we better be prepared to be crapped on. If the worst happens, we don't want to be anywhere near big cities. If we can meet Garth in the middle of Nebraska or Iowa, we might be far enough away."

"Far enough from what?"

He thought about it for a second, unsure if he should say it, but with her, he wasn't going to lie, or even water down the truth. She deserved to know what he was worried about.

"The real-life end of the world."

Basel, Switzerland

"Speak English?" Lieutenant Colonel Ethan Knight asked the Swiss guard at the border checkpoint.

"Yes," the guard replied.

Ethan handed the other man a packet of orders. "This has the authorization of your government. We are to proceed across the border and check on the status of an international operation in Geneva. Specifically, at CERN.

"I'll check on this and be back. One moment, please." The guard walked into a small building. Three additional guards stood nearby, carefully studying Phil and Task Force Blue 7. They had to get out of the German Fox and stand behind it.

"Are they going to let us through?" Phil whispered to Ethan.

It was a little after 10pm.

"They have to. The OpOrd laid all this out. We're good."

Phil could tell by his tone of voice Ethan was full of doubt. They were dependent on bureaucratic paperwork during a time when the chain of command was inconsistent at best. NATO. CENTCOM. JSOC—all just letters, now.

But he was hopeful that one last order had managed to get through.

"Here we go." Ethan stood a bit stiffer as the Swiss

border guard came out of his shack.

"Your orders have been confirmed. The Swiss Army recognizes your right of passage. Good luck."

Ethan glanced at Phil as if to say, "That was easy." Before he got back in the German armored personnel carrier, he looked at the guard again.

"Can you tell us if you know of any trouble up in Geneva? We're heading there, as I said, and it would help to know if your security services have reported anything unusual."

The guard had been serious for the whole encounter, but now he seemed to relax. "Who is to say what is unusual? I've met six Jews fleeing Nazi Germany today. We also picked up a family fleeing from Franco's Spanish Civil War. *Those* are unusual."

"But nothing in Geneva? No big explosions reported? Maybe a missing super collider?"

The guard shook his head. "I've heard of nothing. It is quiet."

"Thank you," Ethan replied.

As they got back in the Fox, Ethan pulled him aside and whispered, "Be on the lookout, now that we're in Switzerland. I believe what the man told me, but there's a reason we're being sent on this mission. Let's assume there are terrorists inside our target, so we don't let ourselves walk into a trap simply because some guard says we have nothing to worry about."

Phil nodded. "I've been on high alert since I almost died on the metal highway back in Bagram."

They sealed the back door, and Ethan spoke to them all.

"My route shows two hours, thirty minutes, people. Get some rest. After we reach the target, who knows when you'll next get a chance to sleep?"

FIFTEEN

***Search for Nuclear, Astrophysical, and Krono-
metric Extremes (SNAKE). Red Mesa, Colorado***

Faith invited the leadership team to look at her data in
the comfort of one of the conference rooms. Despite his
protests, she brought Donald in a wheelchair because she
needed all the sharpest minds to review the information.
She wanted their support. In that regard, she realized she
wasn't much different from General Smith. He relied on his
own scientists to back up his plan too.

Unfortunately, as soon as they were all together, they
wanted to talk about the President's speech.

"Do you think we're going to war?" one of the computer
guys asked the group.

"He didn't exactly exude confidence," a woman in the
back added. "I thought he was certain another country was
going to launch, and he was begging them not to."

Bob replied to his team members. "No one would
launch now. There's no point to it. We've seen the effects of
what our experiment did, and it's clear how time and
magnetic fields are bending all over the planet. They might

136

launch the missiles and end up hitting themselves in the face. It's a huge risk."

If they were going to talk about the speech, Faith had to admit something about the past that troubled her. "What if Hiroshima's nuclear bomb comes through time and appears over Denver?"

The twelve people seated around the table looked at her, dumbfounded.

Bob seemed to consider that for a moment, then made it about him. "Or what if a nuke dropped directly on us? The people out there have no love for this place or the scientists within."

She chuckled, desperate to keep things from becoming only about ego-driven Bob. "There's a huge leap from rock-throwing to nuking, okay guys? I didn't call you together to talk about what might happen out there. We have to deal with what we know in here. We've been working down in the tunnels doing what analysis we could, and I think we have a lead on an answer."

Faith tapped her laptop, and the screen displayed on a whiteboard on the front wall. The same graph she'd shown Bob and Sunetra now displayed for the larger teams of computer modelers and physicists.

"This is what we believe is happening between the two super colliders. The four links between them are the controls. We know they guided the feed of energy when the experiment started, and even when the first one went offline, we don't think it changed the appearance." She tapped the keys to show the shape generated by the experiment.

One of the computer guys whistled. "Yes. It looks like a new energy field is being generated around the Earth."

"A torus-shaped energy field, slowly upsetting the

Earth's normal magnetic field," Faith continued. "It's the only thing that makes sense."

The graphed object on the screen was shaped like a sphere, but there was a tunnel through the middle. The simulation showed the movement of energy from one end of the tunnel at CERN through the pipeline, and then its exit at SNAKE. From there, the energy shot up and wrapped around the Earth in all directions until it joined up again at CERN. It appeared as if the Earth was trapped inside a balloon, except for two holes above the super colliders.

"This is a closed loop," she noted.

Donald stared intently at the data on the screen as if it took a massive amount of concentration to stay focused.

Sunetra picked Faith's explanation. "We still aren't able to say for sure what kind of energy we're dealing with, but my team, with Donald's help, made basic light magnitude comparisons of each of the four beams. When we shut down one beam, video feeds at the others showed how they grew in brightness by about one-third."

"They compensated," a woman physicist suggested, arriving at the same conclusion Faith had.

"Indeed," Sun answered.

Faith spoke slowly. "You now know what we know. The thing we still can't answer is what will happen if we remove all the cabinets inside the SNAKE loop. I believe they will keep compensating, but the mystery is what happens when the last one is pulled. Will that cause the closed system to collapse and return the planet to normal, or will the energy continue to flow unimpeded through the link between CERN and SNAKE over the surface of the Earth?"

She smirked. "This is where you guys come in. You have to find the answer."

The mood in the room shifted now that they had a clear

problem to solve. Several team members opened laptops and instantly began tapping in data.

"Have we figured out what's going on at CERN?" Donald finally asked.

She shook her head. "General Smith said there is a team going in to find out, but they are still an hour or two from getting there. We have to be patient."

A computer team member leaned over the table to see her. "Is the general going to wait until we know more about CERN before shutting off the boxes? Does he have any plans we need to know about?"

"He said I would have the final say. I think he was surprised when I was right yesterday. I told him not to remove the links until we knew more, but he was in a hurry."

Faith glanced to Donald. "Dr. Perkins, do you have any thoughts on what's going on here?" She pointed to the screen. Much of the meeting had been set up to avoid the need for Donald to go down into the dingy tunnels. Someone his age had no business poking around down there, but she valued his insights.

"My first thought from looking at the model is the tunnel you've drawn should not be in the middle of the sphere, but closer to the edge. SNAKE and CERN are about twenty-five percent of the way around the circumference of the Earth, meaning the tunnel would sit closer to the edge of the sphere."

She didn't want to argue with him. She'd explained to the others that her diagram and simulation were crude approximations.

"Can we shut down the system?" she asked with some frustration in her voice.

Donald looked at her seriously, then at the screen, and

finally back to her. "Have we heard anything from CERN?"

She almost cried at hearing him repeat his own question.

Her friend and mentor's brilliant mind was no longer as sharp as she had hoped.

I-80, Wyoming

After walking Mac and making sure he did his business, Buck waited with Connie and the members of his convoy, but not for long. His nervous energy at the mere thought of being trapped in the line spurred him to think of an exit strategy.

"Let's get back to our trucks," Buck suggested to them when he couldn't wait another second. "I have an idea."

Beans, Eve, and Monsignor stood there for a few moments, looking lost.

"I'll explain on the CB," Buck prompted, giving them a thumbs-up and making the first move to return to the driver's seat.

"Roger that, Buck," Monsignor replied. The others broke up and went back to their rides.

He and Connie jogged Mac back to the truck. Connie appeared confused, but she didn't question him until they were back in the cab.

"What do you have in mind?" she inquired. "Are we going to turn around?"

He'd been ready. "I will if I have to. We can't sit here, possibly for hours, and do nothing. Would you mind looking in the road atlas to see if there are any alternate routes in this part of Wyoming?"

"Sure, Buck, but what if there's not?"

He was almost certain there weren't. They hadn't

passed a major intersection in twenty or thirty miles, at least. It seemed unlikely there were too many parallel highways in the remote landscape. They also couldn't go to the north, since the buffalo herd was going that way.

"We'll see."

The Peterbilt was already running, so he adjusted himself in his seat, belted himself in, and put it in gear. He'd left plenty of room between himself and the car ahead, so it was a simple maneuver to get out of the line. He guided his truck to the left and into the breakdown lane as he'd done at the water crossing. There were no cars in the westbound lanes, so he could turn around if that was his decision, but he didn't want to risk going across the median again unless he had a good reason.

It wasn't very courteous, but he drove alongside the two rows of parked cars and got closer to the front like he was butting his way there. The rest of his convoy fell in behind, giving him confidence he wasn't acting alone. When he reached the line of buffalo trotting over the highway, a few of them moved away, as if he might continue into the herd and run them over. However, he put on the brakes and waited at the edge.

Dust and debris floated everywhere around the windows of the cabin, making it difficult to see more than a hundred yards into the thick of the passing mass of animals. There was also a dull roar, like a waterfall of hoof clops right on top of them.

Buck looked at Connie and spoke at a high volume. "Hold your ears."

She put her hands over her ears, but then appeared to change her mind. Both hands went over Mac's floppy ears.

They smiled at each other.

Buck engaged the air horn and held it for twenty seconds.

"Come on you bastards, move!" he shouted.

He let off, then blasted the horn in many short, sharp, shots.

A disturbingly small number of buffalo veered away from his noisy truck, but it had no effect on the larger horde. His faint hope had been that he'd blow his horn and effectively part the waters in front of him, but it was a no-go.

"Fuck," he said in disappointment. "I don't want to wait here."

"Can we push through, do you think?" Connie suggested.

He looked ahead, knowing the force of Mother Nature was not to be tested. Three feet of fast-flowing water could sweep his semi away in a flood. Five feet of fast-moving buffalo would knock him and his friends over with no problem.

"Maybe if we used the cars as meat shields," he suggested with mirth in his voice.

"I don't think you'll have much luck with that," she replied flatly.

He sobered up. "No, I guess not. And no, I don't think we can push these things out of our way, but I had to try." He put the truck in park. "Will you look up those routes? I'm going to step outside and see if the end is out there. Then again, as long as they keep moving, they'll pass. If they stop, then we can bump them out of the way. I think my cool attempt to blast them locked us into going forward."

He opened his door but didn't get down. He closed it, then hopped up onto his hood. For a brief moment he looked in at Connie and the excited Golden, but then he jumped up on his roof and stood tall.

"Come on, guys," he called out to the brown shapes inside their dust cloud. "Get this over with."

He peered into the thick of it, sure there was an end but unable to see it.

Near Georgetown, Delaware

The garage door went all the way up, and still Garth remained on top of the taxi. A lone man came out of the shadows of the junk-filled garage, looking a lot like a zombie.

"Hello," Lydia said in a happy voice. "We're spray-painting!"

"I can see what you're doing, little lady. But why are you doing it in my driveway?" The man wore baggy jeans that hung off his skinny body. His shirt was similarly too big, like he'd shrunk. When the man walked into daylight, Garth got a look at his sallow old face.

He was about a hundred years old.

Garth clambered down. "I'm sorry, sir. We ran out of gas and turned into your driveway because we didn't want to be targets up on the road."

"And you didn't think you might be targets down here? What if I was a criminal?"

"Are you?" Lydia asked naively, as was her way.

The old guy laughed, then rubbed a red bandana over his almost-hairless scalp. It was hot and humid, and he appeared to instantly boil over with sweat. "I served in Italy in Dubya Dubya II. That was the last violence I ever did in my life. No, I'm no criminal." He held up his finger. "But! I'll defend my turf."

"We mean no harm, sir," Garth reassured him. "I want to get out of here more than you want us gone."

"I'm Elwyn. Don't worry about time. You two seem like

cute kids, not like them damned drug addicts who come to my door asking if they can use the phone. That's why I don't answer the door anymore. They always want to come in and scout the place for loot. Then, if they find something they like, they return when I'm not here to get it."

Garth was horrified. "My dad warned me about those people, but I never thought it was real. Do they ever come back?"

Elwyn laughed. "The joke's on them. I have nothing of value inside. The mobile meals people come in and give me my food, and folks from the food pantry drop off goods, too. But it's been a long time since I've owned anything worth fighting for, 'cept maybe my wedding pictures. Would you like to come in and see photos of my dear wife Mary Jo, God rest her soul?"

His mental alarms began to rattle.

"Sure, we'd love to," Lydia said without hesitation.

Garth looked at the half-painted taxi, then at the old guy. "We'll finish painting, then we'll knock on the front door. Will that work?"

Lydia stopped in her tracks as she walked toward the man like she'd done the wrong thing.

"Suit yourself," Elwyn said with resignation. "I'll get out some braunschweiger and swiss. We'll have a nice lunch."

"Sounds great," Garth lied.

The hell I'm going inside some old dude's house.

He got busy painting before there were any more surprises.

SIXTEEN

Canberra-to-Sydney Train, Australia

Destiny tripped over some vines and almost slammed her head on the side of the rescue train engine. Becker put it in her head that it was about to leave without them, so she passed the man and ran like her life depended on it. The engine's diesel motor roared, and the horn blared over and over, but even that wasn't enough to stop her from hitting the side because the jungle rubbed right up against the metal.

Becker tumbled into her.

"We're here!" he screamed over the noise.

She motioned for him to precede her to the stairs, which he did. The giant wheels of the train were in motion, leading her to believe they were about to be left behind.

"Hurry!" she cried.

Thick vines and giant tree trunks surrounded them. Some of the largest trunks pressed up against the metal exterior of the engine, so they had to run around the base of a couple of trees before they reached the entryway.

"There's no carriage," he said with sudden realization. "It's just the engine."

Destiny looked at him for a moment, wondering what was going through his mind, then pushed. "Get on."

Becker hopped up on the step and opened the door at the front of the engine, which was pointed back toward Sydney.

"Don't leave!" he shouted to the person inside.

The engineer was a frumpy-looking woman in her mid-thirties. Her blue jumper and non-matching trackies made Destiny wonder if she was even an official employee.

"I can't," the engineer replied as they climbed into the small engineer's compartment. "I think I backed into these trees and got stuck. Am I on a siding or something?"

"No. This is the main line," Becker exclaimed.

Destiny took some time to consider. The trees had been close to the outer skin, but she assumed they had been there when the train pulled up. "The trees and the tracks seemed merged here. We have to get out, like right now."

The engineer nodded excitedly. "That's why I was blasting the horn. I wanted to leave, but where are the other passengers? They can ride in the back."

"It's only the two of us," Becker reported.

The engineer's name tag said Gladys. Destiny assumed she was going to ask a host of questions about the missing people, but she wasn't fazed. She hit some controls, and the engine groaned with the rise in power.

"Grab a chair and hold on," Gladys said in her engineer voice.

She and Becker pulled down a pair of jump seats attached to the side walls, facing each other across the cabin. The pumping sound of the motor increased quickly, as if the train were going at high speed, but they weren't moving.

Gladys looked at Becker, then worked the control board again. The straining motor died back, then the engine vibrated and creaked.

"We must be hung up on a tree," Gladys declared. "We've got to bully our way past it."

The motor roared to life again, and the engineer leaned forward like her added weight on the throttle was going to make the difference. The frame shuddered, and the metal wheels squealed below her feet.

"Come on!" Gladys yelled.

The motor revved for a few seconds, then the whole machine lurched forward. Destiny used her legs to steady herself on the seat.

They hit something else, but they had a little momentum now. The warping and ripping of metal became much louder, but Gladys seemed prepared to rip the whole engine apart as long as they got free.

The powerful spotlight shined into the vines and leafy growth of the forest. Enough of a path remained clear, like a deep, dark mine shaft through the jungle.

"We're pushing through," Gladys declared.

The jungle outside felt raw and primal, but Destiny found comfort in the reflective surface of the tracks. The twin beams of steel were the only link to civilization. Gladys followed them for many minutes, until the suffocating forest backed off a little. To Destiny, it felt like they'd escaped from being sucked into the primordial past.

She shivered despite the warm interior.

"Get us home," Destiny declared, "and I'll never badmouth Trainlink again."

. . .

Near Georgetown, Delaware

Garth finished with the sixth can of black paint, disappointed in the results. Lydia had done a great job covering the taxi company information on the side of his door, but the rest of the vehicle looked like toddlers had splashed watercolor paints over the yellow base. It was about ninety percent black, but long streaks of yellow were everywhere, and the roof was almost entirely unpainted.

The only positive was that it no longer looked like a taxi. The top plastic sign was broken, and all the words on the side doors were covered.

"It will have to do," he said, disappointed. In his head, he had envisioned that the car would look as professional in black as it had in yellow.

"We did a fair job," Lydia added. "It could use some work here and there, but I think it is pretty good for my first time painting with spray."

He gained some perspective. "Yeah. It's not perfect, but it does what we need. If we look like a dumpy car, fewer people will be interested in stealing it."

"You must live in a world of criminals," Lydia remarked. "You always worry about them."

"They aren't everywhere, but it only takes one to ruin your life. Better safe than sorry, my old man says. I'm trying to make sure you don't have to walk ever again."

"Thank you," she replied.

She smiled at him like he'd saved her life, which made him feel proud. They looked at each other for a long moment, and he was drawn once again to the simple girl's complex green eyes.

"Are we going inside for lunch?" she asked. "I'm quite hungry."

That brought him back down to reality. "Would it make

you mad if we skipped lunch?" He spoke quietly. "I don't trust him. Who waits for an hour to come outside? He's up to something. Even if he isn't, I want to get moving while it is still daytime. I'm going to get in the car and leave."

She looked hurt for a few seconds but then became stoic. "I trust you."

They split apart and walked to their respective doors. He slid into the driver's seat and turned the key.

At first, nothing happened except for a whining sound.

The second time he turned the key, the engine let out a short sputter before stopping again.

"He's there," Lydia croaked.

Garth only gave him a cursory glance. Elwyn was inside his garage but moving slow. He twisted the key again, willing the motor to start.

It cranked for a few seconds, then caught.

He banged on the steering wheel. "Yes!"

The motor roared to life. He immediately put it in reverse, then hit the gas.

The car didn't move.

The emergency brake.

Garth pictured himself in a slasher movie. The old man was the killer, gun in hand, moving in his direction...

He kicked off the brake and looked over his shoulder to see where he was going, but then he took a chance and peered into the garage. The old man was there, holding out his hand as if to wave goodbye.

Garth took a second to wave, uncertain if he was doing the right thing after all, but then he gave it some gas and slowly reversed his way up the gravel drive. He was no expert at going backward, but he tried to convey the sense that he knew what to do, if only for Lydia's sake. When he reached the road, he did his best to look both ways, but then he goosed the gas and backed out onto the blacktop roadway.

He turned so the car faced away from the looters.

"We can finally relax," he advised her. "We don't stick out like a sore thumb, anymore, and people won't constantly flag us down for a ride. With this disguise, we might be able to get home before nightfall. All we have to do is get back to the ferry."

"I can't wait," she said happily.

He drove forward, almost positive he'd thought of everything.

I-80, Wyoming

Connie and Buck sat side by side on top of the Peterbilt. She'd come up after he showed her how. The herd of buffalo continued across their path, and the brown dust blew everywhere around them like they were inside the herd.

"You aren't very good at patience, are you?" She sneezed a few times in a row.

"Bless you!" he replied.

They had to speak loudly to hear each other over the clopping of hooves on the concrete.

"Thanks," she replied with a sniffle.

"No. I hate waiting more than anything. For years, my job has depended on moving the ball forward. Get to the next truck stop. The next town. The next state. Ever since I left Modesto, I've been forced to go slow, and now we're stopped. It's a hundred times worse because Garth is counting on me to get back home."

He pointed indiscriminately at the galloping mass. "And stuff like this could delay me for days."

"Well, I want you to get to Garth as soon as you can, so don't doubt that for a second. However…" Connie scooted closer. "I don't think it'll be days. You're not bad company to keep in the meantime."

Buck smiled, remembering their almost-kiss in the water, but he didn't dare lean over to repeat the attempt because there was nothing romantic about sitting in the dust cloud.

"If Garth were here, I'd pull off the highway, find an out-of-the-way patch of forest, and live off the land until everything got back to normal. I can hunt. Fish. Trap. But each time things like this happen," he gestured to the buffalo, "it proves time is broken, and maybe there is nowhere to hide. It also seems to be getting worse."

"Uh-huh," she replied before sneezing one more time. "I was thinking the same thing. Ever since yesterday morning, we've seen amazing things, each bigger than the last."

"Bless you again, by the way. And now the threats have gone all the way up to nukes," Buck explained. "What can be worse than that?"

Connie seemed to take it as a challenge. "Zombies. Plague. An extinction-level meteor impact. A—"

"I get it," he interrupted with a laugh. "I've listened to books about all of those. But there's something about nuclear war that seems to be worse than them all. I think that's because it is so preventable. If a giant rock hits the Earth from space, you say it's terrible but unavoidable. If we blow ourselves up, all you can say to describe it is 'stupid-level event.'"

Connie leaned over the windshield as if to slide down. "Come on, let's get down to Mac and see if your fancy truck can filter this air. I'm breathing in God-knows-what filth from those animals, and I think I might be allergic."

The blowing debris seemed to get thicker, but when he looked to his right, the dust cleared a little.

"Hey!" He nudged her before she slid down the windshield. "Look!"

Connie halted and turned to where he pointed.

The herd of buffalo was still incredibly massive, but the thick stream of running animals was now about half as dense on the right side of the highway. There was suddenly less dust in the air, and visibility improved to the point that he saw to the horizon in that direction. "This is the end."

"The end?" she replied hopefully.

"Yeah! Let's get down. I've got to tell the others to be ready. Once the last animals cross, we have to lead the whole highway, or we're going to get stuck here until everyone else passes."

"That is *not* going to happen," she insisted before sneezing once more.

SEVENTEEN

Search for Nuclear, Astrophysical, and Krono-metric Extremes (SNAKE). Red Mesa, Colorado

Faith and her team worked for two hours, using her theory of a second energy field wrapped around the planet. She opted to stay in the conference room and work on her laptop, but most everyone else went either to the computer lab or the physics lab, which was essentially another computer lab filled with supercomputers.

She looked at her watch every ten minutes, certain she was about to get a call from General Smith about the team sent into CERN, but no joy.

"Mind if I sit for a while?" Bob asked as he hovered at the door. "We're hitting brick walls in my lab. None of this makes any sense."

"Funny, coming from the guy who set it all up," she replied dryly.

"Ha, ha. I get why you would say that, but I'm serious. None of the effects we've seen around the planet can be explained by shifting magnetic fields. Yeah, it would affect anything dependent on having a correct relationship with the natural field created by the planet, but it wouldn't bring planes from the past, it wouldn't shift the weather, and it certainly wouldn't change the landscape. Did you hear Salt Lake is filling up?"

Faith absently tapped her keyboard. "I hadn't heard that."

"Yeah, I-80 is under ten feet of water. Closed, maybe forever."

"What's your point, Bob?"

"I don't have a point. Well, maybe I do. I think you're wrong."

She pushed back from the table. "It took you long enough to work up to that. Do tell."

"Your energy-field scenario looks a lot like a magnetic field, and the magnetic field of the Earth is being upset by something, but I don't believe the link between CERN and SNAKE is purely magnetic. If it was, we'd be able to measure it with precision, like any other source of magnetic interference. The Four Arrows experiment was designed to tap into dark energy."

"So this is a dark energy field?"

"I don't know. Possibly. The problem is, I can't enter it in my equations because we don't know enough about it. Hell, the experiment was designed to give us clues to its existence inside the mass of the planet. If it had been successful, we might have been able to measure it and explain its properties. That knowledge would have really helped with our issues."

She laughed without mirth. "So, if your experiment wouldn't have broken the world, we would know more about the root cause of what *did* break the world? Talk about a closed loop!"

He sucked air through his nose. "Please don't start. I've said I was sorry. I'm only trying to help."

"We'll have our come-to-Jesus moment after this is all over. If you don't think we're dealing with a magnetic field, I need you to tell me where I went wrong. What the fuck is going on here?"

"Faith, you have to understand. I can't measure energy that defies classification and avoids our existing equipment. Aside from the brightness of the beams, I can't even quantify what we're looking at."

She shared his pessimism. "I understand that you supported this thing and then installed it without my knowledge, and you aren't sure what it does. How does that work, Bob? You personally are responsible for everything that is happening out there. No one else, *you*. I need you to figure it out, and I need that to happen right fucking now."

Her cell phone vibrated in her pocket. When she pulled it out, she saw the name on the screen. It was from her office phone, which meant it was the call she'd been waiting for from General Smith. "We may know something more."

"Hello?" she said.

"Ah, good. The phones are working," the general remarked. "I've been trying to call you for ten minutes."

"What is it, General? Any news?"

"Yes. I wanted to inform you that my team is inside Geneva city limits. They are approaching the facility now. We should have some answers inside the hour."

Her stomach did a somersault. She wasn't sure what answers would help her, but anything would be better than what she had.

"Very good. I could use more information. I'm running on fumes here," she said in a measured voice.

"Yep." General Smith hung up without saying goodbye.

She hung up too.

"That's it?" Bob asked. "Did he hang up on you? Kind of a dick thing to do."

"No, it's fine," she replied. "His team is going in. We'll know our colleagues' fates soon."

Geneva, Switzerland

Phil Stanwick stood next to the Fox armored personnel carrier and looked through a pair of binoculars. It was just after midnight, but the place was well-lit, with many overhead lights.

"What do you see?" Ethan asked.

Phil scanned the campus of CERN, noting the numerous low, flat buildings in the mile-long arrowhead-shaped property. The driver had brought them to a hilltop with a perfect line of sight to most of the grounds.

The long front side of the place was lined with a tall hedge along a busy suburban roadway. Farmland and houses surrounded the rest of the property, making it easy to discern if anything was damaged or destroyed, even in the darkness.

"It looks like nothing is wrong. I don't see any people running around. There are cars parked in the lots. The civilians I can see are standing around or walking between buildings like nothing out of the ordinary is going on."

"That's my assessment, too. It's almost like they don't know they are the focus of an international missing person alert."

Phil focused the lenses of the binoculars. If terrorists had taken over the facility, they might want people walking around so things looked normal, but he'd expect furtive glances from the hostages or telltale shifts in blinds from upper windows as the overseers kept watch. He saw none of that.

"Something is going on," Ethan went on to say. "No one has come into or out of the parking lots since we got here."

"Like there's an experiment in progress?"

"Bingo."

"Do we proceed?" Phil wasn't in charge, but they had one job to do, and he expected the other colonel to order it.

Ethan nodded. "We don't have enough men for anything fancy, but I'm not going to drive in the front gate and allow us to get ambushed. I want to split the team. You'll take three men on foot. Go in through the hedge running along the border of the property. That will give you concealment, and you can be ready in case we need support."

He's assigning me the duty of reporting to HQ if he gets killed.

They spent fifteen minutes driving in a long route out of the direct view of the campus. The driver brought the Fox down the roadway next to the hedge, then pulled onto the dark sidewalk as far as possible between two light posts.

"This isn't going to be very stealthy, but there isn't a better option," Ethan remarked as the back door opened. It was the least exposed approach. It wasn't decent cover since bushes didn't stop bullets, but they wouldn't be out in the open.

Phil ignored the Swiss traffic and scrambled into the tangle of bushes that signified the edge of CERN's property. When he and the other three men were in position, he radioed for Ethan to move the Fox.

After it was gone, he got the sensation that something big was about to happen. It was at odds with the normalcy of local traffic or the birds chirping in the nearby bushes and trees.

The others' expressions showed the same worry.

"You guys feel that?" he asked quietly.

"Yes," a corporal named Barry Grafton replied. "My hair is standing up straight on my arm. Look." He held out his bare wrist to prove his point.

Phil did everything he could to fight the unsettling feeling. It was like he was being watched by a hidden camera while also holding two live wires that must never be joined. One misstep could kill him.

"This wasn't in the brief," Grafton added.

The other two chuckled nervously.

"We're all on edge. Have you ever trained doing MOUT when everything was normal except a major case of the willies?" He smiled at his fellow soldiers. "We have it easy. Knight has to go into the parking lot and walk up to the front door." He tapped his M4 to signify why they were there. "So let's find a position we can live with, then get ready to support their arrival."

They'd arranged it so Phil would have three minutes to get set up. Right on cue, the Fox's engine roared, and it bashed through the hedge about a hundred yards to the south. The driver kept the speed at about twenty miles per hour, but he drove right for the front entrance of the main building. The path took him over a pristine lawn and through a small executive parking lot.

"Ten seconds," Phil relayed.

Private First Class James MacIntire set the M249 light machine gun on its bipod and aimed it at the target building. Their role wasn't to crush the opposition, but if the Fox got into an ambush, they would be able to provide covering fire so the truck could back out of the kill zone.

"He's pulling up to the door," he relayed. "We have bystanders watching." Phil leveled his M4, although it seemed small and useless given the powerful energy he imagined was swirling around them.

"Showtime."

I-80, Wyoming

Buck popped the Peterbilt into gear when he saw daylight between most of the buffalo trotting across the highway.

"We're not waiting until they all cross?" Connie said with reservation.

"No, we're going to push into the back of the herd and lead the procession of vehicles behind us." To that end, the Peterbilt lurched through the first few gears and stuttered forward.

"Break 4. Follow me. Don't fall behind." Buck had three trucks trailing him, and he couldn't afford for one of them to get pinched by the traffic. Most of the people were still out of their cars talking to each other, so he was confident his plan would get them ahead.

Ten seconds later, his tail gunner checked in. "Sparky here. We're all moving with you."

"Roger," he shot back before putting the mic in the cradle.

"Holy shit," Connie exclaimed as they headed into where the buffalo were still clearing out. "Where is the highway?"

Now it looked like the interstate had been draped with a rocky blanket. Millions of hooves trampled over the roadway and kicked up rocks and dirt as the animals crossed the lanes.

The tires of his truck crunched the rocks like they were on a primitive gravel road.

"Probably a few cow pies out here, too." Buck laughed.

"Yuck. Remind me never to follow a herd of buffalo," Connie declared.

"There's safety in the middle, but you get rocks and dust in your face. That's why you want to be in the lead. The frontrunners probably don't know how good they have it."

"Or maybe they do," Connie surmised.

Mac stood on his hind legs next to Connie. He'd been disinterested in the mammoth herd of animals until there were only a few left, then he whined and panted like he wanted to go out and play with the stragglers.

Connie settled him down. "We'll get you a friend soon, but we can't stop here." She wrestled him off the sill of the window and guided him back into the space under her legs. At first, Buck imagined he was pissed at being denied a view of the buffalo, but he laid down, curled up, and sighed a few moments later.

"Good boy, Mac," he said aloud.

We're both putty in her hands.

He laughed to himself. Being at the mercy of the redhead cowgirl was the last thing he had ever expected, and he was certain Mac hadn't seen it coming, either.

The heavy truck cut through most of the debris with no problem, but the deeper he got into the path of the herd, the more frequently he had to maneuver around the remaining buffalo still trying to get across. Much like driving in snow, his tires slid and shifted on the debris.

"Whoa!" he said when the steering wheel grabbed in his hands like the tires wanted to go hard to the left.

A baby buffalo hopped off all four feet to avoid getting branded by Buck's bumper.

"Sorry, lil' dude!"

Buck looked back and saw his friends sliding around on the rock-strewn pavement too. None of the cars had begun to move, even after they were hundreds of yards across. Some of the rocks kicked onto the roadway were almost as large as soccer balls and would be hazardous to smaller cars.

"See?" he said while purposefully looking at his side mirror. "We're doing them a service. We get to go first, but we have the job of smashing the rocks and clearing the way."

The situation improved as they neared the far side of the stragglers. There were fewer rocks in the lanes, and only a few of the slowest buffalo still plodded across the roadway, desperate not to fall too far behind their herd.

Brown rumps shuffled to the north, destined to disrupt whatever towns and highways were in that direction. The cumulus-style dust cloud would herald their arrival.

He scanned the horizon, suddenly aware he would see other herds if they were out there. Getting stopped multiple times by more buffalo was something he wished to avoid, so he had to stay vigilant.

The phone rang in its cradle.

"It's working again!" he shouted.

"Who is it?" Connie asked with excitement.

"Garth!"

EIGHTEEN

Near Georgetown, Delaware

"I feel like a million bucks," Garth said as they drove through the quaint tree-lined countryside in rural Delaware. His broken window created a harsh draft inside the modified taxi, but it felt good to be alive and safe on the open road.

"You would be John Jacob Astor if you had that much money," Lydia replied.

He looked at her, wondering what she was thinking. The name meant nothing to him, but it sounded like she was serious. However, before he could ask a question, he was distracted by her long blonde hair blowing in the wind.

"You took off your bonnet," he remarked casually.

She smiled at him. "Yeah. When you opened my window, however you did that, I was overcome by the fresh air. I love how the wind feels. I've never gone this fast in a wagon!" Lydia leaned her head out the open window a lot like a dog would, and the wind made her hair flow and whip.

Once they left Elwyn's place, Garth had opened her

window to clear out the fresh paint odor, but he hadn't anticipated what it meant for the pioneer girl.

He forced his eyes back on the road. There weren't many cars on the two-lane highway, but his dad had reinforced the idea that he should always keep his eyes on the road no matter what.

Seconds later, he pulled out his phone, held it up next to the steering wheel, and pressed the button to activate voice command, doing it all without looking down.

"What are you doing with that?" Lydia shouted in the wind.

"Calling my dad. He and I have been playing phone tag all day. 'Call Dad.'"

Lydia shifted in her seat. "I love tag! You will have to show me how to play with your telephone."

Garth chuckled to himself as the phone rang on his dad's end.

"It's ringing!" he said excitedly.

The phone rang many times, for at least a minute, and he assumed it was going to fail as it had before. However, he held on because any ring was better than none. If he was patient...

Finally, there was a click, and a voice said, "Hello?"

"Dad?"

"Garth! Hell, yeah! I'm so glad to hear your voice."

"Me too," he said, keeping one hand on the wheel. "Where are you?"

"Didn't you get my texts? I'm in Wyoming. We were stuck behind a huge herd of buffalo crossing the highway, if you can believe it. I sent you a picture of it."

"I think our texts aren't going through all the time. I'd remember if you had told me about buffalo."

They traded stories for a few minutes. Garth told him

about his idea to paint the taxi so it wasn't a huge target. He also explained his dilemma with getting gas, and his dad seemed pleased to hear how he had figured it out.

In return, his dad shared his stories about Utah and Wyoming.

"So, Dad, I've got my gas and a like-new ride. I'm heading home this afternoon. I do have Lydia with me, but I *promise* she'll sleep in a separate room."

Buck laughed. "I trust you to do the right thing. You are a man now." He hesitated like he wanted to say more.

"Dad?"

Buck turned serious. "Son, listen. They are talking about this blue light as if it has made all of the world's military equipment go haywire. The President came on the radio and said some nations are thinking about using nukes because they might soon be obsolete."

Garth held onto the wheel as if losing his grip would result in a fiery wreck. "Dad, are you *serious*? They would really do that?"

"I'll be honest with you, Garth; I don't know. I've talked it over with Connie, and we both agree it is unlikely. However," he stressed, "we're two civvies out here in Bumpkinville, Wyoming. We have no idea what's happening back in civilization. We can't say it is impossible."

"What should we do?" Garth replied, his voice cracking on the last word.

Lydia was now back inside the window and watching him. He figured his change in tone must have been obvious.

Buck went on. "You are safe in Delaware?"

"Yes. We came on the ferry to this state, and we haven't gone far from the landing, but we aren't exactly there right now."

Dad spoke in a muffled voice to someone else, presumably his friend Connie. Garth was interested to know more about the mystery woman because he'd seldom seen his father with a companion.

Not since Mom died.

"Hold on. Connie and I are looking at the atlas. Do you have a map with you?"

"No. I brought the tent and sleeping bags, but I don't have any maps."

"Shit," Dad said under his breath. "I should have anticipated that in my bugout bag. A basic map of the US would have been easy to stick in there."

Connie said something he couldn't pick up, but his dad seemed to repeat it.

"Interstate 64, Garth. Go south all the way through Delaware and Maryland on... Highway 13. Can you remember that? It will take you to a long bridge over the bay, and then you'll be in Virginia. You will literally run into Interstate 64. Take it west. That will keep you well clear of Three Mile Island and any fallout from it."

"South on 13. West on 64. Got it."

"I'll have to get back to you on where we're going to meet, but I want to stay away from all the major cities." His dad paused for a full five seconds. "In case the worst happens."

Garth watched the road, unable to reply right away.

"You good, son?" Buck asked, his voice thick with worry.

His first reaction came out of nowhere: anger. He didn't want to head west, away from home. Away from his best friend. It wasn't only dangerous, it was a colossal disturbance in his existence. His dad had an elaborate plan to ruin Garth's entire life. It was pure Dad being Dad.

But he choked down that first instinct and tried to think

about Dad's position. He was doing his best to get back home.

No, he's doing his best to get to me.

"Are you positive I should leave New York? I'm sure I can get this taxi back home. We can leave if it looks like any war is starting. I'll listen to the radio religiously."

"I know you could make it. I have no doubt of your skills, after what it took to get out the first time. But if there is a war, even a small one, New York is going to be a target. You'll have maybe fifteen minutes of warning, assuming the radio is working. You'd never get out of the city in time."

"This is crazy," Garth reasoned. "I've never driven much before, much less a thousand miles."

Dad laughed in a sympathetic way. "Before a few days ago, you didn't drive at all! There's nothing to it. I could do a thousand miles in one day if I didn't keep running into bull-shit, sometimes literally with this herd. Once you are on the interstate, keep your eyes on the road, don't interact with people if you can help it, and drive west. You'll do fine."

"All right. I trust you know what's going on. I can do this, Dad. If the cell towers are working again, I might even have the internet. I can use online maps to find my way west. That will make it easier."

He felt a little better knowing his dad had faith in his abilities.

"We're going nowhere fast out here," Dad replied. "Keep your phone close, but if all else fails, head for the sunset, okay? Drive west. We'll drive east. Get yourself a map next time you get gas and take bypasses around big cities, right?"

"Got it. How do I get gas?"

Someone spoke to Dad, and his muffled reply suggested

he held a hand over the phone. When he finally came back on, he sounded excited. "We're through the herd and back up to highway speeds, so we're going to make up some time. I'll be back to you in a jiffy, okay? We'll keep in touch for where we're going to meet up."

"Okay," he said, still driving. "We'll be fine. Talk to you soon, Dad."

"Love you, son. Keep the wheel-side down, okay?"

Garth laughed. "Love you, too. Will do."

He hung up and thought about the grave turn the conversation had taken.

Lydia watched him as if waiting for her orders.

He frowned. He'd had his mind set on going home and showing Lydia all the things that were important to him. Maybe even cooking for her, but all that was gone after one short conversation. Dad was right, though. If the shit had hit the fan, staying away from city dwellers was the key to surviving. Garth turned to look at Lydia. At least he wasn't alone. She was a survivor. "Looks like we're heading west."

I-80, Wyoming

"When it rains, it pours." Buck almost set his phone back in the cradle after talking to Garth, but he caught sight of the text notification. "It looks like I've got a text message from Mr. Williams."

Connie didn't miss a beat. "Who is—"

"My boss. Well, more like my manager. He arranges the pickups and drops for the shipping company I contract with." He handed her the phone. "Can you read what he says?"

There were only a few cars on the highway, mostly from

westbound turnarounds who had peeled off from the long line of vehicles waiting for the buffalo herd to clear out. Still, he wasn't going to text and drive.

"It says, 'Buck, I've had ten drivers give up the ghost in the last two days. I'll lose my shirt on the insurance payouts alone. Please tell me you are going to get our load to White Plains.'"

He glanced at Connie. "He used my nickname. It's literally the first time he's ever done it. I think he's desperate."

She smiled at him. "What did he call you all the other times?"

"My real name is Blake," he said as if she'd pulled out one of his teeth.

"Aww. That's a cute name." She reached down to Mac, who remained in a ball at her feet. "You have such a cute daddy."

Buck clenched his jaw and pretended to be mad. In truth, there wasn't much she could say that would make him angry at her.

"So, anyway..." Buck drawled. "I talked to him right after the blue light hit, and I told him I would get this through for him. Do my job, basically. That's what I've been telling our friends in the convoy too, but I made the statement before I saw the full effects of the blue energy wave. And before the red wave, and that was before there was a whiff of nuclear war."

He stopped talking and stared straight ahead.

"Buck? You there?" She seemed to know when to pull him out of his reverie.

After a long sigh, he chanced another look at her. "I can't believe the world has come to this, but I'm considering not pulling this load to White Plains, especially if Garth meets us out on the road. Best case, I delay my delivery for a week or two."

"And worst case?" she asked.

"Worst case is something bad happens with this nuke issue, we meet Garth, then find a comfortable patch of woods to call our own. Try to make the best of whatever resources we can find, and if the world eventually gets back to normal, we come out."

She sat back in her seat and crossed her arms as if getting comfortable for a long ride. "There is an upside, you know?"

"I'd love to hear it," he remarked without enthusiasm.

"We'll have all the chili we can eat."

That struck a gong inside his psyche.

I'm not a thief!

The more he thought about it, however, the more he realized she was being practical. If there was a calamity, he was sitting on a gold mine of survival rations. The metal cans would last a long time. They could get him and his people through the worst of what might be a tough slog.

"And I've got a can opener," he said, deliberately chuckling.

The thought made him look at his trailer in the side mirror. The container practically glowed in the sunshine, but his mind was playing tricks on him again. The endless supply of chili was a fantastic resource to have, but it would also make him a mountain-sized target if people found out what was back there.

"Text a reply to Mr. Williams, please. Tell him I'm still on the road and will do everything in my power to get the shipment to White Plains."

It was a powerful admission to know he probably couldn't make good on that statement, but family came first. After he had Garth back in the fold, he could worry about coming through for his boss.

But not a second before.

NINETEEN

***Search for Nuclear, Astrophysical, and Krono-
metric Extremes (SNAKE). Red Mesa, Colorado***

Faith finally had enough data to go to General Smith
and present her case for how energy flowed inside the
powerful bubble surrounding the Earth. She strode down
the hallway with confidence, until she saw Benny the
reporter leaning against the wall as if waiting for news to
drop in his lap.

"Hey! Dr. Sinclair. You have something for me?"

"Not right now," she replied, sounding chipper. She
didn't want to give him any reason to doubt her. "But I
might have news soon."

Benny blocked her way, although it didn't appear delib-
erate. "Thanks, by the way, for helping my wife come here."

Faith stayed there for a moment. "She's doing okay? No
problems getting in?"

He shook his head. "Nope. They didn't even give her a
once-over to collect her phone, like they did for me. I guess
they didn't think she was a reporter." Benny winked.

"Is she?" Faith whispered.

"Naw. I'm just being silly." He scanned the hallway. "This place has become too serious, if you ask me. It's great I'm here, but hardly anyone is willing to talk to me, as if I'll get them fired."

"Everyone's paranoid," she agreed. "That's the price of having a general of the Army in your house."

"Maybe," he replied.

When Benny didn't volunteer anything more, she made to leave. "I have to go see the general. Hang around, okay? If he clears me to say anything publicly, you'll be the first one to know."

"And the only one!" he added as he stepped aside.

"That's our arrangement," she assured him.

Faith walked past several more offices until she got close to the one being used by the General. His aide stood outside the closed door, which usually meant the general was inside.

Pull it together, Faith.

"Hello. Is the general available? I have some data to show him."

The aide smiled while he checked a digital tablet. "I'm showing he is free in a few minutes. Will that be okay?"

For once she wasn't in a life-or-death rush.

"Yes. I can wait."

"Very good," the man replied.

She looked back at Benny. He remained in the same spot, but he had his eye on her. With luck, she'd have a good meeting with the general, get the okay to tear into one of the Four Arrows boxes, and then have something interesting to share with the reporter. It would relieve everyone in his audience to know there was a solution being worked out.

After waiting a few minutes, the guard let her in.

"Hello, General Smith," she said in the presence of the aide.

The old soldier waited until his helper had shut the door, then addressed her informally. "Come in and sit down, Faith."

He had his top buttons undone, and he was covered in sweat like he'd been doing hard labor since she last saw him on the parking lot. He got up and strode toward the plastic chairs in front of his desk.

Faith looked him up and down because he was a mess.

"I know. I'm soaked from running around outside. Don't tell anyone I'm a normal human," he joked. "It would ruin the image."

"The rumor I hear is your nickname is 'Obi-Wan,' after the *Star Wars* movies. Were you out there working your magic?" The relaxed mood caused her to lower her guard and try a little small talk.

"Who told you that? I've been trying to stamp that nickname out for years. Back in Iraq, I—"

The ground shook under her feet as a fiery orange light erupted from the parking lot. She was sideways to the windows, so she turned in that direction to see what it was.

"Down!" the general bellowed.

He slammed into her.

"Shit!" she yelled as she fell.

The glass of the windows shattered and allowed the full fury of the explosion into the room as she dropped to the floor. The roar was deafening, and it got momentarily hotter, but the impact with the floor hurt her the most.

Tiny pieces of broken glass splashed against the back wall and fell to the floor as a cascade of tinkling crystal. She shielded her head from the flying shards.

She gasped for air as powerful gasoline fumes filled the office.

"What the hell was that?" she yelped.

General Smith had his arm draped over her midsection, and for a few seconds, he didn't move. She thought he might have been injured, so she tried to shift it away.

"Don't," he said. "We need to stick together. Go for the door."

The smoke made it hard to see inside the office, but it wasn't completely dark.

"This way," the general declared as he used his arm to push her toward the hallway door.

"I'm with you," she replied as best she could.

"Watch the glass," Smith announced as he began to crawl toward the door.

"Can we get up?" she asked with obvious fear in her voice.

"Stay down!" he ordered. "We don't know who's out there. We may be targets."

Oh, shit.

They made it over the broken glass and through the door.

His aide was absent, and the hallway was filled with chaos and screaming.

He got her situated on the inside wall, away from any windows.

"Was it a bomb?" she inquired.

"Damn right it was a bomb. Someone blew up a car out on the lot." He picked at his scalp as if checking for shrapnel.

"I don't want to stay here, sir. I've got to get my people out of this hall."

He stopped his self-triage. "Stay low, and go with me

down the hall." He pointed toward the research area, which was at the end of an intersecting hallway. "We've got to get everyone deeper into the facility."

It wasn't dignified to be crawling the hallway in her blouse and dress pants, but she followed the general without complaint. Along the way, she checked on some shaken people, including Benny.

"You okay?" she asked the reporter.

He rubbed his head like he was hurt, but there was no obvious blood or bruising.

"Yeah. Fine. A wheel came through the wall about five feet from my head, and I saw my life flash before my eyes."

She smiled. "We were at the front windows. The glass could have cut us down, but the general knew enough to push me out of the way."

"Wow. Two damned miracles. Hey, can I report this?"

"No!" the general snapped. "We have to know who did this first. They might be waiting for reporting to determine if they killed anyone of importance."

She and Benny exchanged glances, but she wasn't going to argue with the man who had saved her.

Before she and General Smith could move on, an armed contingent of soldiers ran into the hallway and came right up to her and the general.

"Are you okay, sir?" one of them asked.

"*We're* just fine," she snarked.

European Laboratory for Particle Physics (CERN), Switzerland

Phil watched intently as the Fox drove up to the front steps of the main building at CERN. The driver parked it so when the back doors opened, they were shielded from the target by the body of the six-wheeled truck. Two soldiers hopped down from the back and took up positions at the rear corners. The rest of the unit went past them and bounded up the well-lit marble stairs.

Ethan went up too. He walked through the double doors like he owned the place.

"Now we wait some more," Phil said quietly.

He'd begun to think the energy disturbance was simple nerves. Maybe the bomb blast at his command bunker back in Bagram had done more damage than he wanted to admit, because it was unusual for him to feel such anxiety during an op.

"Sir, look at this," Corporal Grafton whispered.

Phil didn't want to take his eyes off the mission. "What is it?" he said without turning around.

"I'm getting more of that static. I can actually see a blue spark if I hold two pieces of metal close to each other. It's like my whole body has been dragged across a shag carpet and now I'm super-charged."

He glanced back as fast as he could. Sure enough, there was a two-inch line of electrical charge between the barrel of his rifle and a spare mag he held in his hand.

"Ignore it," he suggested. There was nothing to be done about it while they huddled in the cover of the leafy hedge.

Grafton's radio came to life. "This is Blue 7 actual. We're inside. Situation appears normal. Rally on me. Over."

Phil went to key the mic and noticed that a burst of static came off his fingers as he touched it. "This is Blue 6. We'll be there in two mikes. Out."

"Shit, I don't know what's going on, guys, but this electrical discharge is pissing me off. We're going to cross this parking lot and rejoin the unit. If your hair starts standing on end and your helmet rises with it, try cinching it down, okay?"

"Hooah," they all replied.

The three men prepared to move out, standing and adopting fields of fire while engaged in movement to contact, even if the contact was supposed to be friendly. Phil planned their route. Ethan said everything was good, and he had no reason to doubt him, but it was his job to plan for the safety of his men. As far as he was concerned, there were snipers in every window across the lot.

"Keep your eyes on those windows and report if you see a weapon, but do not engage. My order only unless we're fired upon, and then I want you to make them sorry they were ever born. Follow me," he said dryly as he stepped out of the hedge and headed for the nearest parked car.

The crackling of electricity was as loud as a swarm of bees by the time he made it halfway across the lot, but he followed his own advice and kept it to himself.

What did I get myself into?

I-80, Wyoming

After hearing from Mr. Williams, Buck became interested in the news again. He and Connie listened to the radio. She pressed the preset button each time a broadcast went to commercial, so they kept up on multiple sources at the same time.

All of the old news was still being discussed, including the Presidential speech and the time anomalies, but he soon became consumed by a story only mentioned on local Wyoming stations. Sections of Interstate I-25 in eastern Wyoming were being closed off for construction projects.

"This ain't good," he said when he heard the words "I-25" again.

"What does it mean? Are they doing construction on the whole highway?"

"We've heard reports of closures in three towns now. I figured it was more buffalo crossing up there, but they didn't mention animals."

Buck reached next to his seat for the atlas.

"So? Maybe time is out of whack, and construction is happening all at once."

He briefly gave her a smile. "Yeah, it's one possibility. Here, open this to Wyoming. Let's take a look."

She grabbed the atlas and flipped it open. "What do you want to know?"

"Interstate 25 goes through Denver. That's a fact. I bet if you follow it north through Wyoming, you'll find it goes into Montana, and probably close to Great Falls."

"The air base on the news is in Great Falls, isn't it?" she asked while leafing the pages.

"Yep," he answered.

She paged through the atlas until she had Montana and Wyoming bookmarked with her fingers. As she switched back and forth, he began to wonder if he remembered the geography correctly. Since it was his job, he wanted to sound like he knew his stuff.

"Well," she said with hesitation, "you are right and wrong. I-25 goes through most of Wyoming, but then it turns into another highway."

"Does that highway go to Great Falls?"

She traced her fingers on the page. "It winds around, but you can get there. I-25 is the only major interstate linking Colorado and Montana, though. You think that airbase has something to do with the road shutdown?"

He wasn't sure he was right, but the pieces seemed to line up.

"Yeah. Malmstrom is in Great Falls. They've been talking about it being on lockdown, but they don't give any other information. Now the main highway between the base and that SNAKE place near Denver is being shut down for construction. If I were running an operation between the two cities, I'd make sure I owned the interstate."

She put her elbow on the armrest and held her chin while looking over to him. "We're heading right for I-25, Buck."

"I know." He sighed.

TWENTY

Princess Anne, Maryland

"Garth, can I ask you a personal question?"

They sped along Hwy 13 going south, and he kept it at the sixty-five-miles-per-hour speed limit. Lydia had her window most of the way up because the blast of air between the two open front windows was too much even for her.

His window was still broken, however, so they both had to speak loudly.

"Sure, go ahead."

She shifted in her seat, pulling one leg under her body so she sat on it, allowing her to face him.

"If we can't get me back to where I came from, could I stay with you?"

"Like, get married?" It fell out of his mouth.

She shrugged, seemingly unconcerned about his etiquette fail. "I will need to find somewhere to stay so I don't become a burden."

Secretly, it was flattering, but he was only fifteen. He imagined what it would be like to walk into Mrs. Anderson's math class and have to explain that he was married to a pioneer girl who dressed like it was 170 years ago. It would be deliciously scandalous. Sam would never talk to him again, or maybe he would. "Take my eyes off you for two minutes and look what happens?"

Not to mention what his dad would say.

"I, uh, don't know what will happen, but I promise you won't be a burden to my dad or me. He will make sure you get somewhere safe, maybe with family living in our time. Hell, I wonder..."

His mind journeyed down a strange road that led him to imagine the possibility he was her descendant.

Yuck. Gross.

"Your last name isn't Meadows, is it?" he asked.

She smiled. "My family name is Masterson."

Phew! Not related.

Upon reflection, he couldn't quite grasp why that was important to him. He didn't want to marry her, certainly, but she was pretty in her own way. If she wore modern clothes and learned a few things about modern life, such as using smartphones, he wouldn't be embarrassed to be around her. He found that he wouldn't mind that at all.

And he wouldn't be embarrassed. She needed a knight in shining armor to protect her from his world, and that was the most embarrassing thing of all.

"Anyway, you wouldn't be a burden. Girls, uh, *women* today can do whatever they want. You could go to college and be a doctor if you felt like it."

"Wow," she said in a distracted way.

The roadway was lined with tall, straight trees until they ended at the edge of a new town. A tasteful brick welcome sign greeted them.

"We're entering Princess Anne," he announced. "I think we should try to get some more gas. Two gallons didn't get us very far, and the line shows we are sitting on empty already. I hate stopping so much."

She giggled. "You amaze me, Garth. We've crossed more land in the past hour than Pa and I would have crossed in two days with our wagon."

"I think I would have killed myself if I had to move so slow."

Lydia huffed. "You shouldn't talk like that. It brings bad luck."

"No, it's a joke. I never would do it. It only means I hate it more than anything."

"Oh, well, still. I would hate to see you hurt yourself."

Once again, he imagined being in school and explaining the weird things she said. Sam would never let him live it down. He'd look for ways to confuse the poor girl with modern sayings. Not because Sam would be mean about it, but because he was always joking with everyone. And then Garth would have to fight him.

Where did that come from?

The town of Princess Anne came up fast, and he saw a few gas stations right away. However, he picked a location closest to one of his favorite fast food joints because he wanted to show the pioneer teenager real modern dining.

"I've got a treat for you," he said as he pulled into the lot. "Wait just a minute."

Garth stopped next to the drive-through order board, giddy with anticipation. "If you think those candy bars were good, wait until you taste this. We can eat in the car."

He ordered and drove around the side. Lydia leaned almost over his lap as she tried to look inside the drive-through window. The smartly-dressed workers moved from station to station, doing their jobs.

"Wow. They are making our food?"

"Yeah, sort of. The food is already there. They assemble it, I think." A couple of schoolmates worked in fast food restaurants. He'd heard horror stories about cleanliness, but he wasn't going to ruin the moment. He figured she probably ate with her hands over campfires, so this couldn't be any worse.

The clerk took his money and handed over his order. Garth maneuvered into a parking space. The gas station next door looked extremely busy, so the food gave them an excuse to wait for things to die down.

"I give you...the Big Mac." He pulled the cheeseburger out of the bag and handed it to her with a couple of napkins. "This is my favorite burger in the whole world. I hope you like it."

"It's huge! How do you eat it?"

He laughed uproariously because it was all coming together. They'd made good time, put some miles on the taxi, and were heading for Dad. He let himself enjoy being with Lydia. But most of all, he wanted to see her face when she got a taste of it.

Garth pulled out a second burger he'd purchased for himself. "Like this." He squeezed the top and bottom buns so all the materials in between squished a bit tighter, then stuffed it in his mouth.

"Ahhh," he mumbled with a full mouth. "So good."

She looked at him sideways.

He nodded emphatically, his eyes pointed at her sandwich.

Lydia studied her burger, then followed his lead. She stuffed it between her hands, then took the biggest bite she could.

A moment later, her eyes lit up.

"I told you!" he bubbled excitedly.

She exaggerated her chewing like she wanted to get done as fast as possible. When she came up for air, her radiant smile gave him hope that she found it as satisfying as he did.

"This is the best thing I've ever tasted," she cooed. "Thank you for getting this for me, Garth. You really are a provider."

She tore into the rest of her burger with grunts and sighs rivaling his own enthusiasm. He joined her in the ritual with glee, but his mood was tempered somewhat by being so close to the gas station.

He wondered how many times he'd have to fill up the tank two gallons at a time before he made it to his dad.

I-80, Wyoming

Buck and Connie listened to the radio for another thirty minutes as they continued toward the eastern half of Wyoming. The terrain became slightly hillier, but it remained desolate. He was starting to doubt he'd make it into Nebraska by nightfall because of all the stoppages and slowdowns of the day. He decided that, if nothing else, he wanted to get past the I-25 intersection at Cheyenne, because he worried they'd shut both highways down at the same time.

He led the convoy, doing eighty miles per hour.

"Buck Rogers, you got your ears on?"

He plucked the CB mic from its holder. "Yeah, Sparky, come on."

"I-70 just got shut down a hundred miles on each side of Denver. Glad we didn't take the southern route to the east." Sparky laughed.

Buck looked at Connie, then at Mac. His decisions during the past few days had been lucky.

"Did they say why they closed the boulevard down there?"

"Road construction," Sparky deadpanned.

He grinned at Connie, then spoke to the other driver. "You don't believe that, do you?"

"Hell, no. Something is going on. First, a bunch of the 25 goes down for construction. Now the 70 is being worked on. It ain't right, to be sure, but I'll be damned if I know what's going on."

"Let me know if you hear anything more about I-25 closing." Buck placed the mic back in its cradle and glanced between the road and the radio.

"Roger, Rogers," Sparky replied, using the last part of Buck's handle.

Connie had her feet back up on the dashboard, and she held Buck's phone in her lap. "Well, I guess we're heading into more trouble. I may never get hold of Philip."

He watched the yellow-striped line ahead, unsure how to respond.

"I believe you, by the way," she went on. "I think he did just fine in the Iraq War and is alive and safe here in 2020." She held up the phone. "I've been sneaky about it, but I've been trying his phone number all day."

"Nothing?" he asked.

"Not a damned thing. It rings and rings. That doesn't sound right, does it? I'm sure he would have an answering machine or someone, a neighbor maybe, would get sick of a phone ringing all the time."

She sighed heavily. "All I want is to hear his voice. I want to know what he's doing with his life. I want to know he's living his dreams and being a good person. Is that too much to ask?"

He smiled. "It's what every parent wants."

"I was so nervous when he went overseas. For me, it was only a few months ago, but for him, it's been seventeen years. Do you think he hates me for leaving him?"

"Fuck, no!" he blurted. Then, with more restraint, he added, "No one could possibly hate you."

"Thanks," she replied sadly. "I guess I'll never know."

"Hey, you can't be sure of that. This whole thing with the blue and red lights might be like a storm passing overhead. It could clear up tomorrow, and everything will go back to the way it was. It's what we're hoping for, right?"

More than ever, a selfish part of him wanted her to remain, even if the rest of the world went back to normal.

"Somehow, I don't think it's going to work that way. Maybe the universe doesn't allow family members to talk to each other when one of them skips through time."

She sniffled.

"I'm sorry this is happening to you," he said in a respectful tone, "but you and I are a team now, right? You've said you needed me a few times. Well, I need you, too. Someone's got to yell at me when I drive through floods and cut across medians."

He laughed, hoping it would spark a response in her.

"Yeah, maybe. I am lucky to be with you, and I know Phil is a strong young man. Whatever he's doing, he'll be wonderful at it. I'm a mom. I'm programmed to worry."

"You're not alone. I worry about my boy all the time, too. He's a good kid, no doubt, but he has a lot of maturing to do. Now he's with a girl..."

Connie guffawed. "Still on about girls, are you? What is it that worries you so much about us ladies?"

He glanced over, to find her wiping away tears.

"It's not the girls I fear. It's my boy. He's right at the age when he's going to discover the wonders of the fairer sex, and I'm afraid he's going to get so distracted by this Lydia person that he drives into the Atlantic Ocean instead of heading west to meet us."

"Don't we make a fine pair?" She grinned. "We're both worrying about things we have absolutely no control over."

"I have a lot of time to think while I drive. It's probably led to more lost sleep than I could ever make up. I'll try to get out of my head while I'm with you."

"Well, I do know one thing that can take your mind off the heavy stuff for a while." She dropped her feet off the dash and brushed her red hair back a little. He'd been caught off-guard and couldn't imagine what she had in mind.

He caught a twinkle in her eye, but then she called, "Mac!"

The Golden barked and hopped off the rear sleeper bed.

"Give me paw," she said.

The dog looked between Connie and him, then held out one of his paws.

"Good dog!" Connie gushed.

"Have you been secretly training him?" he asked with amazement.

Connie reached up above his head and pulled down one of the remaining dog treats. Her perfume wasn't as strong after her time in the water, but it was still there.

For a few miles, he forgot about his worries while Connie practiced the trick over and over with Big Mac. By the time she was done, he did it without hesitation. She'd started working on getting him to do left or right paw when the CB crackled to life.

"Buck Rogers, I have news," Sparky called.

Buck knew by the tone of voice it wasn't going to be good.

His brief moment of happiness was over.

TWENTY-ONE

***Search for Nuclear, Astrophysical, and Krono-
metric Extremes (SNAKE). Red Mesa, Colorado***

Bob ran up, out of breath. "Faith! Holy shit! Are you all right?"

Faith heard his voice, and recognized his face, but had trouble replying. She'd mostly recovered from the car bomb outside the window, but her ears wouldn't let go of a high-pitched squeal. She patted both ears to try to get them to pop and clear up while she and General Smith waited in an interior room.

An Air Force guard ran up behind Bob. When he saw the general, he stopped. "Sir, this man ran through our cordon at the end of this hallway."

"I had to make sure she wasn't hurt, you twit," Bob snapped back without looking at the man.

General Smith busily conferred with some of his men but dismissed the guard with barely a glance. "He's fine. Thank you, son."

The guard glared at Bob, then spun on his heel and left the room.

"I didn't know you gave a damn," Faith said to Bob when it was just the two of them. Her ears weren't getting any better, so she picked through her hair, amazed at all the tiny pieces of glass stuck in her tangled locks.

"Geez, c'mon. I don't want anyone to hurt you. I'm supposed to be your only bad guy."

It touched Faith to know her ex had a tiny bit of compassion, but he'd have an uphill battle if he expected her to forget everything he'd done leading up to the crisis. However, before she could answer him one way or another, General Smith was in her face.

"Doctor Sinclair, I need you to walk with me. Alone."

The general gestured her away from Doctor Stafford.

"You sure you want to go with him?" Bob asked, as if his date was being stolen at Homecoming.

"I'll be fine. Go check on the others." She hadn't heard of any deaths, but her staff was shouting about injuries in the hallway. She wanted to go out and check on them herself, but she had to stay with the general. Once he had done his job, she could do hers.

When Obadias had her alone in the hallway, he began talking in a conspiratorial tone. "Faith, do you have any idea who could have done this? The car is totaled. We're trying to figure out who it belonged to and how it got on your lot. In the meantime, it would help to know if you have any enemies."

She chuckled. "Where do I start? Radical environmental groups have been at our throats since we started up, and they've been angry at CERN for years before that. Those are the people who think what we do is going to open a black hole and swallow the Earth or something."

They looked at each other for a moment. She realized what she'd said.

"No, this isn't a black hole, general. We could measure that easily if it was. Rest assured, the Four Arrows experiment didn't open one."

"Well, okay, then. I feel better knowing that." He put a knuckle to his chin. "But no one else? Does anyone on the inside feel slighted by or vindictive towards what you're doing here?"

"No. Well, I'm not aware of any. Why would one of my own people do this?"

"I don't know, but it's the typical logic in these situations. No one from the outside could have come here this fast, you know? Not unless a terrorist group was based in Denver and rushed to action as soon as SNAKE was mentioned on the news."

"Not likely," she agreed.

They walked down the hall until they came to the circular ring around the experimental chamber. She looked down at the clean room, which was currently empty and running at low power. Most of the facility was working on the math regarding the energy flowing through the collider and up into the atmosphere.

"You've got to think of all the possibilities, Faith. You know the people working for you far better than anyone else. Even with formal interrogations, it would take forever to weed out a malcontent. There has to be someone you'd consider a threat."

"I have hundreds of employees here. I haven't even met them all."

"Faith!" Bob cried out behind them.

"Not him again," the general mumbled.

Bob ran up, holding his phone.

Smith stopped him before he made it the last ten feet. "I insist we be left alone, Doctor."

191

Bob ignored the general and ran up to Faith. "You won't believe this! There's been another explosion."

"I didn't feel one," she replied.

"Where?" the general demanded.

"In the super collider tunnel. Cameras went offline at Transition Point Seven." Bob peered directly at Faith. "A Four Arrows box was there."

"My men!" the general exploded. He'd put guards on each of the boxes.

"Guys, there's something else. The guards have been chased away from the remaining two boxes. Someone is down there, and we don't know what they're doing."

"Dammit all to hell!" The general went over to the stairwell to the tram station. "I'm going down there."

"I'll go with you," Bob announced.

"No!" Faith insisted. "I need you up in the control room. Find Sun. If all the boxes are destroyed, there is no telling what's going to go wrong. I need someone I can trust to manage things up there."

"Shit, Faith. This ain't right. I can't let you go alone."

She smiled. "I'm not alone. I've got a four-star general watching over me."

"I don't care who, but one of you needs to come with me right now to open the tram doors and drive the damned thing." The general started down the stairs.

Bob stood still while she and General Smith hurried away.

There was no romantic goodbye, but she felt a little like it was a farewell with Bob. If the terrorists blew up the other two boxes, all of reality could unravel. There was no way to know for sure what would result, but she was confident it wouldn't be anything good.

"Take care of yourself," she said as she went into the stairwell.

"Yeah, you too," Bob said slowly, disappointment tingeing his words. "I'll watch over things here until you get back."

"You always wanted to be in charge," she allowed. "Now's your chance."

"Not like this," he said in a quiet voice.

She went through the doors and didn't look back. Her flats slapped on each of the steps as she ran as fast as possible to the bottom, but when she entered the station, the *Silver Bullet* wasn't there.

General Smith faced her. "I don't suppose there are other tram cars on the line?"

"There are two, one for each hemisphere." She trotted to the tracks and looked to the right. "There's a sister station about a hundred yards that way." She pointed down the lighted tunnel.

"I'm not too proud to run." General Smith hopped into the tram pathway, which was a smooth slab of concrete bracketed on each side by long metal magnets, which acted as the tracks. Without waiting a second for her, he jogged away.

"Me, either," she assured him as she got onto the tracks.

Ahead, the wedge-shaped back of the tram engine pointed right at her.

Please don't move.

European Laboratory for Particle Physics (CERN), Switzerland

When Philip walked into the lobby of the research facility, it reminded him of being in a library. Ethan conversed in hushed tones with two overnight security guards at the front desk. The sparkling-white floors and metallic walls bounced and warped the echo of the voices.

There didn't appear to be any urgency in the conversation, so he strode up to the desk to listen in.

Ethan saw him and waved him over. "The guards have made a phone call to the director. He should be here momentarily. At first glance, they say we've wasted our time, because nothing unusual is going on."

"Did they say anything about a failed experiment?"

The other man shook his head. "Nope. *Nada*."

"Do we report in?"

Ethan looked at Corporal Grafton. "I want you to report to Battalion. Tell them our first impression is that nothing is amiss. The facility is intact. No reported problems. Waiting for the director. That's all."

Grafton took off his radio to make his report.

"What are we looking at for time?" Phil asked. "Did they say when the boss is going to get here?"

"No," Ethan replied. "But he *is* in this building."

"You want a perimeter?" he inquired quietly.

"Yeah, go ahead. Give the men something to do while we wait. Have them pair up and keep eyes outside and down the two main hallways just in case."

After setting the men in place, Phil checked on Grafton. "You get HQ on the line?"

"Still trying, sir."

"Very good." He went back to the main desk to advise Ethan of the delay, but then a scientist walked up to the Colonel.

"Hello, I'm Dr. Tomas Eli. Can someone tell me what the bloody hell all these guns are doing on my campus at this late hour?"

"I'm Lieutenant Colonel Ethan Knight, sir, and with all due respect, we're the least of your worries."

"Then why are you here?"

Ethan pulled out a piece of paper. "I've got some questions that must be answered, okay?"

The doctor crossed his arms and shifted his glasses as he assumed a defensive stance, arms crossed and leaning backward.

"Do you have any knowledge of the Four Arrows Project, a covert attempt to piggyback on experiment 7HC?"

"Four Arrows? No. But I do know of 7HC. We ran the experiment a few days ago."

Ethan kept reading.

"Do you know the whereabouts of the American, Doctor Kyle Johnson?"

"I do not," the scientist deadpanned.

"Why did you say it like that? You seem upset."

He removed his glasses and pinched the bridge of his nose. "We've been trying to track him down for days. He and his team walked off the floor at a crucial moment during 7HC. We haven't seen them since."

"But you said everything is okay?" Ethan wasn't reading from the card.

"And it is. We have over twenty nations represented here at CERN. Each one can come and go as they please. I'm sure the Americans had something important going on, but it doesn't change the fact that they left without warning during an international experiment."

Ethan seemed to think about the next question because he stared at it for a good ten seconds. "Final item here. By executive order of the President of the United States, in cooperation with the Swiss Federal Council, we have been ordered to evacuate and shut down all power to your facility."

Doctor Eli's face dropped before he recovered, clenching his jaw and glaring at the lieutenant colonel.

I-80, Wyoming

Sparky's voice came out of the tinny speakers. "Buck, there has been a terrorist attack in Red Mesa, Colorado. At that messed-up science place. It's all over the news. You should—"

The audio kicked off. Buck couldn't tell if it was because Sparky had stopped or his radio gave out, but he soon didn't care.

"Oh, shit," he mumbled.

A rush of dizziness clouded his vision, and he desperately gripped the steering wheel to maintain consciousness.

"Buck, it's happening again..." Connie's voice might as well have been over the horizon, it sounded so far away. "The red."

The yellow line down the middle of the dual highway lanes became a tunnel in his vision. The rest of the world was dark, save for a red tint on the remaining pinhole.

He fought to keep the truck on the line, although he tapped the brakes to slow the truck.

Don't pass out, you dumb lug. People depend on you.

The intense buzzing sensation in his head passed as quickly as it arrived. When his vision firmed up, he adjusted the wheel to make sure he was in the lane, then he looked at his side mirror.

Fuck me.

Sparky's blue Mack shot off the highway into the median.

"He's tipping," Buck said dryly.

"Who?" Connie replied weakly.

It happened in slow motion. Sparky's truck tore into the soft ground between the lanes because he came in at an angle. The direction of the wheels was controlled by the force driving them into the dirt, and they yanked his entire rig to the left. A competent driver would steer into the turn to avoid putting so much stress on the frame, but Sparky either didn't or couldn't.

The truck's front left tire continued to dig into the dirt, and nine of the eighteen wheels were soon off the ground.

At the same time, the roadway behind his rig filled with white smoke as the other two semis locked up their brakes to avoid leaving the highway with Sparky.

Finally, the giant Mack truck fell over. The fifth wheel sheered under the extreme stress, and the kingpin separated. The entire tractor-trailer seemed to wring itself out like a wet towel. The front half was yanked left with the tractor, while the back half swung right with momentum. Eventually, the whole warped box trailer split open like a sleeve of crackers. Pallets of boxes hemorrhaged out the sides.

Buck finally stomped on his brakes and brought his trailer to a safe stop.

Smoke and dust whipped past his windows. None of the three trucks were visible as he glanced back because of the debris in the air, but his immediate concern was for Connie and Mac.

"You okay?" he asked her.

She sat straight up in her chair, held there by the seatbelt. A second after he hit the e-brake, she shucked off the belt and reached under the dashboard.

"I'm fine." Mac sat up and gave her a lick on the hands. "We're fine."

"You sure?" he asked.

"Yeah, go," she replied with insistence. Somehow, she knew exactly what he was going to do.

"I'll be right back."

He jumped down from his truck and was greeted by a disaster. Sparky's rig was on its side between the two directions of the interstate. Eve had jackknifed her red Peterbilt, so her cab faced backward. Monsignor was between the other two, stopped, but holding onto his steering wheel like he'd barely dodged the twenty-six-inch shell of a battleship.

Everyone, please be okay.

TWENTY-TWO

Princess Anne, Maryland

Lydia patted the white cloth hanging from a belt at her midsection. "I'm stuffed. Do you eat this much every day?"

Garth laughed. "I could eat that meal for breakfast, lunch, and dinner and not get tired of it. Something about a Big Mac always makes me want another one."

She held up the cup of soda. "And this fizzy drink? Uh, soda? You consume this all the time too?"

He scratched his ear. "Well, not always. Dad doesn't let me have it on school days. Says it makes me lose my concentration. He also doesn't let me have it after dinner. Says it keeps me up at night. However, Sam's parents aren't as strict."

It struck him how often he did the opposite of what his dad told him to do.

Garth drove off the McDonald's lot and pulled up to the gas pump in the station next door. He made up his mind to go for broke and try to buy a full tank of gas. As much as it impressed Lydia to go for forty miles on those two gallons, he didn't want to spend every half-hour faking his way into gas stations to buy a few drops of fuel.

"You stay here," he said after turning off the engine. "I'll be right back. This time I want to go in and out without any trouble, okay?"

She nodded enthusiastically. "I will stay here with my drink. It is so delicious."

He got out, then looked back into the car. "You are drinking Sprite, which is one of the tamer sodas. When I think you're ready for it, I'll get you the good stuff. It's called Mountain Dew."

Lydia grinned. "It sounds like a heavenly place. I loved seeing the mountains."

"No, it's not really from there. Well, maybe it is..." It went on his list to check the next can or bottle he found. Maybe it was made in Colorado or Wyoming?

"Be right back," he assured her.

The convenience store had been crowded while he and Lydia ate lunch, but now the congestion had ebbed a bit. There were a couple of biker-looking guys at the soda fountain, an elderly woman studying the candy aisle, and a couple of teenage boys in baseball uniforms grabbing large boxes of Twinkies and Ding Dongs.

He walked up to the tattooed dark-haired woman behind the counter with all the confidence he could summon.

"I'd like to buy fifty dollars of gas on Pump 1."

She held out her hand and he gave her a fifty-dollar bill, which was the change he had from his earlier purchases. Dad's bugout bag had included four crisp hundred dollar bills, which at first seemed like a fortune, but after the motel and miscellaneous purchases, he now realized how fast he'd gone through most of the first two.

"You're golden," she said dismissively.

He stood there for a few moments, unsure what it meant. He'd been prepared to argue his way through the transaction.

I guess I look older in Maryland.

Grateful for the luck, he shot out the door and went back to the car. Lydia remained exactly where she'd been, sipping soda through her straw. When he reached in to unlock the gas tank door, she waved at him like he'd been gone for a week.

"Hiya, Garth! I'm loving this!" She pointed to the drink.

"Wouldn't you know it? You just said their motto."

"I'm going to fill us all the way to the top. They didn't ask for ID or anything in there. We should be out on the highway and making great time in a few minutes."

"Wonderful!" she exclaimed.

He spent an additional moment looking at her through the window. Her glowing eyes and excitable demeanor reminded him of kids who'd come home from a night of trick or treating on Halloween. She was hopped up on sugar.

She was the only thing on his mind as he gassed up.

Was it harmful to give her so much sugar so fast? Did he have the right to deny it to her? If he'd gone through time from a land of eating leaves and berries and ended up here with giant burgers and pounds of chocolate, he'd want to dive in. He figured it was best to let her go crazy with it.

When the machine kicked off, he noticed he'd only spent forty-eight dollars and a few cents, but he'd told the lady he would spend fifty.

What would Dad do?

Garth looked around, unsure. The other drivers were busy with their own fueling situations and had no interest in him. Dad had never explained this procedure, but he'd seen him mess around with the handle, like he wanted to put more gas in the tank after the pump had stopped. That was what Dad would do here, he figured. Get every cent of fuel he could.

"What the hell," he mumbled.

He pulled the handle and squirted more gas into his tank, but it shut off a second later. The amount on the pump hardly moved. After trying it a few more times, he figured out it was a safety measure to keep people from overfilling their tanks and spilling it on the pavement.

After hanging up the pump and securing his tank door, he went past Lydia again. "I'll be right back. I have to go inside again to get change."

"Fine and dandy!" she replied happily.

As he walked back in, it struck him how easy it would be to blow some more money and buy the Mountain Dew he had promised her. It would be a good drink for doing a lot of driving, but he figured that much sugar and caffeine could hurt Lydia, so he resolved to wait until the next gas station to introduce her to it.

Once inside the swinging doors, he had a moment to orient on the register before his brain short-circuited. A red flash seemed to come from inside his eyeballs, like he'd been zapped by electricity. In the next instant, a dizzy feeling overwhelmed him.

"Whoa!"

He and several other patrons fell to the ground, and a plastic cup tumbled in the next aisle. The sound of sloshing liquid was accompanied by cussing.

The feeling didn't last long. His head was soon back to normal, but he took some time to sit and recover.

"I need to pay and get out of here," he mumbled.

After he got to his feet, Garth helped the two teenage boys to theirs. They collected their boxes of goodies, then followed him to the front counter.

A man in a fancy black suit was already there.

Wait up. There's two.

He blinked several times, not sure if he saw double.

Garth figured out there were two of them, but one was on the other side of the counter.

He lined up behind the first man in the suit, but something about him was off. The posture of the guy was confusing, like he was leaning against the low counter and whispering to the tattooed clerk. The look on her face was unabashed fear.

Danger!

A breath caught in his throat. His body begged him to run away, so he went backward.

"Watch it, dude," one of the baseball players said when he ran into him.

The suited man heard the voice and spun around to see who it was.

Garth's eyes went directly to the man's pistol.

Central Station, Sydney, Australia

It was noon when the engineer brought the engine into the station to deliver the abandoned passenger and the engineer trainee. The trip had taken about twice as long as it should have because every station along the way had lots of people wanting a ride and no carriages to carry them. Gladys insisted they stop at every one and inform the passengers of the problems with the rail lines.

She wanted to scream, but there was no faster way to get to Sydney.

Finally, after what felt like a full lifetime to Destiny, Gladys guided the train to the end of the same walkway where she'd jumped on to catch it during departure. She hopped up, ready to run out the door.

"Thanks for coming to get us," she said to the engineer to be polite. "And thank you for coming with me through those woods," she told Becker.

"I admit that I wanted out of there as much as you did." The young man looked at his feet before asking, "Will you be all right?"

She held out her hands. "I have no baggage, so I'm just going to get a cab and head out. You two should get home, too. After what we saw last night and at those other stations, I don't think the trains will be running much longer."

"I won't be driving one," Becker answered.

Gladys opened the door. "They told me I was going to be awarded time-and-a-half for working this continuous shift, but now I think it's laughable. They're going to have to throw ten times that amount at me for me to head back down those tracks."

Destiny shook hands with both of them, then hurried out the door and down the steps. As she reached the platform, the wave of dizziness came back like a ninja out of the night. It slapped her with a red pulse of energy right behind her eyes.

Destiny woke up and found she'd fallen to the concrete.

"Not again," she mumbled.

The wave passed as quickly as before, and she sprang to her feet to see if anything had changed.

Becker was on the floor inside the cabin of the engine.

"You okay?" she called.

He propped himself up. "I think I packed my dacks, mate."

She hoped he hadn't really soiled his pants, but wouldn't blame him. It was a creepy sensation.

"What is going on?" he pressed. "Was that what happened to us when our engine disappeared?"

"No. Back then was different. This time it was sharp and had a red glow. Did you see it?"

Both of the train employees nodded in agreement. "Red lasers burned my eyes," Becker added. "Like fucking aliens."

"No, it's not coming from the stars. These headache-inducing dizzy spells are being caused by something on the other side of the planet. An experiment gone wrong."

"How can you possibly know such a thing?" he asked.

"Because my sister is in charge of it. She told me weird things were happening with time. Back in Canberra, I saw animals that had been extinct for tens of thousands of years." She watched as he stood up. Gladys recovered in the engine behind him. "The Opera House is gone, not destroyed. It's as if it were never there. Time has come undone."

"What can we do?" he asked in a timid voice.

She shrugged. "Hell if I know, but I'm going to find out. See ya round, okay?"

Destiny pulled out her phone and dialed Faith as she walked into the main terminal. She didn't worry about the exact time zone conversion, but she guessed it was early evening in Denver.

"Come on, dammit! Pick up!"

She had to know how much worse life was going to get, and Faith was the one person she trusted to tell her the truth.

. . .

I-80, Wyoming

Buck had chosen not to pull over, thinking it wouldn't matter. Eve's rig was almost sideways because it had jack-knifed, and Monsignor was next to her. Cars would not be able to get by them.

The smoke and dust had mostly blown away as he hustled into the median and ran alongside Sparky's Mack. It had been tossed to the side, so the driver's window was in the dirt. However, the glass of the front windshield had imploded completely, giving him easy access to the interior.

Sparky was still buckled in, and he smiled from behind the half-deflated airbag.

"Just had a helluva ride," he said. "I blacked out and woke up sideways."

"I almost zoned out, too," Buck admitted. "Eve had issues, but she kept the wheels down."

"I'm assuming my load is gone?" the other driver said despondently.

Buck nodded.

Sparky thought for a second. "Well, shit."

"On the bright side, you're alive. That was a big wreck, hoss."

"Don't do anything unless you're going to give it your best. Apparently, I went all-in, because I never scratched a bumper until today."

Buck held out his hand. "We have to get you out of there. We have to keep moving. Think you can get out?"

Sparky moved his arms and wiggled his fingers. "Looks like I'm fine. Let me pop the belt and gather a few things, and I'll climb out this new door I've made in the windshield."

Buck drew a deep breath. He'd only met Sparky the day before, but he'd come to appreciate the other driver as the lynchpin of his team. It would have been terrible to lose him to something so random.

After watching Sparky unclick his belt and crawl out of his seat, he ran over to Eve's red rig. Monsignor was out of his truck, helping direct her so she could straighten out her trailer without running off the highway.

"You okay, ma'am?" he called up to her.

She smiled tentatively. "I film myself around the clock. It makes for good promotional materials when I'm recruiting. However, I'm going to delete this accident. I've never jackknifed like this. It's rookie material."

"You know, whatever it was that made us all black out, you may have caught it on film. You should hold onto the tape."

"We'll see how I feel when we get to safety."

"Fair enough," Buck agreed.

"You got this?" he asked as he walked up to Monsignor.

The young guy had a thousand-yard-stare. "I'll get her out of here, don't worry about it. Is Sparky good?"

"Yeah. He's banged up, but there is no blood. I'm not sure how he did it, but he said he blacked out. Maybe it helped save his life." Since he spent his life on the road, he'd heard every story about crashes there was. Sometimes, people who fell asleep at the wheel or drove shit-faced drunk got into accidents and survived simply because they were too out of it to brace themselves and break something. Sparky had been saved by the same debilitating dizzy spell that had made him crash.

Buck realized they were now a truck short. "Hey, can you or Eve take him in your rig? I'm already plus one."

"I'll take care of it," Monsignor monotoned.

"Hey, driver!" Buck yelled.

The other man seemed to snap out of his daze.

"Relax," Buck suggested in an even voice. "You look like you're in shock."

"Yeah, maybe I am. I watched Sparky go into the dirt, and I almost rammed into him when I had an episode behind the wheel. I thought the bomb was going to go off." He pointed to his shiny fuel carrier. His biggest fear was blowing up with it.

"You're good," Buck assured him. "We're all alive. Get her pointed in the right direction, put Sparky in a seat, and let's get the hell out of here. Four-wheelers are going to whiz by here in minutes."

Monsignor gave him a thumbs-up.

Buck ran back to his Peterbilt, already thinking about what had to happen next. Once they were all in their trucks and going east, he'd have to balance the need to go faster and get beyond Interstate 25 with the need to keep it slow in case they experienced more of the dizzy spells.

He jumped up on his side step and reached for the door, but his vision went back into that dark tunnel. A blood-red explosion took place at the end of those pinpricks of light, and the dizziness flooded his consciousness.

This time he couldn't hold on.

TWENTY-THREE

Search for Nuclear, Astrophysical, and Krono-metric Extremes (SNAKE). Red Mesa, Colorado

Faith and the general arrived at the alternate tram station after running down the tracks. She made it to the locked doors a few seconds before he did.

"You must work out," he huffed.

"I ride my bike when I'm not solving time anomalies. Here, I've got it open."

He walked into the compartment as if he were the captain of the ship. He went directly to the control panel at the front. "Show me how to drive this, and you can go."

"No, that's not how this works. We're partners, remember?"

"Doctor...uh, Faith, we don't have time to argue. This is going to be dangerous."

She hit the panel for the doors, shutting them both inside.

"Hang on, sir." She gently pushed him aside and hit the aptly-named Go button. It accelerated slowly as she'd seen it do many times, but once it was at sixty miles an hour, she held her hand dramatically over another lever. "We're chucking off the safeties. I assume you're good with me doing so?"

She didn't wait for an answer. After flicking it off, she pulled out a small foldaway chair from under the switchboard. "Normally, this is all automated, but a driver can take control manually. We used that feature when we had to stop in between stations during the inspections. Now I'm going to use it to get us thirty miles down the line in six minutes."

"Do whatever it takes," he ordered.

She experienced the exhilaration of acceleration. The square lights along the wall of the tunnel flashed by like they were under a strobe light.

"We're passing the safe cruising speed," she deadpanned. "One hundred miles per hour."

"You said it can go faster?"

"Oh, yeah," she said with a quiver in her voice and a lump in her stomach. They were in a sixty-mile tube traveling over one hundred miles an hour.

What could go wrong?

"One-twenty-five," she announced.

The car accelerated at a nice even pace because the magnetic system wasn't like a combustion engine. There was no mashing the gas pedal.

"Two hundred," she said with some trepidation.

The lights now appeared as a solid line of white through the windows on both sides of the car. Their eyes couldn't see each individual box anymore.

"What is this tram called?" General Smith asked out of nowhere.

She turned back to him despite the speed of the maglev train. "*Little Scraggy.*"

"What the f—"

He was caught short when they burst through the first station. For a split second, they saw orange flames and bright light.

"Damn!" she yelled. "I forgot, all the safeties are off. Normally we would have stopped at every station."

"That's where the bomb went off, wasn't it?" he asked.

They both looked behind them, although the station was long gone.

"Yeah. We were lucky the track wasn't hit, or we'd be goop on the walls right now."

General Smith ran his fingers through his thinning gray hair. "My God, we're going to be too late. They aren't playing around."

"Three hundred miles per hour," she reported. "This is top speed, sir."

"Can you rig it to go faster?" he asked.

"No. I've got it at maximum power right now. There's nothing we can do to change the physics of this device."

"Wouldn't that be nice?" he asked.

The ride was as smooth as glass. It almost seemed like they weren't moving at all because the lights outside now appeared as one thick block to a point far down the tunnel.

His phone chirped, and he picked up. "Go."

He listened to the person on the line, then said, "Dammit!" and hung up.

"The second box has already been blown. There's only one more."

"Did they say which one blew up?" she asked. "I need to know where we're going because I have to decelerate before we get close."

"They are going in order, apparently. The next one up ahead is gone."

She looked at the sixty-two-mile ring as a clock. The main offices were at six o'clock. The box they took offline yesterday was approximately in the 4 o'clock position. They'd just whipped by the stop at 7, which was on fire. Now they'd learned the Four Arrows box at the 10-slot was gone. There was one left at the 1 o'clock location.

"We have to cross twelve o'clock and go into the other hemisphere."

"And?" he asked.

"General, if the *Silver Bullet* is still on the tracks, we could run into it. That would never happen with the safety on, but we don't have..."

Her hand hovered over the throttle.

"Keep going," he said without emotion. "If they get the last one, we're dead anyway, right?"

She wasn't sure how to address that. She'd come to believe there was something to be said for turning off the mysterious boxes, but her way depended on understanding the inner workings of the containers and shutting them down according to the internal specifications. Blowing them all up couldn't possibly be the solution, could it?

"I guess we're going to find out." She ignored her instinct to slow down and focused intently on the edge of the curve in the tracks far ahead. If there was something blocking them, she was going to drop the power, even if it wasn't going to save them.

When she saw the fire at the next station, she almost powered down, but there wasn't anything on the tracks. The orange glow of burning materials rushed by in a flash, and they were on their way to the last intact box.

Another place I could have died.

Faith stared ahead and kept her hand on the power button constantly. She did that for another minute before she'd had enough. "Sir, at this speed, we'll get to the thirty-mile marker any second. Once we cross over, we have to start the slowdown so we can stop before our destination."

"That was it!" she blurted. The map on the console switched from green to red, indicating they were in the other hemisphere of the ring. *Little Scraggy* didn't belong on the other side.

"Wait until the last second, then stop us," he commanded. "We don't have time to fuck around."

At three hundred miles an hour, she could go all the way around the sixty-mile loop in about twelve minutes, so they were covering a lot of ground in not a lot of time. She didn't wait very long before dropping power, which served as a slowing mechanism.

They'd bled off about half the speed when the station appeared from around the distant bend in the track.

"Oh, shit."

She hit the brake button, which jerked them forward in their seats. It was designed to use the magnets of the levitation system to slow the train, but she saw in an instant that it wasn't going to be enough.

"The train," General Smith pointed. She saw it, too.

They lost more speed, but the *Silver Bullet* got larger every second.

"I have to cut power," she said as she popped open a panel flush with the top of the console. Inside was a bright-red button with an electrical bolt with a line through it. She hit it without any further thought.

All the power went out and the maglev system shut off, canceling the magnetic repulsion that kept them floating on air, which in turn dropped the bottom of the car onto the concrete. The added slowdown slammed her against the control board.

"Hang on!" she screamed over the sound of metal grinding on pavement. She groped around for a seatbelt, but the ends had fallen to the sides of her seat.

Faith sucked in a breath and held it.

The *Silver Bullet* approached like Death incarnate, but there wasn't anything she could do except watch it.

I-80, Wyoming

Buck picked himself up off the pavement, disappointed that he'd been unable to retain consciousness. After one quick glance back at Sparky and Monsignor to make sure they were getting up, he climbed into his rig.

Mac looked over his shoulder, then went back whining next to Connie.

"Connie?" he said as he shuffled over to her.

"Phil? I'll drive you to school. Wake me up after you eat breakfast."

He chuckled, then softly rubbed her hair. "Hey, Connie, it's Buck and Big Mac."

His Golden barked once as if to assure her he was there.

That brought her back to the Peterbilt.

"Oh!" she exclaimed when it was clear he'd been listening to her. "What did I say?"

"You said something about—" He made a snap judgment not to remind her of her missing son. "You said you secretly wished I'd bought you that green T-shirt and a Skoal ball cap, and then I think you were talking about how you were going to put me into one of your books as the pivotal hero."

She rolled her eyes. "I'll put you in a story, all right, but you'll be the one with the ugly shirt and hat, not me. It's the benefit of writing your own stories."

They both noticed his hand on the side of her head. He was going to pull it away, but she reached up and held it closer to her.

"Buck, I admit it. I'm getting scared. Whatever is happening, it's making things worse."

He relaxed with his hand in hers. "We've got to keep going. Garth is counting on me, no matter what. Shit!"

Buck had to pull away from her.

"What is it?" she asked with surprise.

He pulled out his phone, but it had rebooted itself and was in the middle of a restart.

"Dammit. I sent Garth out on the road. What if he blacked out and ended up wrapped around a tree?"

The CB lit up. "Buck, we're ready to roll. I'm riding with Eve. Monsignor said he didn't want me to blow up with him if we crashed again."

"That's right," the other driver chimed in. "I'll drive in the back and leave a mile between us, if it works for you? I'm afraid I'm going to kill someone."

Buck hated to have any separation in his convoy, but the threat was real. He had to drive fast enough to get to Garth before driving became impossible. It was probably prudent to keep the man with the flammable truck as far away from the others as possible.

"Fine with me," he agreed.

"What's our mission?" Sparky asked. "We still aiming for Nebraska?"

He thought about it for a second. It was late in the afternoon, and they were still a hundred miles from the target truck stop in Nebraska. However, they were getting close to Cheyenne and the I-25 intersection.

Buck keyed the mic and spoke slowly. "Our first task is to get to the other side of Cheyenne. I want to put ourselves on the eastern side of 25 before they shut it down. Once we make it there, we can plan how far we want to drive tonight."

"Cheyenne is about thirty miles away," Connie said in a contemplative voice. She'd pulled the atlas onto her lap while Buck was on the CB.

He glanced over to find her looking at him with watery eyes.

"What is it?" he asked.

"Buck, what are you going to do if you black out again? We could end up sideways if you pass out doing seventy miles an hour."

"I've got this," he said with as much positivity as possible. "I'm going to put this rig on cruise control and keep it pointed down the long yellow lines. I've got perfect wheel alignment, too. I'll keep a light touch on the steering wheel. If I black out, it will only be for a few seconds, right? The truck will stay pointed in the proper direction, and we won't go off the roadway. It will be a snap, now that we know what to plan for."

She thought about it for a few moments. "I trust you."

He did everything in his power to believe his own words. The Marine in him wasn't going to stop for anything on Earth, and he did make a good case for avoiding the effects of another blackout, but he couldn't plan for buffalo herds, closed highways, or floods.

"Let's make this happen."

European Laboratory for Particle Physics (CERN), Switzerland

Phil and Ethan watched the orderly evacuation of the administration wing. Because it was the middle of the night, there weren't many people inside. However, Dr. Eli hung around the desk asking questions the entire time.

"So, you are saying SNAKE believes we are still broadcasting power through thousands of kilometers of the Earth's mantle? We are somehow linked together? And that link is causing time distortions throughout the world?"

Phil nodded. "I saw it for myself in Afghanistan. Soviet-era tanks appeared from the 1980s. They were forty years out of time."

"And I've witnessed a plane landing from the Korean war," Ethan added. "Not to mention hundreds of news items on the networks. I still can't believe you don't know about all this. It's everywhere."

Doctor Eli leaned against the security desk. "I haven't heard of this because it isn't happening. Let me show you the world is fine, and maybe we can skip the shutdown?"

"You can try," Ethan agreed.

The doctor stepped around the desk to the computer, then he looked at Ethan and Phil like he was unsure about something. "You aren't going to shoot me, are you?"

Both men had their rifles slung over their shoulders to keep them close, but the scientist still seemed terrified of them.

"We're here to save you," Phil assured him.

"Good," he replied, sitting at the terminal. "Let's see what we can see."

He typed for a few seconds, then leaned back in his chair, victorious. "See? Nothing!"

Phil walked behind Dr. Eli's shoulders to look at the screen. It was set to the international section of one of the big news websites.

"The lead story today is about us Brits still trying to figure out Brexit. Imagine that. There is also something about an actor who is in rehab down in Australia. Oh, and your Yankees won their tenth game in a row. Not sure how it's international news, but I think it speaks to my point. There is nothing unusual going on."

The doctor continued with an impassioned plea. "You have to stop this. There is no need to take us offline. All it will do is interfere with our systems!"

Phil and Ethan looked at each other. Phil thought the other man was going to call in for clarification of his orders, but the resolve on his face didn't change.

"Sir, can you power down from this terminal?"

The hope on the doctor's face evaporated. "I just showed you we're okay. There is nothing wrong!"

Ethan was having none of it. "Doctor, you will shut this place down immediately. My orders are to take you offline and report what happens, so that's what I'm going to do."

"But—"

Ethan grabbed the man by the collar and pulled him close. "Dammit! Don't you get it? I don't trust you, *or* this place. Websites can be faked, but I saw that old plane myself. Phil saw those tanks in person. Every plane in the world has been grounded, and the entire US military is skedaddling back to America. My superiors believe it can be fixed by you shutting down this place, so you're going to do just that."

Ethan pushed the doctor up to the keyboard.

"Fine. I'll shut everything down except the cryo. If that warms up—"

"Shut it down. I don't want an ounce of electricity anywhere within a square kilometer."

The doctor began typing but halted for a second. "You know, electricity doesn't have any weight. It can't be put into an ounce."

Phil thought Ethan was going to lose it, based on the look of frustration on his face, but he simply patted the doctor on the shoulder.

"Get the power off, and you can joke around all you want. In the meantime, I'm trying to save the world."

Phil watched as the man's fingers danced on the keyboard. A minute or two later, the lights in the building turned off and the emergency lights came on.

"Those are battery-powered," the doctor said, continuing to type. "But the collider and the cryo magnets are powering down. I hope you're happy."

Ethan looked at Phil. "Get HQ on the line. We have to see if this worked."

TWENTY-FOUR

Princess Anne, Maryland

"Well, what do we have here? A hero?" The man with the gun pointed it at Garth's face. It was so close he saw into the metal barrel.

"No, uh, sir. I was only here to get change for my gas." His eyes refused to stop focusing on the gun.

"Turn out your pockets, kid. I'll take whatever money you have while I'm knocking over the joint." The man wore a black suit; that much he noticed when not looking at the pistol. He also sported a black felt hat like something they wore in the old days.

My gun.

He entertained the idea of reaching into his pocket and pulling out the PX4 Storm and blowing the guy away, but the dude's pistol was already in his face. It was an impossible-to-win scenario.

"Are you going to kill us?" one of the baseball boys asked.

The man laughed, and Garth finally looked at his face. He was about the same age as his dad, with slicked hair set under the black topper. The guy had white teeth and a thin mustache, which helped him piece together where he might have seen people like him.

"You're gangsters!" Garth blurted. "From the 1920s."

Garth's entire inventory of knowledge about gangsters came from a single movie he and his dad had watched about Prohibition times. Aside from the gunfights, he didn't particularly like it, but his dad had enjoyed seeing the bad guys get their comeuppance.

The greasy man eyed him warily, then reached down to Garth's open pockets.

"Holy Toledo! Frank, this kid is carrying a piece!" The gangster grabbed his subcompact pistol and stepped back. "It's some futuristic thing. Look."

The gun was small enough to sit in the man's hand like a kitten. There was a cat calendar on the wall behind the counter, which gave him the idea for the comparison.

Both men laughed. "Guns are dangerous, kid. I'll keep this for you." The man shoved the little gun into his pants pocket and kept the large revolver trained on Garth's face.

"Um, you can have my wallet, but please don't take my phone."

The guy opened the wallet and seemed disappointed. There was no money in the billfold, though there was a library card and his school ID.

"You have no money?" the man asked with anger.

Garth shook his head. "I spent it all on gas. It cost fifty dollars to fill my tank."

"Fifty dollars?" the man cried out. "You spent fifty on gasoline?"

"Benny," the other man in the suit called out. "Keep it together. This kind woman is giving me the money in her drawer. There is more than you can imagine."

The robber looked at Garth's phone next. "This isn't a gun too, is it? You called it a phone, but that's impossible."

"It is," Garth replied. "You can call people on it and talk to them. They are common as can be in the year 2020." After spending time with Lydia, he was mentally prepared to meet people from a different time.

"2020? You think it is 2020?" For the first time, Garth thought the man looked like he wasn't in control.

"Oh, it *is* 2020, for sure," Garth replied. "There's a calendar right there behind the counter."

The second bad guy shoved the clerk aside, then pulled the cat calendar off the wall. "Benny, take a look. We're being played good."

Benny took the calendar from his friend and looked at it. For one fraction of a second, Garth considered going for the man's gun, but he didn't think he had a chance. Even if he succeeded, the guy had his Storm as a backup, and the other man behind the counter could take a hostage.

Just get out of this alive.

"Something about this isn't right," Frank added. "The money—it's got to be counterfeit. The pictures and years are all wrong."

The man named Frank held a white money bag as he backed away from the counter, but he looked terrified.

"You guys got dizzy, didn't you?" Garth suggested. "We all did. It messed up time."

Benny stepped away from the counter to be with his friend, but he still held Garth's wallet and phone.

"Please, I need my phone," Garth practically begged.

The men didn't appear to be in the mood to negotiate.

"You people are crazy," Benny said. "It can't be 2020. That's a hundred years off. And this can't be a phone. And you can't be real."

The gangsters shuffled toward the front door. Each kept their revolvers on Garth and the two ballplayers, despite the other patrons hovering in the wings.

"Okay, this is what's going to happen," Frank spoke up when his back was to the front door. "I want everyone face-down on the ground. Whatever year this is, you are about to learn the calling card of the Mackey Brothers."

Everyone hesitated to comply. For Garth, it seemed surreal to be held up by gangsters, and he wasn't sure they were serious.

"Get down!" Benny shouted. He pointed his giant revolver at everyone he saw.

Garth dropped to the floor, and the others followed.

"I'm sure you've heard of us," Benny went on. "We always pick one person at random and shoot them in the head before we leave. It's usually the last person to get down on the floor and shut up."

Garth was already on the ground, but he chanced a look at Benny.

"I promise," Benny said, glaring at Garth. "It won't hurt a bit."

I-80, Wyoming

Buck, Eve, and Monsignor drove their three trucks toward Cheyenne, leaving a huge gap between Monsignor and Eve, as he had requested. Buck was happy to be moving, but they were only a few miles from Sparky's crash before Connie gave him some bad news.

"Garth's phone is ringing, I think, but he isn't answering. It went to voicemail, but I didn't say anything. Would you like me to call back for you?" She held his phone.

"No, I'm sure he's fine. I wouldn't want my dad calling

me every ten minutes either. It might make him lose concentration for whatever he's doing right now. We'll try him again once we're safe."

He didn't tell her that trying over and over and getting no answer was also stressful beyond words for him. He needed to focus on the road and the people around him before anyone else rolled over and got hurt. However, he had every intention of calling him once the immediate threats were managed.

He turned on the radio to get information about what was coming up.

"We can now report the shutdown of Interstate 76 between Denver and Fort Morgan, Colorado. Numerous arterial highways are also shut down outside the Mile-High City. Folks, national authorities are still not saying why these closures are necessary, but something is happening inside this zone. Reporters in Denver say there is nothing unusual, but residents are getting scared and the panic is spreading, as you can imagine."

Buck changed to a local Wyoming AM station. "Ten minutes ago, the Wyoming Highway Patrol broadcast a warning they were shutting down further portions of I-25 in the southeastern part of the state due to a maintenance emergency. We're still trying to get information on where the shutdowns are taking place."

"I was right," Buck responded.

"About what?" Connie replied.

"This maintenance bullshit. They are taking ownership of the highway between Malmstrom Air Base and Denver, like I said before. Something is coming down the highway, heading for SNAKE. That's what this is all about."

"You think it had to do with the terrorist attack on SNAKE?" she inquired.

The news had been painfully brief on the cause of the explosion, which told him something too. "I have to admit, I'm the king of conspiracy theories, but wouldn't it be fitting if the Army was transporting a nuclear bomb from up north so they could blow it up at the wayward lab?"

"That's nu—" She stopped herself.

"Nuts," he finished. "I know. But why else would they do it this way? You're an author. Can you think of alternatives?"

"Aliens? Maybe they have a special unit that only deals with aliens, and they need them there in a hurry."

"I like that one," he admitted.

"Hey, either way, though, why aren't they evacuating the people from the city? They wouldn't leave them there if aliens came down or if they were going to blow up a bomb, would they?"

"I did my time for Uncle Sam and saw some pretty fucked up orders, but even I don't think our leaders are capable of such a thing. We wouldn't nuke our own city. Never. As for aliens, I don't believe in them, so that's easy to write off."

Connie harrumphed as if insulted her idea didn't suit him.

"Perhaps another alternative is staring us in the face. We just experienced two bad episodes with the blackouts. Maybe things are getting worse, and the Army is sending soldiers to SNAKE to fix it?"

He shook his head to clear out the confusing thoughts.

"Right now, it doesn't matter. We have to get beyond Cheyenne, and then whatever is going to happen won't be our concern."

Connie rubbed Mac's ruff as he sat tall between their seats.

"I guess you're right," she finally agreed. "I'd like to be far away from whatever it is. These shutdowns remind me of an infection. The area of disease spreads out in larger rings. We have to get clear of that."

They approached a green road sign with the mileage for cities ahead. Connie read off the numbers. "Cheyenne, 20. Sidney, Nebraska, 121."

"Strap yourselves in," he laughed. "We're about to find out what's going on with these closures." He made a production of giving his Peterbilt extra gas.

"As long as you don't pass out," she cautioned.

He backed off the gas again, sure her warning was sound.

TWENTY-FIVE

***Search for Nuclear, Astrophysical, and Krono-
metric Extremes (SNAKE). Red Mesa, Colorado***

Faith's ribs felt like she'd been kicked by a mule, and the strong coppery taste of blood filled her mouth. She'd fallen to the floor of the tram and was on her back, but she considered herself extremely lucky to be alive.

"Faith," the general whispered. "We made it. I can see the last Four Arrows box. It hasn't been blown up."

The tram car's lights were out, but the station provided enough illumination to see the warped interior of the *Little Scraggy*. The door on the side of the car was halfway open, like it was trying to unload passengers one last time.

"Come on," the general said as he slid down the floor and out the door.

Her phone rang with Dez's ringtone, but she silenced it for the moment. There was no time to explain what she was doing.

"Right behind you," she called a second later.

When she made it outside and stood on the platform, she got a good look at what had happened. The *Scraggy* had rammed the other engine, but their pointed noses had served to guide them apart, like two arrows passing each other. Both trains had come off the guide rails, and the force of the moving engine had pushed the *Silver Bullet* to the front part of the room, but both were mostly intact.

"They built them well," she remarked.

The general didn't answer. He moved toward the target like a lion stalking its prey. She followed as best she could, although her legs seemed to be filled with Jell-O, shaking with each step.

Calm down, lady. You survived.

General Smith walked over to the steps to go up and over the collider ring, but he stopped when he saw to the other side.

"Son, step away from there!" he shouted, and darted over the top.

Faith hopped up and filled the space he'd just abandoned. A young man with cropped hair sat on the floor next to the Four Arrows box.

"Stay there!" the man shouted back. With lower volume, he continued, "My pack is loaded with C4."

General Smith halted about twenty feet from the man. He put up his hands, too, because the guy had a semiautomatic pistol.

"You don't have to do this," Faith yelled, seeing her opportunity. "It won't matter if you blow it up or not. Each box compensates. The last one will just disburse the energy into the ring." It was a useful lie. She had no idea what would happen if the last box was shut down, but it was one of her team's working theories.

"What's your name, soldier?" Smith asked the man.

"Call me Ed. I'm not with an official unit. My group is...classified."

"Are you with the outfit out of Malmstrom?"

The man looked up. "Shit, there goes the secret. How did you know that?"

Faith moved next to the general. She vaguely recognized the young man. "You work here, don't you? Facilities and maintenance, I think."

He nodded. "I had to learn the insides of your facility. It's how I was able to walk this down the emergency exit stairs without arousing any suspicion."

"Where are my men, Ed?" the general asked.

Ed pointed up. "They are safe in the woods. I chased them out with the threat of using this explosive pack on them. Oh, and I took their radios, so they are probably jogging through the forest to find their way back to SNAKE's main entrance. I expect they'll be along shortly."

"And the others?" Smith asked.

"I'm sure the others took care of your men, too. We're not killers." Ed seemed to notice he was holding a firearm. "Usually."

"So, why haven't you done like the other two and blown this up already?" she pressed.

General Smith glared at her and shook his head as if she'd done something wrong.

Ed still remained seated next to the cabinet. "They got them, huh? I appreciate the intel."

"Shit," she mumbled.

"It's okay." Smith spoke loudly to her while taking a half-step closer to Ed. "He could have blown up this box when we made our noisy arrival, but he didn't. That tells me he is having second thoughts."

Ed chuckled. "Yeah, I've spent enough time here to know you scientists are the real deal. You believe that if this

229

last box is wiped away, so too will all of history be. I'm trying to square that with my orders."

"What were your orders?" Faith asked in a respectful tone. "As the lead scientist here, I don't want you to do this. I am telling you, there will be horrific consequences."

"When you work for my group, you learn not to ask too many questions. Even knowing our name can get you a 2am visit from the Bullet Fairy. It's simply the way things are, you know?"

"No, I don't. I do things in the open for the betterment of humanity. I don't work in the shadows."

"What about this bad boy? Didn't you know what it would do?" Ed patted the cabinet next to him.

The general sidestepped closer to Ed but spoke to Faith again. "I told you we had members of his special unit arrested and rounded up so they could be brought to SNAKE. They are on the way from Malmstrom."

"They'll never make it," Ed asserted.

"Son, the US Army and Air Force are on top of it. We're working with the Feds—"

"You couldn't even keep three of us out of the bowels of your precious facility. We are small but tenacious in keeping our interests secret."

Ed shifted like he was going to stand up.

He's going to kill himself.

Faith's heart started to pound a staccato, threatening to burst from her chest. She knew why the man had delayed blowing up the box. He wanted an audience.

The general spoke to her, "Faith, I want you to—"

He sprinted the last fifteen feet toward Ed.

The gun went off, causing a loud boom in the cramped space of the subterranean room. She was surprised at the turn of events, and for a second had no idea what to do. She could only watch.

General Smith flung himself into Ed's gut and shoved his head into the concrete wall next to the cabinet.

Ed reeled as the general's fist slammed into his chin.

"Fuck you!" Ed shouted during a countermove.

She imagined the gun between them, although she couldn't see it. The general remained hunched over from the impact and struggled with the younger man like he was trying to get the gun.

The other man had been caught between sitting and standing, which put him at a severe disadvantage. Before he could get upright, she swallowed her fear and ran toward the battle.

She had no weapon, and there was nothing lying around to use as one, but she got right into the mix by using both of her hands to pin Ed's arm to the wall.

"His gun!" Smith grunted.

"You two are going to regret this!" Ed spat at them.

She couldn't even control the one arm, but she did see the gun because it was pointed away from her toward the Four Arrows box.

Faith didn't know how to change the outcome of the fight, but saw her opportunity to do some damage to the struggling man pinned to the wall by General Smith.

Obadias jammed his knee into the other man's crotch.

"Oomph!" Ed reacted to the pain.

The impact opened a small space between the two men, giving her an opening. She bent over, bared the wrist holding the pistol, and bit down with all she had.

Ed screamed and dropped the pistol.

The general punched Ed in the eye socket, which seemed to hurt him as much as Ed.

"Get it!" Smith shouted.

Faith slipped on something wet.

Blood.

She didn't have time to figure out where it came from. She fell to the floor to get the gun, only to get kicked in the cheek by Ed, then her leg was accidentally stepped on by the general.

They paid no attention to her.

The gun was close to the cabinet, so she had to slide around the back of Smith's legs and then reach for it.

Ed tried to kick her again, but she snatched it before he landed a blow.

"Shoot this bastard," Smith said in a tired voice.

She struggled backward on her knees, then stood up. She too was exhausted by those few seconds of life-or-death struggle. Still, she didn't feel right shooting the man.

Smith didn't let her think about it. "Goddamn it, *shoot!*"

Ed returned the favor and kneed the general in the groin. The general winced in pain, then crumpled. He desperately hung onto the other man, but stopped fighting, as if he'd run out of gas.

Ed sloughed off his backpack and fiddled with it, seemingly ignoring her.

"I'll shoot," she said with determination.

"I can tell you won't," he replied as he gave Smith a big shove to the ground.

General Smith was covered with blood. The gunshot had struck him in the chest, but she couldn't figure out where.

She took a step back but kept the gun trained on Ed. "I don't want to, but I will. Tell me why you are doing this." Her hands shook like it was twenty degrees in the room.

"Orders, ma'am. This experiment is over. My bosses

want no evidence it ever took place. It really is that simple. I've put a sixty-second timer on this. If you run now, you can get out."

Ed tossed the backpack at her.

She fired the weapon and hit him in the middle of his throat.

The pack slammed into her and she tried to catch it out of instinct, causing her to bobble the gun and the canvas bag at the same time.

Ed fell to the pavement like a soggy bag of garbage.

She stood there shaking for a few seconds, amazed by the terrible damage she'd done.

"Good work, soldier," Smith croaked.

Before she realized what was going on, Smith yanked the pack from her clutches and hobbled past the Four Arrows cabinet, leaving a trail of blood behind him. He headed for the storage area of the station, which was the farthest point from the cabinet and the collider ring.

"General!" she shouted. "You've been shot!"

He yelled over his shoulder, "Faith, *RUN*, dammit! Listen to me this one time, please."

Somehow the injured man sprinted.

It was impossible to stop him and she didn't want to die watching, so she took off at a limping run in the opposite direction, toward the tram tunnel. She passed the tram and practically fell into the gap beyond. She imagined a giant clock ticking away the seconds, the sound pounding in her head.

Or maybe that was her heartbeat. Faith jumped into the tunnel and kept hobbling. She heard the explosion at the same time that the ground shook below her.

Then the air was sucked from the space.

. . .

Sydney, Australia

Destiny was unable to get a hold of Faith as she walked through the half-empty station. Since most trains were out or had simply vanished, as Becker and Gladys had explained, there were almost none left to carry passengers.

Before she left, her brain was filled with the red light again. She held onto consciousness this time, although most people in the terminal crouched or fell to the floor. It was both horrible and fascinating to watch.

Faith, you're killing me, sis.

She ran out while the people recovered, grabbed a taxi, and went to the Sydney Harbor Foundation. Her anger at how they had left her in the woods had ebbed, because she now understood the madness out in the world. She admitted they had done the right thing by taking care of the larger group, even if it meant she was left behind. However, she needed to maintain the appearance of anger to help her get out of Australia.

She walked into the mostly empty office like a conquering Julius Caesar. Her clothes were dirty and torn from a sweaty and dusty couple of days.

Rodney Blaskowitz was the guy she'd talked to earlier about using the *Majestic* to transport animals to America.

He spoke as soon as he saw her. "You said you were going to call me back! I've been waiting for hours. Those flashes are crazy!"

She rushed up and hugged Rodney. He was old enough to be her father, and she didn't particularly like the guy, but he represented a tiny piece of stability in her topsy-turvy life.

She pulled away after a brief squeeze.

"Oi. What was that for?" he asked.

"Rod, I'm sorry I didn't call. I've been fighting to get

here since the middle of last night when we spoke. Forget the flashes of red. Do we still have the boat?"

"Sure, I guess. Why? What's going on?

"You don't know?" she said with surprise. "The world has turned inside out. Train engines are disappearing. Train tracks are gone. Jungles are where they aren't supposed to be. And the animals... You got my pictures, right?"

He held up his phone, although it was turned off. "Yeah, you sent me some amazing photos."

She took a steadying breath, then looked him square in the eye. "We have to go to America. You. Me. Whoever else can fit on the boat. But we have to go right this minute. It might already be too late."

"Too late for what, Dez? What the hell are you going on about?"

Her desire to go to America was mostly based on a desire to see her sister. If the world was going to fall apart, she didn't want to be alone.

She spoke like she was on speed. "I've not gotten proper sleep in three days. I've been left for dead in the fire. I swam to escape it. I've been shot at. I've shot a pre-historic bird. A jungle almost trapped me. Things are mad outside. I want to rescue some of these Aussie animals and take them to American zoos before they are all killed here."

Rod didn't look convinced. "I saw the pictures, Dez, but I can't believe they are real. The bosses didn't think they were real, either."

"They aren't giving us the boat?"

She had to do it through proper channels because the boat would need to be piloted, and they would need fuel to get all the way to America. There was no better reason for a naturalist society than the preservation of rare species. Unless Tasmanian Tigers were showing up all over America, she was certain she could build a case for transporting them overseas to good homes—and those homes would probably pay for every drop of fuel to get them there.

Rod shrugged. "They said if you can bring live specimens of these things, they'd drive the boat themselves. But Dez, I don't think they were serious."

She held up her finger to shush him, then rang up Zandre.

He picked up right away.

"Dez! You okay?"

"I'm fine. Made it to Sydney. The train won't be running to Canberra for a long time, but that's no longer my concern. I need a huge favor, and it might save both our lives."

"Sure. After the way my people treated you, I owe you one."

"Yeah, maybe," she agreed. "But listen. I need to take a boat to America. Planes aren't flying anymore. To do that, I need some living samples of extinct animals. We're sure zoos in America will cover our costs, but we have to bring them the good stuff. Can you help?"

"I didn't bag my Duck of Doom, but I'll be happy to go back out and try. Every hour my hunters come back with new specimens, although some guys are getting attacked and injured by beasts we didn't know existed out there. Nasty buggers, those."

She smiled on the phone but didn't tell him what she really thought. The imagery of those asshole hunters getting injured warmed her heart. She didn't like thinking what those same animals were doing to innocent people elsewhere in Australia, however.

"Bring as many as you can—alive—in the next twelve hours. You'll have to drive them here, okay?"

"It will take at least four hours to drive there. That only leaves me eight to hunt. Lucky for you, most of the time will be in daylight, but it's still going to be tight."

"You will save my life, Z. I swear."

"I'll do my best."

"We'll meet at Port Botany. The ship is called the *Majestic*. Please. I need you to come through."

She hung up and turned back to Rod.

"He brings the animals, we go to America. Right?"

"I'm sure the bosses will agree."

TWENTY-SIX

Princess Anne, Maryland

Garth kept his hands over his head while they waited on the dirty floor of the gas station as if they could protect against a gunshot. The gangsters had made it clear they were going to shoot one of the patrons, and he was out of ideas for how to fight back. They had his gun and his phone, so he couldn't shoot his way out or dial 911 for help.

Seconds passed, and the whole time he was sure he'd be the one they chose to off because he'd made the mistake of being close to them when the robbery was in progress.

Sorry, Dad. I let you down.

His eyes were closed as he waited, but a red flash came out of nowhere. It was exactly like the one he had suffered minutes earlier when he fell. Fortunately, this time he was already on the ground.

Other people gasped and whined as the uneasy feeling struck to him, but Garth opened his eyes when a girl screamed outside by the pumps. It sounded a lot like Lydia.

If he was going to get shot, he figured it wouldn't matter if he looked up, so he gave it a try.

"They're gone!" he shouted as he sprang to his feet. The two black-suited men were messing around with his spray-painted taxi. Lydia stood outside her car door like they'd kicked her out.

One of the baseball players sniffled. "What's happening to my brain?"

He was unconcerned with the people inside the store. Without a gun, Garth couldn't exactly swoop in like a hero to save Lydia, but he wasn't going to stand inside while she was out there.

"He got up," a woman exclaimed from her prone position next to the soda fountain.

"Don't do it, dude," the other baseball player cautioned as soon as Garth went to the door.

He glanced at the boy. "That's my friend. She needs help."

"She's gonna die," the kid said fearfully.

When he stormed outside, the gangsters were already on the run toward McDonald's. One carried the sack of cash like a little laundry bag while the other followed. They wove in and out of cars in the drive-through lane, then went around the building, out of his field of view.

He sprinted over to Lydia, who remained outside the cab.

"Are you okay?" he asked.

Lydia watched the men run too, but when she saw Garth, she pulled him in for a big hug. "Yes. I'm glad you're here. Those two men jumped into your tack-see and tried to drive it away, but they seemed to have trouble starting it. They asked me for help, but I didn't know anything, so they pushed me out. Then we all had that red zapping feeling, and they left your car screaming."

Two goons from the 1920s apparently had no idea how

to operate a modern vehicle. It had taken him a few tries when he had started it in Sam's backyard, too, until he figured out he needed to put his foot on the brakes to get the motor to turn over.

He had only himself to blame for even giving them a chance to steal his ride. Garth had left the keys in the ignition because it didn't occur to him someone would jump in, but that was one more box to tick off his safety list in the future.

"They stole money from the store and from some of us customers," Garth added. "They pointed guns at us, and made us lay on the floor so they could escape." He squeezed her tight after realizing her closeness made his warp-speed heartbeat decelerate back to normal.

"Did they get your money?"

He laughed, finally feeling safe. "No, but they took my wallet and phone. I keep my money in this little pocket." He pointed to the tiny pouch of his jeans above his right-front pocket. "My friend Sam taught me to keep my big bills in there because the pick-pockets on the subway couldn't get their grubby fingers inside. So far, it's worked like a charm."

"Your friend Sam sounds very wise," she said with awe.

"Wise? I guess he's wise in his own way. Most of his knowledge goes to getting into trouble, however. He loves to goof off."

"You mean play?"

"Yeah. Goof. Play. But always in a good way. He's a good guy." He wondered where Sam and his parents were at that moment.

Garth stood there with Lydia while other patrons came out of the store and got into their cars. He fully expected the police to show up at any minute, and he wanted to be out of there in case they wondered how he had ended up with the stolen taxi.

"We've got a full tank of gas, two hundred dollars, and a thousand miles ahead of us. You ready?"

She pulled away but stood close. "Two hundred dollars? You truly are John Jacob Astor. My pa worked his whole life to save enough for a yoke of oxen and a wagon, and it wasn't that much. He would have guarded it with his life. Here you are with an even larger amount in your pocket."

Her green eyes shimmered, and for a moment he reveled in how she looked up to him, but he couldn't pretend to be rich.

"Remind me to explain inflation to you. I learned about it in school. Basically, two hundred bucks isn't that much money today. I couldn't buy a yoke of oxen or a wagon with this money. In fact, I don't even know if it will be enough to get us where we need to go."

He realized he'd need to cut back on the McDonald's, Mountain Dew, and other treats. The only priority was gas to get him to his dad.

"All right, saddle up." He stepped back, intending to go around the car, but she wasn't moving.

"What?" he asked.

"Why did you say that? We have no horses."

Garth smiled. "It's an expression. I guess it comes from your time, actually. It means we need to get in our car, and make like a tree and leave."

Her puzzled look continued. "A tree?"

"I'm sorry. It's another expression. I swear I'm not trying to confuse you. It's the way I talk. We really do need to get out of here."

After thinking about it, her eyes lit up. "Because a tree has leaves! I understand."

She was laughing hard by the time they were both in their seats.

"We've got to be close to Interstate 64, then we don't stop until we reach my dad."

He sped out of the gas station.

"We've got to find him before he becomes a tree and leaves."

She's trying.

They shared a laugh, content for a moment to be alive.

I-80, Cheyenne, Wyoming

Buck expected to black out the entire time he headed for Cheyenne. He talked a good game to Connie, and he hoped his plan of keeping the rig on cruise control would work, but he feared it wouldn't be enough. When he saw the Welcome to Cheyenne billboard, he let out a huge sigh.

"We made it," he declared.

Connie had been studying the atlas, but when she looked up and saw the sign, she reached over and held his arm. "Good driving, bucko. You got us here."

"Thanks. Now all we have to do is get beyond this upcoming interchange." I-25 and I-80 met a couple of miles ahead, and the news reports said 25 was closing down from Cheyenne to Fort Collins, which was inside the zone already closed off north of Denver.

Buck got on the CB. "We're going into Cheyenne. Look alive, people."

Connie tapped the glass of her window, pointing outside. "I'm so sick of this grass. Isn't there anything interesting in this entire state?"

The patchy green grass went from horizon to horizon. There were a few antelopes eating near the fence line of the highway, and far to the south he glimpsed the peaks of the Rocky Mountains of Colorado, but between those two features, there was absolutely nothing.

"Up north you get mountains and cool stuff like Yellowstone, but down here, no. It's boring as hell. But don't worry," he added with thick sarcasm, "we'll get much more of this in Nebraska."

"Ugh. I always thought Wyoming was high adventure and big mountains."

"Every state has its flaws," he replied.

"Not New Mexico," she insisted. "It has mountains, deserts, caves, and wonderful forests. It basically has everything."

He risked a glance to see her joy at thinking about her state. She caught him looking and smiled.

"We're here," he said, changing the subject.

The north-south I-25 highway crossed I-80 on a pair of bridges above them. Police cars blocked the on-ramp, so he couldn't have gone south on the other highway even if he wanted to.

"Looks like we can go right under it," he explained. "I was worried they'd want to block traffic down here, too. So they wouldn't be seen."

"Why would it matter?" she wondered.

"If we knew what was going south…" As soon as he said it, he had a new thought.

He scrambled for the CB as they drove past the black police cruiser. "Guys, I need you to keep going to Sidney, Nebraska. That's our stop point for tonight. I, uh, have to make a quick pit stop under this bridge, but I'm not out of service."

"10-4, Buck," Sparky replied. "Eve and I will hold a parking spot for you at the truck stop."

Monsignor jumped on when he could. "I'll see you there, too. You've gotten us through some tight scrapes. Glad to return the favor and save you a spot."

"Thanks, guys," he answered.

Buck applied the brakes and pulled to the shoulder of the highway, then guided the truck under the bridge carrying the southbound lanes of I-25. He continued on, parking under the bridge for the northbound lanes of the other highway.

"Buck? I see the look in your eyes. You're excited about something."

He put his finger over his lips. "Shh. We're going Marine Recon for a minute. You get Mac on a leash and get him to do his business. I'm putting out some triangles."

The evening air was cool, especially in the shade under the bridge. While Connie dutifully walked Big Mac around, he placed three orange warning triangles about a hundred yards behind his trailer so other drivers wouldn't run into him.

To any onlooker, he had broken down.

He and Connie rejoined after both their tasks were complete. Buck got down on one knee and gave his pup a vigorous head and neck scratch. "You're a good boy. Yes, you are!"

Mac leaned against him, wanting more.

Cars and trucks sped under the bridge, but traffic was light for the most part. He listened as he gave Mac more loving.

"What are we waiting for?" Connie asked after realizing Buck wasn't getting up.

"Vehicles up above," he said quietly. "They just closed the highway up there, which probably means something is about to go by."

244

"And you want to see what it is," she declared with skepticism.

"We're here, so I figured it was worth a look. Aren't you the least bit interested to see why they closed the highway up and down the whole state?"

She considered it. Another big rig flew by, blowing her hair almost sideways on her head, but once it was gone, the underpass became quiet.

Not long after, there was a distinct rumbling on the roadway above them.

"There! I was right. Those bastards are coming through right now."

"Who is it?"

He stood and took her hand. "Let's find out."

Together, the three of them went up the concrete incline and came out between the parallel bridges of Interstate 25. The northbound lanes were empty in both directions, and the southbound lanes were empty to the south, but a line of vehicles was coming over the bridge, heading south as they got up there.

"Got ya!" he bragged.

"What the hell is that thing in the front?" she asked.

The lead vehicle was a six-wheeled military monstrosity. It was painted desert tan, had the aerodynamics of a shipping container, and had a crane-arm on top of the superstructure. Its huge knobby tires purred on the pavement as it crossed the bridge.

"It's called a... Well, shit, you'll never believe this. That is known as a Buffalo. I saw these on my second deployment. They were shipped over because they couldn't be destroyed by IEDs or mines."

"Oh, I believe anything these days. What is it doing here?"

A miles-long procession of military vehicles followed the lone Buffalo. Humvees and light tactical vehicles were near the front, but heavier machines were in the distance.

"They're going to a party," he said dryly.

"What does it all mean? Why did they shut the highway down for all these military people? Is this an invasion?"

"No," he replied quickly. "These are all American. Those are US Army vehicles."

The noise amped up as tan Humvees passed their position. Buck ducked lower at the edge of the tall grass, unsure if they would be spotted but unable to turn away. Somehow, he knew an important event was taking place, although he had no idea what it was.

He stuck his head as high as he dared to get a look at what else was coming up the highway.

"Paladins! I think I see tanks on flatbeds, too. Christ. They aren't fucking around."

Mac pulled at his leash, sending Connie on a brief slide back down the concrete slope. "Buck, I think he's scared. Let's get him out of here."

He didn't want to leave. The military tactician in him wanted to stay and count vehicles until he knew for sure how big this convoy was. He'd put the numbers together and had been right about what was coming down the roadway and where it was going, but he was left dangling when it came to the why of it.

Walk away, Buck. You have more important things to worry about.

He looked down at Connie sliding on her butt with his retriever at her side. The young pup was whining and making it clear he wanted to get away from the noisy highway. Being in the cab of the Peterbilt was one thing for the dog, but being out in the wind and road noise was too much.

He started down the slope and easily caught up.

"Yeah, let's go. We'll catch up with our friends. Get hold of Garth, and get a few hours of sleep." Part of him wanted to skip sleep completely, but he knew that was folly. He intended to be back on the road to Garth before the sun came up.

"Separate beds?" she said in an enigmatic tone.

"Well, I don't want to run out of money, actually. I was thinking of sleeping in the cab tonight." He paused for a second to see what she'd say, but he decided to be a gentleman about it. "I'll sleep in my seat. It folds all the way back. You and Mac can have the bed."

"I see," she replied dryly.

European Laboratory for Particle Physics (CERN), Switzerland

Phil expected Ethan to hear that the power-down worked from HQ, but the look on the colonel's face said otherwise. Phil had spent almost half his life in the service, often in theaters with active conflict, and knew the disappointment of mission failure intimately.

"Grafton can't raise Ramstein," Ethan said to him once they were away from Dr. Eli. "I don't want him to know we're having problems, but we have to find out if this worked. Any ideas?"

"Don't suppose you have a satellite phone?"

Ethan shook his head. "I even tried my disposable cell. Nothing."

The Army didn't allow him to take anything personal on missions, but he often took disposable phones, for emergency use only. Ethan apparently did the same.

"We could have Dr. Eli make a call to SNAKE from his

desk. That might be the quickest way. You might get billed for the call, though." He smiled at Ethan to get him to lighten up. Nothing could ruin an op worse than losing your temper, and the other officer seemed frazzled at being out of contact with his superiors.

"No. I don't trust him. How would we know it was really who he said it was? I think we—"

Ethan froze mid-sentence, and his eyeballs turned up in his head like he was having a seizure.

"What the..." Static energy filled the air, crackling around him and making his hair stand on end. Then nausea and dizziness struck like a baseball bat to the stomach, knocking him off his feet. A blue aura filled his vision as he sped toward the tiled floor.

He passed out the instant before he hit the deck.

TWENTY-SEVEN

***Search for Nuclear, Astrophysical, and Krono-
metric Extremes (SNAKE). Red Mesa, Colorado***

Faith didn't check to see if General Smith had survived
the blast. The noble general didn't do things halfway. He
wasn't trying to save himself; he thought he was saving the
world. He had carried the backpack as far as he could in
those few seconds, and probably cradled it to absorb as
much of the blast as possible.

His only goal had been preserving the Four Arrows
cabinet, and in that he was successful. Even through the
choking smoke in the tunnel, Faith confirmed that the blue
beam still came out of the metal box, presumably main-
taining one last link between SNAKE and CERN.

"Thank you, sir," she got out between unwanted sobs.
"I'll tell everyone you were a hero."

She tried to get her breathing under control. The dead
man was on the floor, not far from the box. He was right
where she had killed him. But the general had decided that
his life and the life of the bomber were fair payment to stop
the destruction of the Four Arrows device.

Because Faith had convinced him not to destroy it.

"And I still exist," she said in a dreamy voice. She assumed one of the bombs had severed the collider ring, which would cut off the flow of energy as certainly as removing all the boxes. However, the general had detonated his backpack away from the collider, and the other two explosions must also have avoided destroying the circle.

I won't know until I get back.

She rang Security on the emergency phone and begged them to hurry out to her, but it took two hours for a rescue team to arrive. She went up the steps of the fire exit and met them on a narrow two-track maintenance path in the woods.

The facilities man drove her back to the main office, but that took another hour. By the time she walked into the administration wing, she hardly recognized the place.

"Faith!" Bob ran up and looked like he was going to give her a hug. Instead, he chucked her on the shoulder. "I can't believe you made it. We saw the two explosions on the cameras, and we saw you and the general blast through those stations on the maglev like you were going for the land speed record."

The hours of waiting had given her plenty of time to work through her sorrow at the general's loss. She was already numb. "Is the collider totaled?"

"No," he exclaimed. "The blasts destroyed a lot of the spare equipment in each station, but the charges were designed to eliminate the boxes, not the heavier metal infrastructure of the ring. Those magnets are like armor around it."

"So, the beam hasn't been cut off inside the ring?" She'd surmised the outcome, but it was nice to have confirmation.

"Same as before. We aren't powering it, but there is still power in the ring."

"From CERN," she acknowledged. "Has anyone made contact with them? Smith said he had people going in. We should have heard something by now."

Bob shrugged. "The military guys have been scarce in here since the bomb went off. They're outside in the parking lot, mostly, keeping people away from the front doors. Locals have been arriving all afternoon to protest."

"Bob, we have to know what's happening at CERN. This is important."

"I know. I really do. We'll ask the soldiers as soon as we can, but you'll never believe what's taking place on the news. Our very own Doctor Shinano is going to speak on a local Denver TV station. They've been trying to get him on for fifteen minutes, but the feed keeps dropping. We're waiting for him to come back on."

"What is he saying?"

Bob seemed excited. "No one knows. The longer he gets cut off, the more we think he's going to say something incriminating. Maybe a rich asshole like him knows what's happened at CERN."

"He's back!" someone shouted.

"Come on!" Bob gushed.

Most of the senior staff was holed up in a computer lab. It didn't have any windows facing the front parking lot, and thus it was protected from rocks, or worse. When she went in with the others, many people waved to her or said they were happy to have her back, but all eyes were on one of the largest monitors.

Faith recognized Shinano instantly. He'd made a brief appearance when the Izanagi Experiment had failed and she'd had to explain to him what had happened, but he'd been absent ever since. She hadn't thought about him again until now.

"I don't have much time," the Japanese industrialist said in passable English. "The US military is outside trying to prevent me from getting this message to you. What I must say is this: My company caused the time distortions being experienced all over the world. Our project was designed to test the limits of quantum teleportation under the guidance of the military-industrial complex of the United States. Unfortunately, we chewed off more than we could bite."

She forgave him mixing up the English idiom.

"The disaster is worldwide, but not absolute. I want to absolve my company and restore some of my personal honor. There are two places you can go to get safe from its effects. The first place is the laboratory here in Denver, which you call SNAKE. The second is—"

The screen went black, as if the station transmitter had been knocked over.

At first, everyone in the room was silent, but after a few seconds, the managers exploded with excited conversation.

"SNAKE is safe?" she asked Bob under all the other talk. "Does that mean what I think?"

"It's what you've been saying for a while now," he replied in an equally quiet tone. "The energy burst you sketched out showed the hole in the bubble around the Earth. If SNAKE is truly safe, as you speculated, then the only other place he could have meant was CERN."

"Dammit." She looked at the TV screen, hoping the man would come back on. "What did he mean? Safe is relative. Did he mean we are safe for now? Are we safe forever? And for the love of God, why didn't he say how to end this clown-suited merry-go-round journey through Hell?"

The chaos of the room didn't bother her, but as the leader, she had to make a decision of some kind. There was one remaining Four Arrows box. The power link to CERN was still active, meaning the general's people must not have succeeded in Switzerland. And he said the criminals responsible for the experiment had been found and were being brought to SNAKE. Who else knew about that?

Dammit, general. What do I do now?

The TV station popped back on. A disheveled reporter sat at a desk with a mess of papers in front of her, but she read from the one in her hand.

"We here at Special Nine News would like to apologize for the unprofessional and dangerous prank pulled on our viewers over the last half an hour. SNN management tried in vain to get this farce stopped, but we were unable to do so. Please disregard what this actor has said. We believe he intended to sow chaos as part of an elaborate psychological experiment. There is nothing to fear..."

"Phew!" Bob blew out a breath as it became clear what had happened. "That makes a lot more sense. It was all bullshit."

Faith nodded and smiled, but she knew the Japanese man well enough to know it wasn't an actor playing him on national television. He believed what he had said, and apparently had done it at considerable risk.

The question was, who *else* would believe him?

Sydney, Australia

Dez sat by the phone through the lunch hour, anxious to hear good news from Zandre. However, when the phone finally rang, it was Rod again.

"Dez! You were right, mate! We have to get to the United States. It's fucking *everywhere*!"

"Whoa! Slow down. What are you talking about?"

"Some guy named Shinano was there! He's singing like a Kookaburra about the end of the world. It's on all the newsies. You were right about the extinct animals. The boat. *The Majestic*. We have to get on board and get to America. The whole world is going to shit, and the only place safe is somewhere in Colorado."

"Let me call you back," she replied.

"Dez, listen. They are taking the boat with or without you. Don't delay."

"What? Without me? Sydney Harbor Foundation doesn't want my animals?"

"No, they don't care about the fucking animals. Don't you get it? The world has just entered a race to get itself to safety. If you want to live, you have to get on that boat right away. They're sailing to America. It's the only way."

"Thanks," she said resignedly. Coming out of the blue as it had, Rod's warning served more to turn her off to the true nature of her employer than it did to get her running to join them. If they didn't care about animals, what were they doing in this business?

And she couldn't abandon Zandre. She'd sent him out looking for her extinct critters. Hopping on a boat and ditching him wasn't something she was willing to do, even if it endangered her life.

She tried to call Faith again, sure her sister would give her better information and tell her if all this was for real, but the call refused to go through. Her pulse quickened as she hung up because it felt like she'd been cut off from her big sister by an impenetrable barrier called "the end of the world." It was difficult enough getting to America on a good day. This was anything but.

"Damn all this confusion!"

She turned on the television to see if she could glean any information about the Shinano guy. Maybe Faith's SNAKE facility would be mentioned, with advice for citizens. That might give her an idea if it was really safe, and whether she could make it there. While skipping channels, Dez looked outside her window to see how the time shifts affected her personally.

The Sydney Opera House was still gone.

It was personal enough.

"I'm coming, Faith. I swear it."

She was already dialing Zandre.

I-80, east of Cheyenne, Wyoming

Buck drove east to catch up with his friends in what was left of his convoy. I-80 was almost empty, and he was worried the Army would chase after him for having seen the mysterious convoy, but he reassured himself that his conspiracy gene was getting the better of him. After all, anyone sitting by the highway between Montana and Denver could have easily seen the same thing. The members of the convoy weren't exactly hiding.

He caught himself looking in the side mirror again. It was only him and the prairie of high-plains Wyoming. He stomped a foot on the floor, wondering what he'd gained with his delay. He had seen things that didn't help him get to Garth, and by seeing those things, he had risked achieving his goal. Buck gritted his teeth and grumbled to himself.

Mac was on Connie's lap once more, as if sensing the anxiety weighing down his two human friends.

"He's up there *again*?" Buck remarked as he glanced at his pup.

"I don't mind. I feel safe with him so near, like he's my security blanket." Connie laughed and rubbed Mac's flank. In return, he groaned like he was in Heaven.

"Mac, you're one lucky dog," he expressed, along with a heavy sigh.

She glanced at him with a sparkle in her eyes. "Really? Why is that?"

"What? Oh, I meant because he doesn't have to worry about the things you and I worry about. Time travel. Army guys. Buffalo crossings."

"And that's all?" she said in a tone suggesting she thought he was hiding something.

"Well..." He hesitated. "He probably doesn't wonder if an Army mom and a jarhead from two different eras could ever end up together."

"Probably doesn't wonder?" She shook her head at Buck's strangled wording. "Should we ask him?"

She held his gaze for a few moments, but then turned and looked out the front window. "Eyes forward, Marine. If you black out, I'm sure our luck will be all bad."

"Roger that," he said in a businesslike voice. It wasn't in his nature to charge the hill without knowing if he could take it, so he didn't know what to say when he didn't experience immediate victory.

"Buck, you get Mac and me to safety, and I guarantee we'll have something to discuss about the good kind of luck. I know I don't look it, but I'm scared shitless you are going to wreck and get hurt because of those blackouts."

He sat up straight. "You're right. I need—"

The CB crackled and Sparky's voice came out, but he sounded distant through the static. Buck had a view several miles ahead and there were no trucks out there, so his friends were beyond the horizon.

"Turn on the news! Buck, did you hear? Are you back there? ...on the news!"

He and Connie shared a meaningful look, then she turned on the FM radio. She flipped a few channels until she found one with talk.

"If you've just joined us, this is what's happening in Denver, Colorado. A man named Sadayoshi Shinano claims to have firsthand knowledge of the experiment responsible for all the odd weather and other, uh, phenomena wreaking havoc across the United States. His bold claim is that the only place safe on the entire planet is in a science lab southwest of Denver."

They played the short message from Dr. Shinano, which repeated what the host had outlined.

"Holy moly," Connie exclaimed after hearing it in full.

The host went on, "The station immediately disavowed this interview as a hoax, but we here at 98.5, The Train, play this for your consideration. Do you think what he says is real, or is this one more confusing anomaly in a country full of them? Give us a call."

"Do you believe him?" Connie asked.

He didn't want to. If there was only one safe spot in the whole world, what did that mean for his son? Would Garth be able to make it to Colorado from across the country? Buck wasn't going to stop and wait for him to drive in, either. He was intent to go east and get to his boy as soon as humanly possible, no matter what the cost. However, would doing so jeopardize Connie's safety?

Buck was tempted to call Garth, but he was so close to the Nebraska border, he decided to wait. Soon they'd be at the Sidney truck stop, and he could make all the calls he wanted without fear of running off the road.

"If it's true, it could be awesome for us because we're so close. If it's fake, it could give a lot of people false hope. They'll do crazy things to get there. That would be bad for us."

Connie rubbed Mac for a minute before finally replying, "Tonight, you and I should take some time to really talk through our options. I've always drawn strength from a higher power. First, with Philip and the war. Then, when we almost died at the hands of those bikers. Now, we're faced with what looks like an even bigger challenge."

He sensed the weight of the radio broadcast and her words, but when he looked over, she had a fiery sparkle in her eyes again.

"But," she went on, "I also draw strength from being with you and your lovable dog. I feel like I can take on the world sitting up here in your big truck. Whatever we do, we're going into it together, okay? I don't care what that guy says, we've got to get your son first. Whatever happens afterward, at least you two will be together."

Buck wanted to stop the truck and swoop her into his arms for saying what she had, but it wasn't the right time.

"You get me," he said. "Not many people do, Connie."

"Nah, you aren't so complicated." She smirked. "You're a man's man. You aren't going to stop before you have your son, except when you pull a bonehead move like stopping to see the secret convoy. And you need me to tell you to cut the crap."

"I do," he admitted. "But now I know they're hiding something from us."

"And?" She paused for dramatic effect. "How does that bring you closer to your son?"

"You get me," he repeated.

"In more ways than you admit." She smiled. "And you'll get me, too. When the time is right."

"I'm at a severe disadvantage in my relationship jousting." He stared straight ahead, the truck speeding up as he wished it to get to the truck stop more quickly.

"Want me to give Garth a call?"

TWENTY-EIGHT

Richmond, Virginia

"We're finally making good time," Garth said to Lydia over the endless wind noise.

"I can't believe the size of your cities. Richmond went on forever," she exclaimed.

"Pshaw! You think Richmond was big, you should see what New York City looks like. It never ends."

"I'd like to see it someday. Do you think we'll ever go back to your home?"

He heard the dreariness in her voice. Once her sugar high wore off, she had crashed hard. That had started on the other side of Richmond, but miles later, she still wasn't out of it.

"Oh, hell yeah. Once we get to my dad, I'm sure things will settle back down to normal. We'll go home together."

"And what will happen to me?"

He'd already established he wasn't going to let her out of his sight, but her tiredness brought out the question once again.

"Lydia, you don't have to worry about a thing. I'm glad you and I ended up together. It's been fun, actually."

"Really?" She maneuvered her leg under herself again to face him. "You're not just saying that?"

He shook his head. "Well, some things I'd pass on doing again, but showing you the Big Mac was awesome. I can't wait to show you other things too, like my video games. At the same time, I've been fighting the urge to, um, kind of ask you..."

"Yes, Garth?" She exuded excitement.

"Well, I've listened to you talk about your time. About how girls marry at sixteen and whatever, and I..."

It became difficult to look at her, so he watched the road.

"I really like you," he admitted, "but my dad would never let me get married."

She stared at him for a few seconds as if interpreting his words, then laughed in a good-natured way.

"Garth, whatever makes you think I would want to get married right now?"

He rubbed his head behind his ear. "I thought that was how you did things in your time? A boy and a girl pair up and they get married. I mean, I want to someday, I guess, but—"

She giggled. "You are such a strange boy. And sweet. But I am in your time, not the other way around. How do you behave around girls normally?"

Awkwardly.

"Well, we do have girlfriends and boyfriends..."

"So do we!" she exclaimed. "Though I never had the chance on the wagon train. I was sad for many weeks after my pa was gone. I guess it never occurred to me to have a boyfriend—not until I met you."

Garth was uncomfortable with the compliment.

"Thanks. I'm glad I met you, too, but we have to figure out where this highway is taking us before we can let our hair down, you know?"

"My hair is already down," she expressed happily. "See?"

The sun had nearly set, but a lone beam came in through the front windshield and caught her blonde hair and green eyes at the perfect angle. For a brief instant, she was so attractive he would have considered marrying her on the spot.

Then the car moved, and the beam shifted elsewhere.

"Yeah, I see," he remarked like it was no big deal. "Without my phone, I don't know how in the hell I'm going to find him."

She clapped. "Oh, another challenge. That's what I love about your world, Garth. There are so many puzzles to figure out."

"Yeah, well, it isn't always like this. We usually spend our time playing games on our phones. Me and Sam play these strategy games, which are...sort of puzzles."

He cracked himself up.

"I guess we do have a lot of brainteasers, but this is a complex world. Still, I'm sure we can think of a way to get hold of my dad. We just have to think of who else has my dad's phone number, and we can call him on a different telephone."

"You don't have his number? Didn't you talk to him all the time?"

"Yes," he admitted, "but all I did was tap or speak his name, and the phone dialed the number. I didn't have to memorize it. Funny, huh?"

"Another quirk of your time I will never understand.

Who else has his number, then? Does the phone maker have it?"

He thought about it for a minute as he drove through the shadowy pine forest of central Virginia. The maker of the phone was some company in China, but the people who ran his cell phone plan would almost certainly have it.

"Lydia, you're a genius! I know exactly how we can get hold of my dad. First thing in the morning, I'll show you."

"Oh, goodie!" she exclaimed.

"Tonight, though, we're going to make some time. I'm not stopping until we have to get the next tank of gas." The needle was only a quarter of the way toward empty, and the digital readout said they had three hundred and seventy-five miles until empty. After the long delays of the day, he was adamant on impressing his dad by driving off a lot of miles now that he had the gas.

"If you had asked, my pa would have given his approval, Garth. He would be proud of you for taking such good care of me when you didn't have to."

It never occurred to him what her father would think of him, but her words touched him deeply. Somehow, the suggestion of doing right by both their fathers made him feel like an honorable young man.

He gripped the steering wheel and peered ahead. They had made it through another day. Whatever was ahead, he could handle it.

"Thanks. My dad is going to love you, too."

Unknown location

Phil woke up on the ground in the shadows of tall trees in a forest. He'd fallen sometime in the morning, and now he was outside, and it was the evening. Perhaps five or six at night. He imagined he'd been out for the better part of a day. Had he been drugged and tossed out of CERN? Had the Swiss police dumped him in the forest to send a message?

"Colonel Knight?" he called. "You there? I think those scientists fucked us over."

His hands pressed against pine needles as he struggled to his knees and looked around. He groped for and found his weapon still strapped to his back.

"They left me with my rifle?" he whispered. If someone was going to dump him in the woods, why would they let him keep his firearm? He could walk out of the woods and go right back to CERN armed—and a lot angrier.

Phil got up and made sure he was solid. The dizziness was gone, and the fresh air seemed to do him good.

"Colonel? Anyone?" He dared not yell, but he wanted to be heard. The large trunks and tall, thin trees with pine boughs at the top gave him no clue where he was. There wasn't a lot of groundcover, either, which offered him a good look at the hilly terrain. Not steep like the side of a mountain, but close.

He chose to walk downhill. The Alps surrounded Geneva, and he had no interest in going higher in elevation toward the snow-capped peaks. Civilization would be in the valley.

After about fifteen minutes, he found a small dirt path with two dusty tracks side-by-side. It was big enough for a four-wheeler, or two bicycles next to each other. It was the type of thing he expected in a Swiss resort during the summertime.

The path went over a small rise, then around a bend.

"Someone is going to fucking pay for this," he muttered quietly. If nothing else, the scientists had stopped him and

Task Force Blue 7 from doing their job. They'd shut down the power, but had never confirmed their success with headquarters. He was pissed, and Ethan would undoubtedly be chewing nails by now.

Phil was thinking about whether he was going to walk back into CERN with his weapon out as a show of force when he came around a sharp curve next to a rocky hillside. He looked up to find three soldiers sitting on a fallen log.

"Hey, guys! I found you!" he said, thinking they were his men.

An instant too late, he realized they were American, but not his unit. He froze in place.

He expected them to challenge his approach or whip out their weapons, but the Air Force airmen continued to sit there.

One of them invited him over. "Did those crazy fuckers threaten you with a bomb, too?"

Phil stood fifty feet away, unsure what to make of them.

"No. I was in the offices of CERN talking to a scientist, then I zonked out and woke up here in the woods. How did you get here?"

"We were guarding the CERN links. We were jumped by a guy with a backpack of C-4. Said we had a minute to clear out before he was going to blow himself up. We couldn't fight him, so we ran. Now we're trying to get back to SNAKE headquarters through these woods."

"SNAKE?" he said sarcastically. "I was at CERN. In Switzerland."

The three airmen laughed. "You must have hit your head. It happens, guy."

He stepped closer. "No. Really. I'm Lieutenant Colonel Phil Stanwick. Two days ago, I fought at Bagram Air Base until I was medevacked to Ramstein. Then I was recruited to go to the CERN scientific lab in Geneva, Switzerland. I blacked out..."

He touched his temple, wondering for a second if he was under hypnosis. Here he was giving away operational intelligence.

"Oh, sorry, sir." The men stood up and saluted. One of them continued. "Well, however you got here, welcome back to America, Colonel. You've made it to Red Mesa, Colorado. We're somewhere at the edge of the ring of the SNAKE supercollider. We're trying to get back to the main offices before dark. Stick with us, and when we get there, you'll see where you are."

Phil strode up and sat on the log close to the three others.

"I think those scientists broke my brain. I don't see how we're going to get back if we're sitting on a log."

Sidney, Nebraska

Buck and Connie caught up with the rest of the convoy, and they all stopped at the Love's truck stop in Sidney, Nebraska, as planned. They shared a few minutes of conversation and wolfed down junk food from the convenience store, but Buck was anxious to get some rest, so he and Connie left the others.

Ten minutes later, it was lights out in his cabin.

"You're thinking about Garth, aren't you?" Connie said from her side of the sleeper bed. He fully intended to spend the night in his captain's chair, but Connie insisted he should get comfortable and lay in the bed with her and Big Mac.

"I don't know why he isn't answering his phone. I think

communications are getting worse. Everything is breaking down."

She chuckled. "No shit, and the price of diesel has gone up, to boot. The pumps here showed $5.49 a gallon!"

"Yeah," he agreed. "The world is going to shit, and that means it's harder to get fuel deliveries. It's a good thing we gassed up in Wyoming, because fuel isn't going to get any cheaper from here on out. We should have enough in the tank to link up with Garth if we can talk to him and find out where he's going to be."

"You told him to drive west on I-64, right? That's where he'll be."

The thought gave him no sense of comfort. Even if they knew for sure he was on a particular interstate, it would be a miracle if they saw him passing in the other lanes. They had to talk in real time.

"I'm sure things will look better in the morning," she reasoned.

Mac flopped around in the gap between Buck and Connie. The small bed was at capacity, and Mac seemed to have trouble getting comfortable between his two humans.

"Whoa, boy," Buck said in a quiet voice as he rubbed the Golden. His hand met Connie's as she also tried to comfort the pup.

"Listen to your daddy," she whispered.

Mac settled down, but Connie kept her hand over his.

"Do you think that man was telling the truth?" she asked in the darkness. "Do we really have one chance? One safe place?"

Buck didn't say anything right away, but he was happy to already have a safe harbor in the chaos. The sleeper cab was an isolation chamber protecting the three of them from whatever was out there. His bubble of safety was what he had to hold onto if he wanted to have any hope of sleeping and recovering tonight, which is what he desperately needed—so he could do it again the next day.

"It's like you said," he replied through a dreary fog. "It'll look better tomorrow."

His hand relaxed Mac, and Connie's, in turn, calmed him.

Tomorrow's the day I see Garth.

Buck fell asleep under the warmth of her touch.

To Be Continued in End Days, Book 4

If you like this book, please leave a review. This is a new series, so the only way I can decide whether to commit more time to it is by getting feedback from you, the readers. Your opinion matters to me. Continue or not? I have only so much time to craft new stories. Help me invest that time wisely. Plus, reviews buoy my spirits and stoke the fires of creativity.

Don't stop now! Keep turning the pages since there's a little more insight and such from the authors.

COPYRIGHT

AUTHOR NOTES – E.E. ISHERWOOD

Written February 27, 2019

End Days is flying off the shelves because of your support. Please keep the great reviews coming as they are the life-blood of independent authors. We can't thank you enough for them.

I love science fiction, but I also love science fact. As a young teen, I spent many hours watching the PBS series *Cosmos*, with Carl Sagan. If you haven't seen it, go get it. The original, not the new one. I recently went back and re-watched the whole 13-part series and it is still wonderfully entertaining and informative. Sagan had a way of simplifying the science so the rest of us could understand it. I still think of his imaginary spaceship plying the stars as he showed the scale of our universe. And, of course, he mentioned time travel...

I happen to believe time travel in reverse is impossible, but not because of any scientific formula. I base it on circumstantial evidence. If mankind somehow figures it out a million years in the future, human nature would ensure those noble people would go back and try to improve the past. The ethics would go out the window, even if every futuristic child was taught how a time change could make them not exist. They'd still try to go back. Bank on it.

Hitler would be like the bug zapper on my back patio, always attracting time traveler mosquitoes, intent on righting a massive injustice in our timeline. And, as was said in this book, if you get a chance to kill Hitler, you always take it. His survival, and innumerable other despots throughout history, tells me we do not gain the power to go back in time and correct our mistakes.

It would be nice if I could slow down time, however. I'd love to have more weeks of writing to make these books a lot longer. There are so many places in the story where I want to delve into the details of the shifts taking place in this broken world, but I'd risk bogging the plot in endless minutia.

Thank you again for reading *End Days*. We've got more adventure coming.

EE

AUTHOR NOTES - CRAIG MARTELLE

Written March 16, 2019

You are still reading! Thank you so much. It doesn't get much better than that.

E.E. Isherwood does it again! We've worked through this one pretty hard. If there are any issues with the military scenes and stuff, those are all on me as that's the expertise I bring to this tandem. E.E. is the main man, though and I can't thank him enough for bringing this story to life.

I think we have a great storyline rolling. The next book could be a couple months away. Will number four be the last? I originally thought it would be but the characters are so compelling and the story so engaging that you, the fans may not want it to end. The jury is still out on this one, but we'll do our best and see where the next story takes us.

The weather has turned – we had a chinook wind pop up and bring warm air. I think we hit 114 days straight below freezing this winter before temperatures jumped up. At three this morning it was 37F, which is crazy for mid-March, but I'll take it. Phyllis was panting a bit during our walk, but she still enjoyed the weather change. She wasn't so keen with all the wind, though, bringing strange sounds and smells from afar.

The key to a great summer is for the temperatures to plunge to ridiculous levels. That will kill off all the freshly hatching mosquitoes. Make no mistake, those little bastards are percolating right now because the first hint above freezing gets them going. If we can get a good -20F day or two, that'll kill them all and then the summer will be far more congenial. I hate mosquitoes. I'll wear long-sleeves and a head net for most of the summer while outdoors.

We didn't get much snow this year, 150 miles from the Arctic Circle. Breakup (the Alaskan term for when the snowpack melts and it happens quickly, over the course of about one week, and that's when the rivers run free once again) looks like it will happen early. Maybe the golf courses will open in May. My old man is coming up in June. It would be cool to get a round in with him on the northern-most golf course in North America. It's only five miles from my home.

But Dad wants to fish, so we have reservations and everything to go fishing. He wants some river fishing for salmon, but I made us an appointment to do halibut fishing and salmon fishing on a North Country charter out of Homer. I want the fish, so we'll have them flash frozen and then bring back home. We love halibut and at $29 a pound in the store, we'll catch it ourselves.

But that's in May. Between now and then, more stories, more universes, and more great things to experience.

Peace, fellow humans.

Craig Martelle's other books (listed by series)
If you liked this story, you might like some of my other books. You can join my mailing list by dropping by my website **www.craigmartelle.com** where you'll always be the first to hear when I put my books on sale. Or if you have any comments, shoot me a note at craig@craigmartelle.com. I am always happy to hear from people who've read my work. I try to answer every email I receive.

Amazon – www.amazon.com/author/craigmartelle

BookBub – https://www.bookbub.com/authors/craig-martelle

Facebook – www.facebook.com/authorcraigmartelle

My web page – www.craigmartelle.com

ALSO BY E.E. ISHERWOOD

End Days (co-written with E.E. Craig Martelle) – a post-apocalyptic adventure

Sirens of the Zombie Apocalypse – What if the only people immune are those over 100? A teen boy must keep his great-grandma alive to find the cure to the zombie plague.

Eternal Apocalypse – Set 70 years after the zombies came, a group of survivors manipulates aging to endure their time in survival bunkers, but it all falls apart when a young girl feels sunlight for the first time.

Undead Worlds Volume 1 – Short story. "On the Rocks"

Undead Worlds Volume 2 – Short story. "Picking it Up in the Middle"

Descent into Darkness – Short story. "The Nine Lives of Captain Osborne"

The Expanding Universe Vol 1. – Sci-fi short story.

Metamorphosis Alpha Vol 2. – A short story set the world's first science fiction RPG

CRAIG MARTELLE'S OTHER BOOKS
(LISTED BY SERIES)

(# - AVAILABLE IN AUDIO, TOO)

Terry Henry Walton Chronicles (# co-written with Michael Anderle) – a post-apocalyptic paranormal adventure

Gateway to the Universe (# co-written with Justin Sloan & Michael Anderle) – this book transitions the characters from the Terry Henry Walton Chronicles to The Bad Company

The Bad Company (# co-written with Michael Anderle) – a military science fiction space opera

End Times Alaska (#) – a Permuted Press publication – a post-apocalyptic survivalist adventure

The Free Trader – a Young Adult Science Fiction Action Adventure

Cygnus Space Opera – # A Young Adult Space Opera (set in the Free Trader universe)

Darklanding (co-written with Scott Moon) – a Space Western

Judge, Jury, & Executioner – # a space opera adventure legal thriller

Rick Banik – # Spy & Terrorism Action Adventure

Become a Successful Indie Author – a non-fiction work

Metamorphosis Alpha – stories from the world's first science fiction RPG with James M. Ward

The Expanding Universe – science fiction anthologies

Shadow Vanguard – a Tom Dublin series

Enemy of my Enemy (co-written with Tim Marquitz) – A galactic alien military space opera

Superdreadnought (co-written with Tim Marquitz) – an AI military space opera

Metal Legion (co-written with Caleb Wachter) – a galactic military sci-fi with mechs

End Days (co-written with E.E. Isherwood) – a post-apocalyptic adventure

Mystically Engineered (co-written with Valerie Emerson) – dragons in space (coming Jan 2019)

Monster Case Files (co-written with Kathryn Hearst) – a ghost-hunting adventure mystery series

If you liked the story, please write a short review for me on Amazon. I greatly appreciate any kind words; even one or two sentences go a long way. The number of reviews an ebook receives greatly improves how well an ebook does on Amazon.

Made in United States
Troutdale, OR
05/05/2024

19654553R00159